DARK WHISPERS FROM THE PAST

THE CHILDREN OF THE GODS BOOK 62

I. T. LUCAS

Dark Whispers From The Past is a work of fiction! Names, characters, places and incidents are products of the author's imagination or are used fictitiously and are not to be construed as real. Any similarity to actual persons, organizations and/or events is purely coincidental.

Copyright © 2022 by I. T. Lucas
All rights reserved.

No part of this book may be reproduced in any form or by any electronic or mechanical means, including information storage and retrieval systems, without written permission from the author, except for the use of brief quotations in a book review.

Published by Evening Star Press
EveningStarPress.com
ISBN: 978-1-957139-28-9

1

JADE

The trees were a blur as Jade's booted feet ate up the miles. Propelled by the rage simmering inside her, she ran faster, pushed harder, and let her instincts guide her through the dense forest without colliding with obstacles or stumbling over them.

Leaving her hunting party behind, Jade veered to the right, leaped over a boulder, and dodged a fallen log. Her speed and agility could only be matched by her second-in-command, who was barely keeping up, while the rest would be left to fend for themselves, including her daughter and Kagra's sons.

Their offspring might be purebloaded Kra-ell and possess the most powerful and ruthless of warrior genes, but they didn't have the furnace of rage to push them beyond their comfort zone. Besides, what Igor's offspring failed to realize was that being a powerful Kra-ell was about more than genes. It was about smarts and honing their brains along with their bodies, and it was about honor and following an ancient code of conduct given to the Kra-ell by the Mother of all Life herself.

Exertion usually took the edge off, but today it failed to burn through the rage, fueling it instead. Her lungs gobbling up the mist and her heart pumping blood into her tiring limbs, Jade added a burst of speed and pushed harder.

Not to be outdone, Kagra sped up as well. Her long lean limbs working in perfect synchronization, her dark braid flying behind her like a devil's tail, she was a sight to behold. Watching her protégé blossom into the leader she'd been born to be filled Jade's chest with pride. She wished her daughter could be more like Kagra, but Drova was her father's daughter through and through. Just like Igor, she pissed on the Mother's teaching and ignored even the most basic tenets of the Kra-ell code of honor.

Despite Drova's lowlife murderer of a sire, Jade had had high hopes for her daughter, but even with all she'd invested in teaching and training the girl, it seemed that her nurture could not outdo Igor's nature.

Thank the Mother for guiding her to choose Kagra even though her second had been a pain in the ass at times. She wasn't a *yes* female, and she challenged Jade left and right, but she was loyal and honorable, and her mind was strong enough to withstand Igor's influence and retain some of its autonomy.

Kagra had always been a strong-willed, capable female, but during their twenty-two years of captivity, she'd become a force to be reckoned with. In a decade or two, she might match or even surpass Jade's power, but it would do her no good. It would only make her even more desirable to Igor, who wanted his offspring to be born to the strongest females, leaving the other captives to serve his henchmen and produce more of them for his army, so they could raid more Kra-ell tribes, steal their females and slaughter their males.

In a way, the weaker ones had it easier, their susceptibility to Igor's compulsion allowing him to subdue their grief and rage and make them more malleable, but Jade wouldn't have traded places with them for anything, not even her freedom. As long as her anger and grief burned within her heart, she would never stop plotting her revenge.

Although she and Kagra were the two most powerful females in the compound, able to retain some of their free will and autonomous thinking, neither of them would ever be able to break Igor's hold on their minds. They would never get free, and their need for revenge would probably remain an unappeased inferno of fury burning in their guts. But as long as Jade still had breath in her lungs and a mind capable of thinking, she would never abandon hope of one day killing Igor in the most painful and horrific way.

How could the Mother have given such an evil male such an incredible gift?

How could she look upon her children and watch her once proud daughters subjugated and exploited?

Perhaps the devil that the humans believed in was real, and he'd been the one who had bestowed upon Igor the power to bend others to his will. The Mother of all Life was supposed to look after her loyal creations and bestow her gifts upon her most deserving daughters, and very rarely on her most deserving sons as well.

"Slow down," Kagra panted beside her. "You can't outrun your anger."

"I can try." Jade continued at a breakneck speed for several more miles, slowing down only when her legs threatened to give out.

Stretching, she waited for Kagra to catch up.

"You're killing me." Kagra put her hands on her hips. "I'm going to throw up."

"You should thank me for pushing you. What's the only way to get stronger?"

Kagra rolled her eyes. "Train, and train, and then train some more until you can't move, and then do the same thing the next day, over and over again."

"You're lucky that I'm too tired to punch you for that eye-roll." Jade stretched her calves and motioned for Kagra to do the same. "We need to catch a big prey to replenish our reserves. I've burned through everything I had, and I'm starving."

"Let's rest a little first," Kagra said. "I'm thirsty more than hungry." She sniffed the air. "I smell water."

As Kagra beelined for the nearest stream, Jade followed.

Karelia was a beautiful region, densely wooded and rich in water and game, but it didn't make living under Igor's thumb any more tolerable. To have her family and her freedom back, Jade would have traded Karelia for a life of near starvation on barren and desolate land.

Anything would be better than the nightmare she was living in, even death. But since Jade was still in her prime, the end of her life wasn't coming any time soon, and even if taking her own life wasn't dishonorable, the option had been taken away from her along with every other personal liberty and right.

For a Kra-ell, the only way to die honorably was either in battle or in a duel to the death, but Igor had made sure that she could do neither, and he'd also closed every other loophole that could lead to her death or that of her charges.

Sitting on the rocky riverbank, Kagra took off her boots and socks and put her feet in the water. "It's as freezing as usual, but it feels good."

"Summer is coming." Jade sat next to her and started removing her boots as well. "It's getting warmer."

Kagra moved her foot in circles, creating little spirals. "What if you push me in? I might wash up somewhere far away from here, and perhaps Igor's influence wouldn't reach that far?"

"Yeah, and you'll be saved by a frog prince who will kiss you and turn you into an ugly toad."

That got a laugh out of Kagra. "I love it when you take human fairytales and parables and turn them on their heads, but I'm serious. I can't jump into the water with the intention of running away, but if you push me, then it's an accident."

"I can't push you because that would be aiding your escape, which I'm under strong compulsion not to do. Secondly, you might freeze to death before you wash up. And thirdly, if you are not back in the compound within forty-eight hours, he will activate the damn collar." Jade pushed a finger under hers, rubbing it against the chafe marks on her neck.

Most of the time, she managed to forget about the titanium circle around her throat, the symbol that marked her as Igor's slave, but when she ran, the damn thing abraded her skin.

"The remote won't work from that far away," Kagra argued. "Besides, I don't think that there are explosives in the collars. The bands are not thick enough to contain anything. I think Igor just put them on us to torment and humiliate us."

"I'm just glad that they don't have listening devices in them. If I couldn't talk freely with you, I would explode." At first, Jade had thought that the collars contained tracking and listening devices, but after cursing Igor out on multiple occasions and not getting punished for it, she realized that no one was listening. "But I bet that he has location trackers in them in case someone manages to throw off his compulsion." Jade lifted the collar of her shirt and tucked it under the metal. "Not that I can imagine anyone strong enough to do that. If you and I can't break free of his compulsion, no one can. He might have put the trackers in just to make us feel even more helpless, and he succeeded. After twenty-two years of examining every loophole and thinking of every way I could kill him, even at the expense of my own life, I know that there is no way out. We are going to die here, and so will our children."

"Maybe they will come for us," Kagra whispered. "The queen was supposed to send more settlers."

Jade sighed. "No one is coming. And even if they did, they wouldn't know where to look for us."

2

WILLIAM

As William took the stairs to Kian's office two at a time, he was proud of himself for being able to do so without getting winded but at the same time annoyed with himself for being predictably late. He'd planned to arrive at least half an hour early, but as usual, he'd gotten distracted, and now he had less than fifteen minutes left before the meeting to discuss with Kian all the issues that were of no interest to the other participants.

"Good morning." He rushed into the boss's office. "I know that I'm early, but I need to talk to you before the others arrive."

Kian smiled indulgently. "I assume this has to do with your recruitment efforts?"

"Yes." William pulled out a chair next to the conference table and dropped into it.

"How is that going?" Kian asked. "Are the increased incentives attracting better-qualified people?"

William chuckled. "Nearly doubling what we were offering certainly helped attract a higher caliber of candidates, but the qualifications are the lesser problem. The bigger one is finding bioinformaticians who are willing to accept work on a secret project that requires them to live in isolation for several months. They are in such high demand that they can pick and choose, and the good ones are more interested in prestige than money. A secret project they can't talk about or even mention will not help their future career prospects because they can't put it on their résumé."

Kian pursed his lips. "It's only going to last a couple of months, and it's not such a daunting prospect given that the isolated location is Safe Haven, which we've turned into a high-end resort. They can enjoy the beach and the gym, and we even hired a gourmet cook to prepare healthy meals for them."

The gourmet cook and the facilities would be shared with Eleanor's paranormals, but William saw that as an advantage rather than a disadvantage. His team would have only three to five members, and that wasn't enough to keep people from going stir crazy from isolation. And since the paranormal enclave was inside the most secure zone, it wasn't a safety issue either.

William pushed his glasses up his nose. "I hope they don't notice the security measures that can put Area 51 to shame. The so-called resort is guarded better than a top-security prison."

"They won't notice." Kian waved a dismissive hand. "We went to great lengths to keep all of it hidden, and if they see the occasional drone, they will assume it belongs to one of the lodge's guests."

"I hope so." William released a breath. "I lined up several good candidates from Stanford, most of them recent graduates, and I'm meeting with them tomorrow and Wednesday."

"Where?" Kian asked.

The boss didn't like him leaving the village without a Guardian escort, and William braced for a confrontation. None of the other council members were forced to travel with bodyguards, and he saw no reason for being singled out.

"The Bay Area, of course. I meant to tell you last week that I would be flying out tomorrow, but I forgot." He hadn't, but he hoped that it would be too late for Kian to insist on a Guardian escort.

Kian frowned. "Your time is too valuable to waste on traveling to interview prospects. You can use teleconferencing to interview them."

That was an angle William hadn't anticipated, mostly because what Kian was suggesting was absurd. He couldn't choose his team members based on a video call interview. As an immortal, he had extrasensory perception that could only be used in close physical proximity.

"My time is indeed valuable, but so is the information we are trying to decipher with the help of these recruits. I've done most of the groundwork via emails and phone calls, but you know as well as I do that there is no substitute for face-to-face meetings."

Kian lifted a brow. "Are you so desperate that you plan on thralling them into accepting the job?"

William wondered whether the boss was suggesting that he do that or warning him not to do it. Kian could go both ways.

"Thralling humans for our benefit is against clan law, and it's also immoral, but I'm ashamed to admit that the thought has crossed my mind." He sighed. "The reason I want to meet with them in person is that I need to get a sense of who they are as people. Their academic abilities are not the only deciding factor. I'll be spending a lot of time with them over several months, and it's important that I get along with them, and that they get along with each other. If I manage to have a team of three to five bioinformaticians assembled by the end of Wednesday, I'll consider it time very well spent."

Kian regarded him with a smile. "Let me guess. Your nineteen-year-old prodigy refused to come to you for an interview, and you hope to convince her to join your team in person."

That was true, but William wasn't going to apologize for wanting Doctor Kaia Locke on his team. "She's my best candidate, but I would have gone even if her parents weren't an issue."

"What's their problem?"

"They think that she's too young to leave home, which is absurd since the girl is an adult and has a PhD. I hope that after they meet me, they will agree to let her join." He waved a hand over his face. "My harmless, nice-guy appearance will finally be good for something."

Kian chuckled. "You *are* a harmless, nice guy. I hope you convince her to join. Is she pretty?"

William shrugged. "I'm not the kind of guy who allows himself to be blinded by physical beauty. Kaia's beautiful brain is of much more interest to me than her physical appearance." Especially since she was nineteen, and William had never been drawn to young women.

He preferred mature females who knew what they wanted and didn't waste time on games.

"Kaia what?" Kian flipped his laptop open.

"Doctor Kaia Locke." William shook his head. The guy was a two-thousand-year-old immortal, but he was acting like a frat boy.

Most men, including the mighty Kian, judged people, and especially females, based on their looks. William wasn't indifferent to beauty, but he deemed exceptional brains and strength of character much more important than a person's appearance.

Kian typed in the name, lifted a brow, and kept reading. "Doctor Locke has a very impressive résumé, and I suspect that under those monster frames, she's a looker."

William had seen Kaia's graduation photo, and even though her dark-framed enormous eyeglasses hid most of her face, he couldn't help but notice her lush, sexy lips, and the secretive smile that hinted at a sense of humor. But since she was only nineteen, Kaia Locke would never become anything more than a colleague.

Taking off his glasses, William rubbed the lenses with a corner of his Hawaiian shirt. "I believe that Doctor Kaia Locke is more concerned with science than she is with trivial things like fashionable frames and makeup."

Kian lifted his hands in the air. "I meant no offense. Are you taking the jet?"

"I don't need the jet to get to the Bay Area. I booked a commercial flight."

Kian shook his head. "I want you to take the jet, and I'm sending a Guardian with you."

That was what William had been afraid of. "Why?"

"Did you forget? We lost Mark in the Bay Area."

William winced as a spear of pain pierced his heart. Given their shared field of expertise, Mark and he had been close, and he still mourned his loss.

He wasn't the only one.

Mark's murder had shaken up their family. It was the reason Kian had decided to pull all of their people from the Bay Area, build a hidden village for the clan, and have everyone living where they were protected and safe.

But that had been four and a half years ago, and a lot had changed since.

"I didn't forget, and I never will, but we haven't heard from the Doomers in months. Lokan says that Navuh is busy breeding the next generation of smart warriors, and until he achieves that, he isn't going to come after us."

Kian leaned forward and pinned William with his intense eyes. "That might be true, but we know that they run drug and prostitution rings in California. You could accidentally bump into a Doomer, and you are not a warrior. Cancel the flight. You're taking the private jet and a Guardian. End of discussion."

Folding his arms over his chest, William glared at Kian. "None of the other council members have to travel with bodyguards." He sounded like a kindergartner, but he really didn't want to have a Guardian going with him on the interviews.

"What do you want me to say, that you are more valuable?" Kian leaned back in his chair, but his eyes were still holding William's captive. "I value all the council members tremendously, for their skills and as my closest friends, but if tragedy strikes, they can all be replaced. No one can take your place."

"I'm training Marcel. He's almost as good as me." That was a gross exaggeration, but Kian wouldn't know that.

"Almost doesn't cut it, and we both know that Marcel doesn't have that extra something that you have. Shai knows every aspect of the clan business as well and better than I do, but he can't take my place for the same reason. I know in my gut when to make a deal and when not to. Things are rarely clear cut, and I don't base my decisions solely on numbers and charts, just as you don't base yours on calculations alone or rely on tried and tested solutions. You think outside the box."

Regrettably, that was true, but that didn't mean that he should be kept in a cocoon. "I'm not going to show up to meetings with a bodyguard."

"The Guardian can pretend to be your chauffeur."

William snorted. "Do I look like the kind of guy who has a chauffeur?" He flapped his Hawaiian shirt, which was two sizes too big on him. He'd lost about thirty pounds since he'd started training with Ronja and Darlene, but he needed to lose at least thirty more, and it would be a waste of time and energy to shop for new clothes only to do it again in a couple of months.

Kian eyed the shirt with a frown. "Get some new clothes before you go. If you want to impress your candidates, and especially Doctor Kaia Locke and her parents, you can't show up looking like a schlump."

3

KAIA

"Don't cry, sweet pea." Swaying on her feet, Kaia held her baby brother to her chest and rocked him gently. "Whoever decided that babies needed to get six vaccines at twelve months old was a sadistic bastard. They should have spread them out over several months."

Her mother rocked Ryan, who was hiccuping between sniffles. "It's better to get it over with all at once."

Kaia strongly disagreed. When she had children, she wouldn't allow them to be tormented like that.

Poor boys.

Throughout the ordeal the twins had been screaming their little heads off, and when they'd gotten exhausted, they'd switched to pitiful whimpering and casting accusing looks at Kaia and their mother for allowing the nurse to give them ouchies.

"Gilbert should have been here with his sons. I don't want them to associate me with needles. I want Evan, Ryan, and Idina to always think of me as the cool, fun big sister."

Usually the nanny accompanied their mother to doctor visits with the twins, but Idina had come down with a cold and couldn't go to preschool, so the nanny had to stay home with her.

Her mother sighed. "He wanted to be here for them, but he had an important inspection at a job site that he couldn't leave to the supervisor. He had to attend it in person."

Kaia twisted her lips in a grimace. "Yeah, I bet."

It wasn't the first time Gilbert had come up with a convenient excuse to wiggle out of performing his less-than-pleasant fatherly duties, which included changing poopy diapers and wiping little noses. The guy was only forty-eight, but he acted like a throwback to the fifties.

He was a great guy, and he loved Kaia and Cheryl as if they were his own daughters, but he wasn't very helpful with the little ones, leaving all the work of raising them to their mother and the nanny.

It would have been semi-okay if their mother was a stay-at-home mom, but she wasn't. Karen Locke was a sysadmin for a large defense contractor, which was a demanding position with a salary to match. It wasn't fair for her partner to leave all the work of managing the household and taking care of his toddler daughter and twin baby sons to her, and by extension, to Kaia and Cheryl.

Well, mostly to Kaia because Cheryl was still in high school while Kaia was home, exploring her employment options.

She'd had offers from several universities and a dozen or so private research facilities, but she was probably going to accept a position at Stanford so she could keep living at home.

Her mother and Gilbert didn't want her to move out, and she didn't want to do that either. How could she possibly leave her sweet baby brothers, Idina and Cheryl? She would miss them too much.

On the other hand, starting college at fourteen and finishing her doctorate at nineteen, all while living at home, meant that Kaia had missed out on the whole college experience. It would have been nice to try something different instead of doing more of the same for the rest of her life.

She stifled a snort. If her memories of her past life as a mathematician were real and not imagined, she was doing more or less the same thing during two lifetimes, or maybe more. What if she'd been stuck in the same groove throughout her soul's existence? She might have gone through many life cycles, and in each of them, she'd been consumed by the beauty of numbers and the endless patterns they formed. All of creation was based on numbers, and it fascinated her, but there was more to life than research, and she'd learned that lesson in her past life as well as in her current one.

Her previous self had been single, childless, and lonely, while Kaia had a wonderful family and was surrounded by love. Losing her father at a young age had reinforced the lessons learned in her previous life, making her hold on to the people she loved because she could never know how long she would have with them.

Maybe that was why Kaia appreciated her chaotic home life and was in no hurry to leave.

"Come on." Her mother slung the strap of her enormous baby bag over her shoulder. "Let's take the boys home."

By the time they got to the car Evan had fallen asleep, exhausted from all the crying, and Ryan had quieted down but was still sniffling pitifully.

After strapping the twins into their car seats, Kaia got behind the wheel. "I guess we are not stopping by the supermarket on our way home."

Her mother turned to look at the babies in the backseat. "Not with the twins. We can order what we need online and have it delivered."

Kaia grimaced. "They always mess things up, and they drive me nuts with all the messages about approving substitutions. I prefer to drop you off and go by myself. The guy from the secret research project is coming tomorrow, and all we have to serve are Skittles and gummy bears."

"I don't know why you agreed to see him." Her mother folded her arms over her chest. "We've talked about it, and we agreed that you are not going to accept his offer no matter how good it is. You are just wasting his time and ours."

"I'm curious to hear more about the project. What if it's about something so crucial and necessary that I would later beat myself up for not being part of it? Besides, the guy sounds so desperate for me to join that he might present me with an offer that I can't refuse."

That was all true, but there was a third reason for her wanting to meet William, and it had to do with Tony's disappearance. Her mother and Gilbert would freak out if they knew that she was getting involved in that, and her mother wouldn't allow the recruiter anywhere near the house if she suspected that he had anything to do with Tony's fate.

Kaia didn't know whether William had been involved in Tony's case or not, but she was desperate for any clues that could help her find out what happened to her friend.

The thing was that William's offer was very similar to the one Anthony had received a little over a year ago. The highly classified research project had been supposed to take four months, and yet no one had heard from Anthony in over a year. It was a long shot to think that William had been Tony's recruiter as well, but bioinformatics wasn't a huge field, and there weren't that many players outside of academia and major research institutions. William could have heard something, or he might know the people who had hired Anthony.

4

KIAN

"Good morning." Syssi walked over to Kian and leaned to kiss his cheek. "Am I late?"

"You're not." He pulled out a chair for her. "Okidu called to tell me that he's stuck in traffic. He estimates Mia and Toven's time of arrival to be eleven-thirty."

She glanced at William, who was never on time, and then at her watch. "I'm a little late. I didn't want to be the last one to get here, but I didn't want to leave Allegra with Vivian without making sure that she was okay with her, so I waited a few minutes to see how they were getting along. I swear that baby understands every word I say. I told her that Mommy would be back shortly and to play nicely with Aunt Vivian. She smiled and waved bye-bye at me."

"My daughter is a genius."

Syssi sat down with an infectious grin spreading over her face. "I know, right?" She turned to William. "How come you're early?"

"I wanted to talk to Kian about my trip to the Bay Area before the meeting. I'm going tomorrow, and I forgot to tell him about it."

"What's in the Bay Area?"

"I'm meeting with several bioinformaticians, and I hope to have a team assembled by Wednesday."

She arched a brow. "You've been looking for people for months. How did you manage to line up several candidates?"

Looking at Kian, he smiled. "The boss has given me a bigger budget and an attractive location to conduct the research. I've also lowered my standards, and I'm willing to recruit greenhorns fresh out of grad school."

"Doctor Kaia Locke is a greenhorn," Kian said. "And yet she's your best candidate."

William nodded. "She is, and if I get her to join, she can shore up the rest of the team."

"I can't wait to meet her." Syssi tilted her head and looked at Kian from under her lashes. "I also want to see the new and improved Safe Haven. Can we go for a day trip? We can fly in the morning and return the same evening."

"I don't see why not." He took her hand. "Turner and William have designed a security system that is nearly as good as what we have in the village, and the accommodations can rival any high-end resort. I don't mind taking you and Allegra for a visit."

High-end was a bit of an exaggeration since the rooms in the original lodge were small, and the ones in the bungalows were only slightly bigger, but he'd approved high-quality fixtures and furnishings, so the interiors were luxuriously appointed.

"I've seen the brochure." Syssi leaned forward and pulled one from the stack on the conference table. "Emmett's hair and beard are epic. And that gown." Lifting the pamphlet, she laughed. "He looks like a prophet."

"He plays the part." Kian took another pamphlet and handed it to William. "We want to attract people with paranormal talents, and I'm not sure whether Emmett's guru persona is going to attract or repel them. But in either case, he needs it to hide how young he looks."

"The prophet look worked for him very well in the past." Syssi spread out the pamphlet. "I don't see why it wouldn't now."

Kian tapped his fingers on the table. "I'm curious. Would either of you have paid money to participate in a spiritual retreat run by a guy who looks like Moses?"

William laughed. "I probably wouldn't have noticed Emmett's outfit, but I wouldn't have wasted my time on anything with the words spiritual or retreat in it either. Those kinds of things don't interest me."

Syssi shook her head. "I wouldn't have participated no matter how its leader looked. I'm too shy to enjoy communal experiences, especially with people I'm not already friends with."

"You work in a lab full of people." Kian wrapped his arm around her shoulders. "You are also surrounded by people in the village, and I don't see you hiding at home."

"It's different." She waved a hand in dismissal. "I know everyone at the lab, and I'm comfortable with them."

"What about the test subjects?"

She chuckled. "They are usually more nervous than I am, so I have to make an effort to put them at ease. Besides, I have Amanda, the ultimate extrovert, to run interference for me if I need it."

"How is it being back at work?" William asked.

"Challenging." Syssi smiled. "But I'm glad that I decided to return to work. I love being a mother, but that's not all I am. I need to get out of the house, and I need to stimulate my brain. Thankfully, I can take Allegra with me, and she enjoys the change in scenery as well, but it has been only ten days, so it's still an adjustment period." She chuckled. "When Annani took Alena and Orion on a trip to see he Sanctuary and later to Scotland, Amanda and I lost our two best babysitters, so we had to go back to work and hire a nanny."

"I know." William pushed his glasses back. "Roni and I ran the security check on her."

"Right, I forgot about that. Anyway, Eliza is great, and Ingrid did an amazing job converting Amanda's office into a nursery."

Kian shifted in his chair, hiding his discomfort from Syssi. She knew that he was worried about her taking Allegra with her to work, but she thought that he was being overprotective.

William's crew had fortified the security measures at the university to include all the walkways around it, so Kian could see the nanny taking the babies for a walk in their double stroller. Unbeknownst to Amanda and Syssi, there was also a team of Guardians parked near the lab's building, ready to deploy in seconds if needed, but it still made him uneasy having his daughter away from the security of the village.

"I'm looking forward to working in the lab at Safe Haven," William said. "But I'm going to miss my lab here and working side by side with Roni. We make a great team."

Leaning back, Syssi folded her arms over her chest. "I still don't know why you decided to do the research there. It would have been safer to keep the journals here and bring those bioinformaticians to the village. You are going to thrall them to forget everything anyway, so what difference does it make?"

"The journals stay here," Kian said. "I had Okidu photocopy each page and scan them into our secure servers."

Syssi let out a breath. "I know that, and I also know that no one can hack the clan's servers, but someone can attack Safe Haven and steal the information from the computers that are there, or just take the servers with them."

5

WILLIAM

"I can answer that," William said. "I worked with Turner to design the security measures, and Safe Haven is now practically impenetrable. We set up concentric perimeter security zones, with the outmost ring starting twenty miles out. We have hidden infrared cameras and sensors installed at all roads leading to Safe Haven, whether paved, gravel, or animal trails. These devices are powered by long-lasting battery packs, and they transmit via the clan satellites directly to the main security room in the village, with a parallel feed going to the security room at Safe Haven. Images of each vehicle's occupants are captured and fed into our proprietary face recognition software and are processed in real time for immediate feedback."

"Wow." Syssi pushed a strand of hair behind her ear. "What if someone is hiding in the trunk?"

William smiled. "We have that covered as well. Infrared cameras scan the vehicles and alert security if they detect hidden occupants. A team of Guardians will intercept the vehicle, stop it, and search it. They will also stop any car whose occupants' faces don't match those that were fed into the system ahead of time. We will have three teams of Guardians with us, so one team is always on duty."

"Is the system already operational?" Syssi asked. "I don't expect any of it to be needed, but the paranormals moved in a week ago, and we are responsible for their safety."

William nodded. "Except for the drones and measures at the lab itself, all the rest is working. The density of the surveillance equipment doubles at every concentric parameter. At ten miles out, the equipment covers all the wooded area regardless of roads or trails. The entire coastline is covered for fifteen miles in each direction, so we are not exposed from the ocean side either. When we assemble the scientific team and start working on the journals, advanced stealth drones with high-power optics and infrared equipment will be monitoring the area around the clock." He chuckled. "Roni hacked into the FAA's servers and instructed them to ignore the drones. We also have battle-grade drones that are ready to deploy on command, and I had one of the noise cannons moved to Safe Haven as well."

He had to admit that the security measures were excessive. It would have been more economical to bring the team to the village, but he saw the merit of having another secure location in case they needed to evacuate the village for whatever reason. Besides, it was good for the Guardians to learn to operate the new systems that he and Turner had designed while the risk of attack was low.

"Wow, my head is spinning." Syssi looked at Kian. "I should have known that your paranoia would kick in big time. Are you expecting a Doomer attack?"

He shrugged. "You never know. The information in those journals is priceless, and since William convinced me that the only way he could get qualified people to work on deciphering them without resorting to thralling or compulsion was to allow them some freedom, I had no choice but to go overboard. Besides, we figured out that it was strategically prudent to have another secure location in case the unthinkable happened, and the village's location was compromised." He looked at William. "Don't forget to power up Armageddon when the team starts working in the lab."

"What's Armageddon?" Syssi asked.

"It's what I nicknamed the lab's security." William took his glasses off, folded them, and put them on the conference table. "The security office, the control center, the servers, the armory, and the lab itself are all located underground, and the entrance is fortified with blast-proof doors. But if the doors are breached, we have a self-destruct button that will detonate underneath the structure and destroy everything inside of it."

Syssi paled. "Are you serious? With the people inside?"

"We have an escape tunnel, but as a last resort, I will blow the place up with everyone inside, including myself, to prevent this technology from falling into the wrong hands."

Shaking her head, Syssi put her hand on Kian's arm. "You should just destroy those journals. I'm starting to agree with the gods on that. Not on the destruction of the Odus, which was barbaric even though they weren't sentient, but the technology to make them. I'm sure that the gods had very compelling reasons for banning the technology. It's not worth the risk."

Kian sighed. "Don't think that I wasn't tempted, but those journals might contain genetic information that could save lives. Along with the code to build the Odus, they might have included the code that's responsible for our fast healing and regenerating. We could transform the world with that knowledge."

"Or destroy it." Syssi let out a breath. "But I get it. That's why I didn't advise against attempting to decipher them. What about the people working on them? How are you protecting the information from being stolen?" She looked at William. "Their minds are not the only way they can copy it and smuggle it out. I'm not a computer expert, and I'm sure that you have it covered, but if you can explain it to me in layman's terms, I would sleep better at night knowing that the information, both the original and the translation, is protected."

Lifting his glasses off the table, William put them back on even though there was no need for anti-glare lenses inside Kian's office. "The Safe Haven lab servers are connected to the village servers via an ultra-secure encrypted link using 512-bit encryption designed by Roni and me. None of the servers are connected to the internet, and they communicate only via the clan's satellite. All traffic between them requires ongoing authentication. Also, each person working in the lab will be issued a fob key that regenerates a new access code every two hours. Without it, everything they see would be scrambled. None of the information is stored locally on the lab's servers, and all files on the local servers, including cache files, are fully encrypted."

Syssi tapped her fingers on the table. "What about their phones? Will they have to surrender them before entering the lab or before being admitted to Safe Haven?"

"They can bring their phones to their bungalows," William said. "But no phones will be allowed in the lab or the rest of the underground facility. Besides, even if they manage to smuggle one in, it would be useless. The underground and its immediate area will have the same protection as the village, so no electromagnetic signals can be broadcast or received there. Only the clan phones will work. On top of that, all cellular and internet traffic from Safe Haven's general facilities area will be monitored in real time by an AI program designed by Roni and me. If it flags anything up, the connection will be severed instantly."

"Wow again." Syssi pretended to wipe the sweat off her brow. "Now I can sleep without worrying about exploding labs. I will just have to contend with nightmares about the end of the world via an army of Odus."

"I will never allow that to happen." Kian took her hand and gave it a gentle squeeze. "Our Allegra will grow up in a world of peace and prosperity."

Syssi didn't look reassured. "You can't make promises like that, Kian. Not everything is under your control."

"Not everything, but with two gods to back me up, a lot is."

6

MIA

As the limo's windows turned opaque, Mia's excitement ratcheted up a notch. It was her first time back in the village since she and Toven had left after her transition.

Orion and Alena had come over to say goodbye before leaving for the goddess's sanctuary, and Geraldine and Cassandra had also visited with their mates, but Mia hadn't seen any of the others in nearly a month, and she missed the sense of community of the village.

"It won't be the same without Annani, Orion, and Alena." She leaned her head against Toven's shoulder. "But I'm glad that Orion is going to Scotland to meet Alena's children. It wouldn't be right for them to get married without doing that first."

"If you say so." He kissed the top of her head. "They are not going to stay there for long, though, and by the time they return, we will be living in the village."

"I'm looking forward to that." She lifted her head and smiled at him. "When they get back, I want to invite them to dinner at our new place. My grandmother will be over the moon."

Toven chuckled. "I can just imagine how anxious she will be about preparing a meal for Annani. In your grandmother's eyes, she is a real god. I'm a broken one."

"That's not true. My grandparents love you."

"And I love them back, but since I don't glow, I'm not a real god."

Toven had lost his glow a long time ago, most likely following the trauma of losing his people, but he was working on getting it back. "You'll find your glow again. I'm sure of it."

"I am too. With you by my side, I feel like a god for the first time in centuries." He smoothed his hand over her arm and leaned to nuzzle her ear. "Especially when you climax and scream, oh god, oh god."

Her cheeks catching fire, she slapped his arm. "I do not."

"Yes, you do."

"Once. I only did that once, you scoundrel."

For the first two weeks after her transition, Toven had been afraid to make love to her, and when he finally had, Mia had screamed his name. She might have added an oh-god or two, but she didn't remember that.

After a month of recuperating, she felt fantastic despite the constant itching and pain of her growing legs. It wasn't as bad as Bridget had warned her it would be, but she had the pain meds the doctor had prescribed to thank for that. Without them, things would have been much more difficult.

"Are you nervous about the meeting?" Toven asked.

"Nope. I'm excited."

Toven had exchanged some emails with Kian and Syssi regarding the terms of Perfect Match's acquisition, and they had teleconferenced with them a few times, but now that Mia was over the first stage of her transition and feeling great, they were going to finalize the terms in a face-to-face meeting.

This time around, though, Mia felt confident, and she wasn't scared of participating. Syssi was going to be there, and the two of them saw eye to eye on things. Also, with both of them being creative people, they had a lot in common and felt a strong affinity toward each other. But Syssi was more business savvy, and Kian was intimidating as heck, so some nervous butterflies were still buzzing around in Mia's belly.

As they entered the tunnel, Okidu looked at her through the

rearview mirror. "No need to fret, Mistress Mia. These are just the village's security measures. We are almost there."

"It's okay." Mia smiled at him. "I approve of them wholeheartedly."

Okidu's smile grew even wider. "I am glad, mistress."

It was hard to believe that the butler was not human, and Mia couldn't help but think of him as a middle-aged British man. Then again, the only other cyborgs she'd encountered had been fictional characters in movies and books, and they had been depicted as very human as well, so she had no real reference for how a cyborg should act, and the same went for aliens, which reminded her of what Cassandra had told her about the Kra-ell living in the village.

Lifting her eyes to Toven, she put her hand on his knee. "After the meeting, I want to visit the café."

"Are you hungry?" He gave her a worried look. "I don't know how long the meeting will take, and I don't want you to wait until it is over. I can call Kian and tell him that we are grabbing a sandwich on the way."

"I'll wait until after the meeting. They've been waiting for us long enough."

"It's almost noontime. We had breakfast three hours ago."

"It's okay." She patted his knee. "I mentioned the café because I want to see the Kra-ell girl working there, not because I'm hungry."

He arched a brow. "I can hear your belly rumbling."

Mia laughed. "It does it all the time lately. I need to watch it, or I'll turn into a pumpkin, and you won't be able to keep carrying me around."

Since waking up after her initial transition, she'd been eating like a horse, but it was never enough, and she was hungry all the time.

"There is no chance of that." He leaned down and kissed the tip of her nose. "Your body is using that fuel to continue your transformation. You are no heavier now than you were a month ago."

"Liar." She leaned up and kissed his lips. "But that's okay. You can keep lying to me."

"I'm not lying." He looked genuinely offended.

Mia rolled her eyes. "I had to order new pants that were a size larger than my old ones. I know that I gained a few pounds, and I'm okay with that. I no longer have to worry about the strain the extra weight would put on my heart." She took a deep breath. "One of the best things about my transition is the peace of mind knowing that I'm not going to collapse all of a sudden. I feel drunk on the tranquility."

"It's the pain meds." Toven winked. "And the extra something special I give you every night, and I'm not talking about earth-shattering orgasms."

"You aren't?" She feigned innocence. "I thought that was your best godly expression."

He tightened his arm around her. "Well, if you insist. I'm sure that they have a therapeutic effect as well."

7

KIAN

"Hello, everyone." Mia waved her hand as Toven carried her into the office. "There is no elevator in your building." She cast a glance at Kian that was part apologetic and part accusatory.

"My apologies." Kian rushed to pull out a chair for her. "It was an unforgivable oversight on my part. I should have held the meeting in my office in the underground complex, which is easily accessible."

He was surprised that Syssi hadn't thought of that, but then she'd been preoccupied with returning to work, hiring a nanny to look after Allegra and Evie at the lab, and finding a new babysitter for their daughter in the village for special occasions like today's meeting.

"That's okay." Toven set Mia on the chair. "I'll go back down and bring the wheelchair up, but if you want to make it up to Mia for the oversight, you can order lunch. She is hungry."

"I'm okay." Mia's cheeks pinked in embarrassment. "I can wait until after the meeting."

"I'll have lunch delivered." Kian pulled out his phone.

"Who are you going to call?" Syssi asked. "The café doesn't deliver, and Callie's place is not open yet."

"I'm texting Wendy. She can send Aliya over with our order."

"I could eat," William said. "Can you please order me a Reuben?"

Kian collected everyone's orders and then waited for Toven to come back with the wheelchair. "What would you like?"

"I'm not picky. Whatever you're having is good for me."

Kian arched a brow. "I'm ordering the only vegan sandwich they have on the menu. Are you sure that's what you want?"

"It's fine."

Unlike Annani, Toven was not a prima donna. In fact, he was more accommodating than Kalugal, who must have inherited his penchant for flair and drama from the same source Annani had—his maternal grandfather. Ahn had been the consummate politician, and according to Annani, his leadership had never been challenged, not even by Mortdh. He'd been the most powerful god, but that wasn't the only reason no one could have imagined any other god taking his place. He'd had that innate something extra, a dramatic flair that his daughter had inherited, and so had some of his grandchildren, specifically Amanda and Kalugal.

Toven parked the wheelchair next to Mia. "Do you want to change seats?"

"I'm fine for now. But if I need to visit the bathroom, I'll need the wheelchair."

"About that." Syssi winced. "None of the bathrooms in the office building are wheelchair accessible."

"I'll carry you." Toven sat down next to Mia and turned to Kian. "Let's talk business."

"Indeed." Kian handed him the draft he'd prepared. "As we've discussed over the phone, you are going to purchase most of Hunter and Gabriel's shares and some of Syssi's. The equity and voting shares will be equally split between you and Syssi at fifty percent each, but they will represent only forty percent of the profit-sharing stock. The founders will retain ten percent each."

Toven's main objective was to have control over the company, but he conceded to sharing it with Syssi as long as it was only the two of them, so neither could make a major decision without the other. The problem with that was giving Hunter and Gabriel a stake in the company without giving them the deciding voting rights. It had been solved by creating two classes of stocks.

After reading through the one-page document, Toven passed it over to Mia. "What do you think?"

"It looks fine to me," she said. "I'm just surprised at how short it is. I expected the contract to be at least as hefty as my medical record."

Syssi laughed. "The final draft will probably be much longer, mainly for Hunter and Gabriel's sake. I'm fine with sealing the deal with a handshake."

"So am I." Toven turned to her. "As long as the main items we agreed upon are spelled out, so there is no future disagreement, we don't need the legalese to complicate things." He smiled. "It's not like we can take each other to court over disputes."

Syssi waved a dismissive hand. "Fates forbid we ever get there. We are both reasonable people, and we are in agreement about the major issues. We can negotiate over the minor details."

"I have a few that are not that minor." Toven turned to William. "The first thing I want to do is bring more machines here. From what I heard, there is a long waiting list of village residents for the two you have, and that's unacceptable. I want to have enough machines so Mia and I can go on an adventure whenever we please without feeling guilty about making others wait."

William cleared his throat. "The demand is high, but I think that four additional machines would suffice. The problem will be finding space for them. Up until recently, we only had two curtained-off areas, but we've added walls, and now we have two dedicated private rooms, but we will need four more."

The rooms in the lab were also tiny and spartan, nowhere near as nice as the ones in the Perfect Match studios.

"Then we need to build a studio in the village." Toven shifted his eyes to Kian. "Since Mia and I will be frequent users, I will cover the expense of building it."

Kian didn't like the idea of Toven financing building projects in the village. He was fine with the god owning half of Perfect Match, but he wasn't ready to give him a stake in the village. Then again, he'd let Kalugal pay for developing and building his section, which was a much bigger deal than a studio, so it wasn't rational to deny Toven.

Still, it wasn't the same. Kalugal had pledged his allegiance to the clan, while Toven was a free agent, and the only guarantee they had of him not turning against the clan was that his children and grandchildren were members.

"I was thinking about charging for the service." Kian leaned back and folded his arms over his chest. "In time, the proceeds will cover the expense. The problem is finding space for a new common building. I'm not willing to shrink the lawn area, or sacrifice greenery for more buildings, but we have vacant residences that could be converted into studios. Most of the houses have only two bedrooms, but we can use two adjacent homes to house the four new machines, or three to house all six. I'm sure that Ingrid can convert them to look just as good or better than the Perfect Match studios."

Toven nodded. "That's an acceptable solution. I also need space for a creators' studio. Mia wants to try her hand at designing environments, and I would like to move some of the work that's now done in the Perfect Match headquarters to the village. I understand that William has many programmers working on different projects, including developing new adventures."

"I do," William said. "They all have workstations in the underground lab, but we are at capacity. I have no people to spare for more projects." He scratched his head. "We have many programmers in the clan, but I could always use more." He looked at Kian. "Can you incentivize computer studies?"

Kian doubted that would help, but it never hurt to try.

He nodded. "I can do that."

8

TOVEN

"I don't want Mia to work underground." Toven uncrossed his arms and draped one over the back of Mia's chair. "That's not an environment conducive to creativity."

"I agree," Syssi said. "Maybe some of your programmers would like to work aboveground? Their productivity might increase."

William shrugged. "It's possible. But I'm going to work remotely for the next several months, and the lab won't function as well without me, so I wouldn't suggest making any changes while I'm gone."

"Where are you going?" Toven asked.

"I'm running a new project at Safe Haven."

"I have an idea." Syssi's eyes lit up with excitement. "After you are done there, we can move the Perfect Match headquarters to Safe Haven. Everything will already be set up, and it would be a waste not to utilize the lab there beyond this one project."

William frowned. "I don't see how that can help. First of all, the lab in Safe Haven is too small to serve as headquarters, and secondly, it's also underground, and for a good reason. It's much easier to secure."

A knock on the door put a temporary halt to the conversation, and as it opened and a very tall and very skinny woman entered with a tray of drinks in one hand and a large paper bag in the other, Toven had no doubt that she was the Kra-ell female who Mia had wanted to meet.

Aliya was lovely, beautiful in an alien way that didn't resemble any of the goddesses he remembered. Had her ancestors come from the same place as the gods?

His father hadn't mentioned another humanoid species sharing their corner of the universe, but he'd hinted that humans were not the gods' first genetic experiment. They had created other intelligent life by combining their genetic material with that of local primitive life, speeding up its evolution to leap over hundreds of thousands of years of natural processes.

Had the Kra-ell been one of their creations?

"Thank you, Aliya." Kian took the bag and the tray from her. "I apologize for dragging you up here."

"It's my pleasure." She looked at Toven and then at Mia. "Hi."

"Hello." Mia smiled at her. "You can blame me for that. Ever since I woke up from my transition, I'm constantly hungry."

"Congratulations on turning immortal." Aliya looked down at Mia's missing legs. "I heard about you, and I've met your grandparents. They are very nice. I'm glad that you're getting your legs back. I don't know if my people can regenerate like that."

As a long moment of awkward silence stretched over Kian's office, Aliya's olive-toned skin went a shade darker. "I'm sorry. Did I say something inappropriate? I'm still learning what's okay to say and what's not, and I don't understand many of the English idioms."

"You didn't say anything wrong," Mia reassured her. "I heard about you too, and I was curious to see you. You are very pretty."

Aliya chuckled. "For an alien."

"For anyone," Mia said. "Your beauty is different, but that's what makes you look so exotic. Is it okay if I draw you? I'm an artist."

"Yeah, I know. Your grandparents told me that you illustrate children's books."

"I also draw for my own pleasure, and those pictures have more mature themes." Mia sent Toven a reproachful sidelong glance. "But no nudes or anything suggestive." She turned back to Aliya. "I like to draw interesting faces."

After Orion had shown her the journal he'd stolen, Mia had asked to see Toven's other journals that contained drawings of his lovers and the comments he'd written to help him remember them. It was a very bad idea for her to see the sheer amount of them, but thankfully, the originals were stored in a safe in Switzerland. He'd offered to show her the scans he'd made on his computer, but after seeing a few pages, Mia had decided to wait until he could show her the actual journals.

Aliya shrugged. "I don't mind you drawing me as long as you don't make it public. I don't like being put on display." She pushed a lock of hair behind her ear, which was slightly pointed.

"I totally get it," Mia said. "I'll give you a copy, and you can do whatever you want with it."

That got a smile out of Aliya. "Awesome. I'll give the picture to Vrog. When do you want to do it?"

"We are moving into the village this Wednesday. So maybe this weekend?"

Aliya nodded. "Let me know when and where." She turned toward the door. "Enjoy your lunch."

"What about your grandparents?" Syssi asked when the door closed behind her.

"They are moving with us," Toven said.

Kian turned to him. "What about their home in Arcadia?"

"They are excited to move into the village," Mia said. "But we've decided to do it in stages. At first, we will spend the weekdays in the village and the weekends back in Arcadia. That way, I can keep seeing my friends until the new headquarters are set up in the village, and we can bring them here."

Kian frowned. "I wasn't aware of any such plans."

"We suspect that they are Dormants," Toven said. "I felt an immediate affinity toward them, and Lisa confirmed my suspicions. I know that's not enough to prove that they are indeed Dormants, but once they start dating immortal males, we will find out sooner or later whether they can be induced or not."

Kian groaned. "I'm not okay with that. We have Safe Haven for trying out potential Dormants. If you want your friends with you, you should consider moving there. You don't have to work in the underground lab. You can work in one of the lovely bungalows we've built there."

Mia turned a pair of worried eyes to Toven. "My grandparents like the village, and the machines are here. The idea was to make Frankie and Margo testers of adventures. What are they going to do in Safe Haven?"

Toven took her hand. "Don't worry. We are not moving to Safe Haven." He turned to Kian. "I will compel the girls to keep the village and its occupants a secret, and since they are both young and attractive, we won't have to wait long for them to find inducers. They'll turn immortal in no time."

Looking like he'd swallowed a bitter pill, Kian nodded. "You will be responsible for them."

"I am perfectly aware of that." Toven shifted his gaze to William. "How soon can we bring four additional machines to the village, and how long will it take to set them up in the homes Kian will dedicate to them?"

"I need to talk to Hunter. If he has the parts and sends them to me, I can have my people assemble them in a week. The setup will take a few more days."

"After you talk to him, let me know."

"I will."

Leaning over, Toven picked up the printed piece of paper Kian had prepared. "Do you want me to sign it?"

"No need. I'll have Edna draft a proper contract, and I will forward it to you for review. If there are no changes, we will sign on that. I'll have the accounting department calculate how much money you will need to transfer to Gabriel and Hunter and how much to Syssi."

Toven smiled. "I'm glad that it's only half of what I originally planned to pay. If you don't mind, and Hunter and Gabriel agree, I would prefer to make it an installment deal. Too much money changing hands at once will attract attention that neither of us needs."

"I agree." Kian looked at Syssi. "Is that okay with you?"

"Sure." She extended her hand to Toven. "Let's shake on it, partner."

9

WILLIAM

"How do I look?" William buttoned up his new shirt.

Pursing his lips, Max nodded. "Not bad. For a nerd, you clean up nicely."

He had to agree. The shopping trip the Guardian had taken him on had been a success. He'd gotten a new pair of dress shoes, three shirts, one pair of slacks, and two pairs of jeans. Everything was either two or three sizes smaller than what he usually ordered online, and he couldn't remember looking that good since he was a teenager.

William had always been more interested in books and learning than running around hunting or playing sports like the other boys, and he loved to eat, so he'd always been a little padded, but ever since he'd dived into coding, the weight had piled on until he'd gone from plump to fat. Hannah had started him on the journey of eating better and moving more, but the biggest change was the result of him joining Ronja and Darlene on their quest for improved health.

He was still a little overweight and had another twenty or thirty pounds to lose, but on his six-foot-two-inch frame, that wasn't a lot.

"Glasses on or off?" he asked the Guardian.

"You don't need them unless you are in front of a computer screen, so why wear them?"

William had been asked that question many times, and the simple answer was that they had become part of his persona, and he felt naked without them. But he'd been told that his blue eyes were pretty, so maybe he should not wear them when he wanted to impress Doctor Kaia Locke?

On the other hand, the interview with her was already making him nervous enough, and he would be even more nervous without his glasses on.

"I look smart with them on." He put the glasses back on top of his nose. "It's a job interview, not a date."

Max snorted. "A date? We don't go on dates. We hunt for hookups." He draped his arm over William's shoulders. "What say you we go clubbing after the interview? You've got new clothes, and you look hot. The ladies are going to be all over you."

William hadn't gone hunting in months, and even though he wasn't as obsessed with sex as other immortal males, the dry spell was too long even for him. That being said, he hated what the others called hunting, but he hated paying for pros even more, so that didn't leave him with many options.

Maybe now that he'd actually put a little effort into how he dressed, the ladies would come to him.

Yeah, right.

He was getting a few appreciative looks here and there, but usually that was the extent of it. On the rare occasions when his lab mates managed to drag him out to a club, no one hit on him, despite his new and improved appearance, and it wasn't because he was too intimidating. He simply didn't exude masculinity like the other immortal males. Or maybe he had a tattoo on his forehead that spelled Mega Nerd and was visible only to women.

William was a teddy bear, or rather that was the impression he gave.

On the inside, he wasn't as soft and cuddly.

Well, that wasn't true. He was a romantic, and he enjoyed being polite and chivalrous, and that made him seem soft.

No female had ever called him a tiger.

With a sigh, he turned away from the mirror and collected his wallet from the entry table. "That depends on how well the interview goes. If she accepts the offer, I will be in a mood to celebrate. If she doesn't, I'll be bummed. I need her."

Max clapped him on the back. "Lay on the charm, buddy."

"I'll do my best."

Max had escorted him before on other out-of-town trips, and he was glad that Onegus had assigned him to accompany him on this one as well. He was fun to be around, wasn't as buff as the other Guardians, and he didn't look like a bodyguard.

Perhaps he could pass for a chauffeur, but that didn't solve the problem either. William didn't want to look like the kind of guy who had one. It was okay for Kian to be driven around, but even he would have gladly given that up if he didn't have to take two bodyguards with him every time he left the safety of the village.

"Do me a favor, Max. When we get to the house, drop me off and park a block away. If they ask, I'll say that a friend gave me a lift and is coming back to pick me up later."

"No problem, but you'll have to leave the earpiece open and broadcasting. I need to be able to hear what's going on."

"I'm not going to wear it. It's going to stay in my pocket."

Max shrugged. "Good enough for me. But if anything smells fishy, put it in. You can claim to be hard of hearing."

"I don't expect any trouble in the suburban family home of Doctor Locke, but if I get ambushed by her or her younger siblings, I'll put the earpiece in."

"Yeah, yeah." Max grabbed the keys and opened the door to their hotel room. "You can never know where danger lurks, and as the boss likes to say, better safe than sorry."

10

KAIA

"When is Gilbert coming home?" Scooping up one of Idina's dolls off the floor, Kaia dumped it into the laundry basket that she was using as a collection bin for the toys her little sister and brothers had left strewn all over the living room. The poor Barbie had fallen victim to one of Idina's foul moods and was missing all of her clothes and half her hair.

"He'll be here." Her mother wiped Evan's hands with a wet towel.

"I know that he will, but the question is when. William is going to get here at seven, and Gilbert told me to wait for him. What am I going to do? Take the guy out for a walk?"

"You know Gilbert. Intimidating strangers and keeping them off balance is something that he actually enjoys doing."

Ryan was still eating, and the nanny was trying and failing to keep the area around him clean.

Kaia snorted. "Yeah, I don't envy the guy. Gilbert is going to give him a military-style interrogation. If he shows up on time, that is."

Her mother, the responsible adult in the house, had come home from work early to get everything ready for the meeting, but Gilbert was still a no-show, and Kaia had no intention of waiting for him. Still, she would have preferred him to be there. The guy had a nose for crooks and lowlifes, and if William was either, Gilbert would sniff him out and wipe the floor with him.

Her honorary stepdad took no prisoners when he was in his family-protector mode.

Kaia wished she had his skills, but despite memories of her prior life, she was still too naive and trusting for her own good.

"Leave the toys," her mother said. "Berta and I will finish cleaning here. You need to change and do something with your hair. It's a mess."

Smoothing a hand over her long wavy hair, Kaia looked down at her stylishly torn jeans. "Why? This is my best pair. They are comfortable, and I look great in them."

"You are a PhD, and you are being interviewed for an important job. You need to dress appropriately even if you have no intention of taking it. The academic world is not that big, and the competition is stiff. If William McLean forms a negative impression of you and talks about it in his academic circles, it could hurt your chances of getting the job you actually want."

"All because of an outfit? That's a bit of a stretch, don't you think?"

Her mother rolled her eyes. "Do you have to argue about everything? Just go upstairs and change into something nice and conservative. The white button-down blouse I've gotten for you is perfect for an interview."

"I look like a nun in it," Kaia grumbled. "But fine. It's worth wearing a nun outfit if it gets me off cleaning duty." She looked at the messy living room and groaned. "Why did I think that inviting him to my house was a good idea? I should have met him at a coffee shop."

She loved her chaotic home, but William would probably be horrified. Hopefully, the twins would be asleep by the time he arrived, or the interview would turn into a circus. Idina wouldn't be asleep yet, but she was okay unless she didn't like the guy. Her little sister had a bit of a mean streak, and she pinched people who rubbed her the wrong way.

Up in her room, Kaia walked into her closet and looked at her selection of clothes. Very few were job-interview appropriate, and the white blouse her mother had gotten for her was one of her only two choices. The other one was a dark blue blouse with ruffles at the sleeves that made her look like an escapee from an Amish community. Another gift from her mother.

Karen Locke was many things, but fashionista wasn't one of them. She had terrible taste in clothes.

Heaving a sigh, Kaia pulled her T-shirt off and shrugged the blouse on. Buttoning it up to her neck, she chuckled at her reflection. "I look like a librarian." Pulling her jeans off, she reached for the only skirt hanging in her closet.

It was calf-long and had little blue flowers printed on the fabric. It wasn't ugly, but together with the white blouse, it was awful.

Gilbert would love to see her wearing it. The guy was obsessed with protecting her and Cheryl's virtue, and he made all kinds of weird rules about having boys over. If either of them took a guy to her room, the door had to remain open at all times.

He was such a hypocrite.

If he was so concerned with their reputations, he should have married their mother, but despite having three kids together, Gilbert and her mother hadn't made things official. Nevertheless, he was very protective of his adopted daughters. Not that anything had been officially done about that either, but he always referred to her and Cheryl as his daughters, and she liked that he cared deeply about them.

That didn't mean that she should dress like a librarian to please him, though.

Perhaps wearing a pair of jeans that didn't have tears in them would be enough to make her mother and Gilbert happy.

Despite how full her closet was, very little of its content was wearable. She'd outgrown most of it and should either give it to Cheryl or donate it to charity. Perhaps her mother was right, and she should get a few work-appropriate outfits, but she hated shopping, and she didn't care much about clothes.

Kaia was most comfortable in jeans, T-shirts, and flip-flops.

After finding a pair of jeans that passed inspection, she pushed her feet into a pair of ballet flats, brushed her long wavy hair and pulled it into a high ponytail, and finished up by spraying a little perfume on her neck.

That was as much prep as she was willing to put into meeting the recruiter. After all, she wasn't going out on a date, and it wasn't as if she needed to impress him with her looks. What was inside her head was much more important to him than the outer packaging.

11

WILLIAM

As Max pulled up next to Kaia's house, William regarded the mansion-sized home with a sinking feeling in his heart.

When Roni had done a background check on Kaia and her family, he'd found out that her mother was a sysadmin for a large defense contractor, which meant that everyone in the household had gone through rigorous background checks, and since Roni hadn't had to dig deep in search of red flags, William hadn't bothered to read through the file either.

Roni had mentioned that the unofficial stepdad was a successful builder and that the family was affluent, but owning a house like that in this neighborhood indicated that they were more than that.

They were rich.

Money was not going to be as important to Kaia and her parents as prestige, and she would prefer a job that would earn her recognition rather than a secret project for which she would get no credit.

"Fancy house," Max said. "To have a place this size in this neighborhood, they have to be loaded."

"It would appear so." William opened the passenger door. "Please, park where they can't see you."

"Yes, boss." Max gave him a two-finger salute.

William waited until the Guardian drove away before walking up to the front gate. It opened before he had a chance to press the intercom button, which meant that his arrival had been monitored. There was a camera mounted on one of the pillars holding up the gate, but it was an older model that was popular for home installations. Still, it wasn't the cheap kind, and whoever had installed it had done a good job.

As he walked through the gate, it closed behind him, and the front door opened.

The intimidating human who stepped out gave him an unabashed critical once-over. "William McLean, I presume?"

"That's me." William gave him his best smile and offered him his hand.

The guy took it and squeezed hard. "Gilbert Emerson. Kaia's stepfather."

Karen Locke and Gilbert Emerson weren't married, but they'd been together for twelve years and had three kids in addition to Kaia and her sister, so the guy was solid, and he seemed to be taking his fatherly duties seriously.

"A pleasure to meet you, Mr. Emerson."

"Call me Gilbert." The guy cracked a smile and draped his arm over William's shoulders as if they were best buddies. "I expected someone older. Are you really the chief scientist of the project, or are you just the recruiter?"

"I'm older than I look, and I'm the chief."

"You must have been a prodigy like our Kaia. Where did you go to school?"

They were still standing outside the door, and the guy was already in interrogator mode. His hostility was evident, but it was coming from a good place. Gilbert was looking out for his family.

William took a step away, getting out from under the guy's arm. "Let's get inside, so I won't have to repeat my life story and credentials for your daughter and the rest of the family."

Gilbert smiled, seeming satisfied for some reason.

Perhaps he liked that William wasn't intimidated by him.

Kaia's stepdad was tall, only an inch or so shorter than him, and he was a little padded around the middle but still handsome. He was in his late forties, had most of his hair, and he had a certain charm about him despite the assertiveness that bordered on aggression and the directness that bordered on incivility.

"I'm buying time for my better half and the nanny to wrestle the twins to bed. We won't be able to talk while they're awake."

Just then, an angry wail sounded, and it was immediately joined by another one. Then the wails turned into a loud demand. "Dada!"

Gilbert dropped his head in resignation. "I've been summoned. Just tell me where you went to school, and I'll leave you to talk with Kaia."

"The University of Glasgow." William let some of his Scottish accent bleed through.

"A Scot, eh?" Gilbert clapped him on the back. "I thought I detected a slight accent."

"Gilbert!" an angry female voice called. "Get up here."

"I'm coming!" He stayed exactly where he was. "So, what is a Scot doing in the Bay Area recruiting bioinformaticians for a secret project?"

"I was offered a job in Los Angeles straight out of college, and I stayed."

"Gilbert!" A tall blond walked out the door. "Invite Mr. McLean inside and go to your sons." She cast William an apologetic smile.

This was unmistakably Doctor Kaia Locke, and she was stunning.

Instead of the enormous glasses she'd worn in her graduation photo, she wore fashionable frames that didn't detract from her natural beauty, and a beauty she was.

Doctor Kaia Locke was dressed in slim jeans that accentuated her long, trim legs and a dressy white shirt that was a little too conservative for a young woman her age, implying an innocence that her eyes belied.

She reminded him of Annani. A young body housing an old soul.

"Hello." He smiled and offered her his hand. "Please, call me William."

12

KAIA

William McLean looked nothing like what Kaia had imagined, and seeing him standing on her doorstep triggered two opposing emotions.

First, her heart sank because the guy had the face of a sweetheart, not a conniving manipulator, so he probably had had nothing to do with Tony's disappearance, and a moment later, excited butterflies took flight in her belly because he was way too attractive for a chief scientist.

Why the hell did the guy have to be so handsome?

Then again, maybe his appearance was misleading. With that guileless, nice-guy expression, he could easily ensnare his unsuspecting victims.

"Please, call me William." He offered her his hand.

Did he omit the doctor on purpose, or did he keep forgetting that he was a PhD like she was?

Or maybe he didn't have a doctorate? Come to think of it, he'd never introduced himself as one in all their online communications.

"Kaia." She narrowed her eyes at him before clasping his hand.

As their palms touched, an electric current zinged between them, sending a pulse of longing to all of Kaia's neglected feminine parts.

She tried to pull her hand out of his grasp, but he held on for a split second too long before letting go. "Just Kaia?" He smiled. "Not Doctor Kaia Locke?"

She shrugged. "I keep forgetting that I'm a PhD. It feels weird to be addressed as doctor. What about you? Do you have a PhD that you are not flaunting for some reason?"

"I don't." He pushed his glasses up his nose. "I'm a software engineer, and I didn't pursue a doctorate. I needed to start working."

Kaia tilted her head. "Didn't they offer you a stipend?"

"Money wasn't the reason I needed to start working." He shifted from foot to foot, reminding her that she was just as lousy of a host as Gilbert and was keeping him on her doorstep instead of inviting him in.

She moved aside, clearing the doorway. "Please, come in. We can continue our conversation sitting down."

"Thank you." He turned sideways as if he was concerned about passing through the doorway with her blocking part of it.

William was tall and slightly padded but he wasn't huge. Maybe he used to be and still retained the habits of a big guy?

An old memory of making the same move in her previous life flashed through her mind. She'd been a large man who had always been self-conscious about his height, his big protruding belly, and mostly about his thick, meaty fingers. Inelegant and unfitting for a mathematician, they'd been the source of endless embarrassment.

Kaia still caught herself looking at her hands from time to time and being pleasantly surprised to see the slender fingers she had in this life. Maybe that was why she gave them much more attention than her hair and even her face, filing her nails and applying fresh polish as soon as the old stuff started peeling.

"The dining room is the safest bet." She led him to the only room in the house that didn't get invaded by her younger siblings.

"You have a lovely home," William said as he followed her.

"Thank you. My stepdad built it. There was an old house on the property when he bought it, but he demolished it completely and built a new one for us."

"He did a very nice job." William pulled out a chair for her.

"Thank you." She smiled and lowered herself as gracefully as she could to the seat instead of dropping into it like she usually did.

His gentlemanly gesture deserved a ladylike response.

These days it was so uncommon for guys to do things like opening doors and pulling out chairs, but somehow it didn't seem odd for a young man like William to act so old-fashioned. He seemed older than his years, and the impression she got was that he was a very kind person.

She wasn't sure whether she should hope that he was the man he seemed to be or hope that he wasn't. If William was a good guy, he wouldn't be able to help her, but on the other hand, it made the prospect of joining his team appealing and not for professional reasons.

It had been a year since Kaia broke up with the only boyfriend she'd had, and she hadn't been in a rush to replace him, but meeting William changed things.

He was at least ten years older than her, if not more, so he might try to stay away, but she saw how he looked at her, and he wasn't indifferent.

It would be nice to have a boyfriend who wasn't intimidated by her academic achievements.

"Do you want to hear about the project, or are we waiting for your parents to join us?"

"Let's give them a few more minutes." She smiled apologetically. "Gilbert will chew my head off if I start without him. In the meantime, you can tell me about my competition. Who else have you interviewed so far?"

"You are my first," he admitted. "The others are not as good, and I really hope that you'll consider joining my team because I don't think the others could do the job without you leading them."

Evidently, William wasn't a skilled recruiter. That had been way too honest, giving her the leverage to demand whatever she wanted in exchange for agreeing to work for him.

"Oh, wow." Kaia flipped her long ponytail over her shoulder. "You're putting a lot of confidence in a greenhorn. Who are the others, if I may ask? I probably know all the bioinformaticians in the area."

William pulled a folded piece of paper from his shirt pocket and handed it to her. "These are the people I'm meeting with tomorrow. I don't know who will make the team."

She scanned the list. "These are all good people." She refolded the note and handed it back to him. "The fact that I got my PhD while being ten years younger doesn't mean that I'm better than them. It just means that I have an unnaturally fast learning ability." And previous knowledge that had been the foundation of her academic success, but that was a secret no one besides her mother knew, and even she thought that Kaia was making it up.

"You're being too modest." William put the note back in his shirt pocket. "I've read your thesis and the papers you published. I consider myself a smart guy, but it took me a while to understand them."

"Are you a bioinformatician?"

He shook his head. "I'm a software engineer, and I enjoy coming up with new programs and new inventions that make life better for people."

If anyone else had said that to her, she would have regarded it as a nice sales pitch, but William looked and sounded so sincere that Kaia believed him.

Then again, she wasn't the best at judging character.

Where the hell was Gilbert? She needed his nose for crooks and manipulators.

No more wailing was coming from upstairs, and even Idina hadn't run in to poke her nose into the dining room. Cheryl had her in the den, and they were watching one of Idina's favorite animated movies, but the moment she realized that they had a guest, the little demon would want to see him.

"It's no wonder that you had trouble understanding my papers. You are not a bioinformatician."

He smiled sheepishly. "I usually don't have trouble understanding papers from fields that are unrelated to my particular expertise, but genetics seems to be written in a whole different language."

"That's because it is. It's the language of life."

13

WILLIAM

*A*s the wailing upstairs suddenly resumed, a little girl ran into the dining room and leaped into Kaia's lap.

"I'm Idina," she introduced herself. "Who are you?"

William was about to answer when Kaia's other sister rushed in. "She tricked me. She said that she was going upstairs to get her teddy bear." She trained an apologetic set of eyes on William. "I'm Cheryl, Kaia's sister."

"I'm William. It's nice to meet you."

"You didn't say that to me." The toddler pouted. "Say it's nice to meet me too."

"It's very nice to meet you, Idina." He offered his hand to the little girl and looked into her brown, cunning eyes. "How old are you?"

"I'm three." She put one small hand in his for a handshake and lifted the other with three fingers up. "How old are you?"

"Idina," Kaia said in a reproachful tone. "That's not polite to ask."

"Why? He asked me."

"She's right." William smiled. "I'm thirty-two."

Idina narrowed her eyes at him. "No, you're not."

Stifling a chuckle, he asked, "How old do you think I am?"

"Twenty-seven."

That wasn't a bad guess for a little girl. When he'd been heavier, he'd looked a little older, and thirty-two had seemed reasonable, but after losing weight, he looked younger.

"I'll take twenty-seven if you're selling."

She scrunched her nose. "How can I sell twenty-seven? I don't have it."

"Enough with the questions." Kaia pushed to her feet with Idina in her arms and handed her over to Cheryl. "You can either go back to watching your movie, or you can go upstairs and get ready for bed."

"I don't want to go. I want to stay here!" The child tried to wiggle out of Cheryl's hold, and when that didn't work, she started kicking her sister.

"Stop it!" Cheryl tried to catch her legs.

"I'm sorry about that." Kaia shook her head. "This house is just impossible. Do you want to go for a walk?"

"Gilbert is not going to like that," Cheryl grumbled while wrestling Idina to stop kicking her.

"I can't hear myself think in here." Kaia walked up to the front door and opened it. "Tell him that William and I are taking a walk around the block. If he wants, he can catch up to us."

"Fine." Cheryl carried the wiggling child away.

As Kaia closed the door, shutting the chaos behind her, William let out a breath. "I love children, but after today, I'm not in a rush to have any. I'd rather be the uncle who can walk out whenever he wants."

"It takes some getting used to." Kaia tugged on the elastic holding her ponytail, releasing her long hair from its confines. "They are at their worst just before going to bed because they are tired and cranky, but other times they are a joy." She smiled. "They are generators of love."

As the wild mass cascaded down her shoulders, framing her pale face in a golden halo, she looked ethereal, but it was an illusion.

He'd met her less than half an hour ago, but in that short time, he'd learned that Kaia wasn't a delicate flower. Her smart eyes betrayed not only a sharp mind but also a strength of character.

"You don't look like your sisters," he said to break the silence stretching between them.

Cheryl and Idina had dark hair and brown eyes, while Kaia was blond with blue eyes and skin that was nearly translucent.

"Cheryl looks like our mom, and Idina looks like Gilbert. I look like my father." She pulled her phone out of the back pocket of her jeans. "He looked a little like you. I can show you a picture." She scrolled through her photos until she found what she'd been looking for and held the phone up to William.

He had to admit that she was right. The young man's smiling face bore some resemblance to his, and their coloring was similar. There was also something in the guy's expression that made William like him. "He's a handsome fellow, and he seems like a nice guy."

"He was. He died when I was five." Kaia turned the phone off and tucked it back in her pocket. "He was also an engineer like you."

"What happened to him?"

"Heart failure." Kaia sighed. "This makes me too sad. Let's talk about something else. Tell me about your project."

William debated how much he could tell her without lying. "You might think of it as a translation project. We have charts upon charts of instructions that are written in what I believe is a genetic code, and to decipher them, I need skilled bioinformaticians."

She arched a brow. "What happened to the people who made those charts?"

"Regrettably, that person is no longer with us." They had never even set foot on Earth, but that was as close as William dared to get to the truth.

"I see. So, the author passed away, and you need someone to decipher what he or she wrote in code."

"Yeah, that's about it."

"Why is it such a big secret? What do you think is in those charts?"

"If I tell you, it's not going to be a secret. I can't tell you more before you sign the confidentiality agreement."

"Can you at least give me a hint? I can't commit to a project without knowing what I'm going to work on. I don't want to be involved in the creation of biological weapons or anything that could be used to harm people."

Without knowing what she was talking about, Kaia was surprisingly close to the truth.

"We suspect that these journals contain information that might revolutionize medicine and help a lot of people, or it might reveal something dangerous that could do the opposite. Until we know for sure what is in them, we can't let anyone get their hands on that information, and if we discover that it's bad, we will destroy it."

"So, I was right. It could be a biological weapon."

"Or a cure-all for cancer. We won't know until we decipher the code and translate the writings."

In essence, that was true. Mass-producing Odus could be a great boon, freeing humanity from all sorts of manual labor, but it could also be a disaster if there was no way to prevent them from being turned into weapons. And if the journals held the secret to immortality, that could create a whole new set of problems as well.

14

KAIA

"But what if a member of your team sells the information after the project is done?"

A signature on a nondisclosure agreement wasn't a fail-proof way to prevent the information from being leaked or sold, and the only way to guarantee that didn't happen was to silence the scientists who had worked on it for good.

Perhaps that was what had happened to Tony.

Perhaps he'd been recruited to work on a secret project, and once it was completed, they'd offed him to keep him from revealing what he'd learned. William didn't look like a murderer, but what if someone else had done the killing, and he didn't even know about it?

"We are not going to allow anyone to take notes out of the lab. I also designed a protocol that will keep the information encrypted at all times. To access it, the team members will get a fob that generates a new code every two hours, and they will have to input it to keep working."

"That sounds very sophisticated." She cast him a sidelong glance. "Did you have leaks in the past, and is that why you are so careful?"

William shook his head. "This is the first time I've needed help on a project that I can't get from my own people, who I trust implicitly. I'm forced to assemble a team of strangers, and I'm doing my best to mitigate security leaks and other problems before they are created."

Again, William sounded so sincere that Kaia had a hard time holding on to her suspicions.

And he was also so damn likable. He gave off a vibe of a big teddy bear, safe and cuddly, and she had the odd urge to crawl into his arms and put her head on his chest.

Was it because he reminded her of her father?

Hopefully not, because that would just be sick. She was attracted to the guy, for goodness sake, and she didn't have daddy issues.

"What if someone has an eidetic memory?" Kaia looked at William from under lowered lashes. "They could walk out of your lab with all the information stored inside their heads. You can't encrypt a brain."

He smiled sheepishly. "I thought about that loophole as well, and I hired a powerful hypnotist to make the team members forget what they worked on."

"Ingenious, but a little out there. I don't believe in hypnosis. Only weak-minded people can be hypnotized."

He frowned. "Has anyone tried to hypnotize you and failed?"

"No."

"Then how do you know that you can't be hypnotized?"

Kaia shrugged. "I was curious about how hypnosis works, so I read about it. People who are suggestible and eager to please are easily controlled by a skilled person who knows how to manipulate those weaknesses. I'm neither suggestible nor eager to please, so I'm not hypnotizable."

William opened his mouth, closed it, and then opened it again as if he'd changed his mind about what he was going to say. "You need to experience it once before deciding that it doesn't work on you."

"True, and I'm willing to put it to the test, but I'm ninety-nine percent sure that I can't be hypnotized."

A smile lifted his perfectly shaped lips. "As long as you leave that one percent open, you're not a lost cause. So, did I pique your interest in my project?"

"You did, but to be honest, I'm probably going to accept the job offer from Stanford. I've gotten better offers from private research companies and other universities, but I want to keep living at home, and that's an overriding factor."

William stopped walking and turned to her. "Do you really want that, or are you doing it because your family wants you to stay home?"

"Both. It might surprise you, but for me, family comes first. I love my siblings, and I don't want to be away from them." She smiled. "Despite the noise and the mess, I adore them."

"I get it, believe me. I love my family as well, but you need to think about your future and what's best for your career."

Kaia laughed. "A project that I can't talk about and a work experience that some hypnotist is going to make me forget will not help my career."

"That's true, but the camaraderie and connection you'll develop with your teammates are priceless, on a personal level as well as the professional."

She tilted her head. "Are you talking about romantic involvement?"

The guy actually blushed, which was adorable. "Not at all, but that can be another bonus. Working and living with your teammates is a unique experience, especially when the project you are working on is interesting and challenging. That's something you won't be able to do later in life when you are married with two and a half kids and a dog."

He wasn't wrong, and a part of her yearned for the adventure and for the change of pace, but a larger part needed to cling to her family and never let go.

"Life is short, William, and job satisfaction is not as important as the people I love and who love me back. Money doesn't motivate me either. I just want to make enough to cover my expenses."

15

WILLIAM

That was a very mature statement from someone as young as Kaia, but then it shouldn't have surprised him. Other than her appearance, nothing about Kaia was young. She didn't talk like a nineteen-year-old or behave like other girls her age.

In fact, her approach to life was more mature than his, and he was ancient compared to her.

Before the lab grew to the mega factory it was now, he'd spent most of his time in isolation, working on projects that fascinated him and filled his mind and his heart. He'd felt lonely at times, but not enough to leave his lab and pursue contact with people. The one time that William had been motivated to take a break from his work was when he'd met Hannah, but after that relationship had fizzled out, he'd dived even deeper into his projects.

Still, he was an immortal, and unlike Kaia, he was not going to run out of time to find his true love and strive for more balance in his life.

Casting a sidelong glance at her, he felt an absurd longing for her to be the one for him, and that made even less sense than his former infatuation with Hannah.

He'd been drawn to Hannah and had felt an affinity toward her because she was a scientist and a fellow brainiac, same as Kaia, but she'd been a mature woman in her late twenties, not a kid.

Kaia was beautiful and sexy, but even acknowledging her attractiveness made him feel like a damn pedophile. Legally, she was permissible, but morally, she wasn't.

Regardless of his hormones deciding to act at the least opportune time, he needed her on his team, and he had to convince her to join, hopefully without thralling her, but he might not have a choice.

"What about the excitement of discovery?" He looked into her big blue eyes. "I live for that. Sometimes I can't fall asleep at night because my brain keeps churning up new ideas or new angles to approach what I'm working on. It's like living on high-octane fuel. I'm always hyped up." He chuckled. "People say that I talk too fast, but that's nowhere near the speed at which my mind works. I couldn't slow down even if I wanted to."

Kaia regarded him with a curious expression on her beautiful face. "I envy you. I don't get excited about much, and especially not about work." Her lush lips lifted in a small smile. "I get excited when my baby brothers learn a new word, or when they try to walk. I get excited when Cheryl gets an award at school. She's so smart, and she has her own Instatock channel for which she produces daily content, but people don't make a big deal out of her achievements because of the shadow I cast, and it makes me feel bad." She pushed a strand of hair behind her ear. "Maybe if I went away for a while, they would start noticing her more."

William's heart leaped with hope. "Then come to work for me. A few months away is nothing in the grand scheme of things, and with your bright star shining somewhere else for a little while, Cheryl will get her chance in the spotlight."

"That's something to consider." Kaia let out a breath. "We should head back. The little ones are probably asleep by now, so my mother and Gilbert can join us."

As they reached the gate it opened immediately, and a moment later Gilbert opened the front door. Standing with his arms crossed over his chest, he glared at William. "Took you long enough."

"Are the little ones asleep?" she asked.

"Yes." The guy diverted his glare at Kaia.

"Then we can talk inside." Unperturbed by the glare, she walked past him.

As the guy stepped aside, letting William in, a smile tugged on his lips, suggesting that the glare had been just for show. He wasn't emitting any hostility either.

When William entered the living room, a pretty brunette rose to her feet and offered him her hand. "I'm Karen, Kaia's mother. I'm sorry I wasn't here to greet you when you arrived."

"That's perfectly all right." He shook her warm palm. "You and your mate had your hands full."

She tilted her head. "Mate? I like that. Is it a Scottish expression? Gilbert told me that you are originally from Scotland."

"You are?" Kaia asked. "I didn't detect any accent."

"That's because I usually hide it." He affected an exaggerated Scottish accent. "I pretend to be an American."

"Don't. Your accent is so sexy."

"Kaia," her mother said in a stern tone.

"It's okay, Mom." She patted her shoulder. "William is cool, and he's not a stick in the mud. You can relax."

Well, that was good to hear. He must have made a good impression after all.

"Please, sit down." Karen motioned to one of the oversized armchairs. "Can I offer you something to drink?"

Whiskey would have been great but inappropriate. "A glass of water would be wonderful. Thank you."

"I'll get it." Cheryl got to her feet and walked out of the room.

Gilbert sat in the armchair across from him and assumed a regal pose worthy of the king of the castle. "So, what have you two been talking about during your walk?" He turned to look at Kaia. "I hope you didn't make any decisions without consulting with us first."

"We talked about William's project and the team he's assembling. I know everyone on his list of candidates, so if I decide to take his offer, I will not be working with strangers."

Talk about surprises. Only moments ago, she'd said that she'd prefer to stay home and take the job offer from Stanford.

Had thinking of her sister living in her shadow been what had made all the difference?

Curiosity getting the better of him, he tentatively reached into her mind, got the shock of his life, and retreated as fast as he'd entered.

Kaia's mind wasn't just her own. She shared it with an older man, or rather thought of herself as one. One moment she examined things as Kaia, a nineteen-year-old girl ready to embark on an adventure, and the next, she examined them from the point of view of a lonely, middle-aged man.

16

KAIA

William looked as if he had seen a ghost. Could the stunned expression on his face be the result of her expressing a tentative interest in joining his team?

To be honest, she'd given him conflicting cues, one minute claiming that she wanted to accept the offer from Stanford and the next giving his offer another thought.

It had been inspiring to hear him talk about the exhilaration he felt when thinking about new ideas or working out a problem with a product or software he was developing. She wanted that too, and then thinking about Cheryl living in her shadow and not getting the recognition she deserved from their mom and from Gilbert and the rest of the family worked in favor of accepting William's offer as well.

Could she live without them for three to four months, though? She would miss the little ones too damn much.

They were growing so fast, and every moment with them was precious. If she went away, would they even remember her when she returned?

"What's wrong?" Gilbert asked William. "You look pale all of a sudden."

He heaved a sigh. "I just thought of a flaw in one of my designs." He forced a smile. "I know it's random and unrelated to what I'm here for, but sometimes my mind just gets away from me and goes galloping in strange directions."

"Kaia is the same way." Cheryl walked in with a tray loaded with soft drinks and an assortment of things to snack on. "Sometimes she just spaces out and doesn't even hear me talking to her. You two will get along great."

William turned hopeful eyes at Kaia. "Are you seriously considering my offer?"

"I am. The position at Stanford will become available only at the end of October, which will give me four months to work on your project if I decide to join. The problem is that I'm not willing to be away from my family for the entire time. I will need to go home at least every other weekend, and I want them to be able to visit me. If you can compromise on the isolation, I'll give it serious consideration."

William's eyes shone as if he had just been informed that he'd won a Nobel Prize. "I might be able to make it work. The project is top secret, but I can make special accommodations for you." He rubbed the back of his neck. "I need to figure out the details, but I will make it work one way or another. I have a feeling that you are the key to deciphering those schematics. The other candidates are capable people, and they might be good, but none of them are as brilliant as you."

His compliments made her feel self-conscious, and Kaia shifted on the couch. "Thank you, but that's an exaggeration, and I'm not being falsely modest. I have a very good command of mathematics, and that gives me an advantage, but it doesn't make me a genius."

Cheryl snorted. "Just take the compliment, Kaia. You have a PhD at nineteen. I think that proves you are a genius."

"I'm not." Kaia folded her arms over her chest. "You think that it's great to be called a prodigy or brilliant, but it's not. It puts pressure on me that I don't want. What if I can't pull off a miracle? What if I disappoint William? I constantly need to prove myself."

"You don't." Her mother took her hand. "You should only do the best you can, and if that's not enough, then it's not your problem."

"True." Kaia let out a breath. "I just want to be normal."

She wanted to go on a date with a guy her age without having to lie about her achievements, but then she also wanted to have something interesting she could talk with him about, and that was much tougher than lying and pretending to be a normal college girl.

She was a freak, and not just because she was smarter than most people or had a PhD in bioinformatics.

"We all want something we can't have," Gilbert said. "And being so-called normal is overrated." He crossed his legs at the ankles and leaned back. "It's damn boring, that's what it is. Right, William?"

"Absolutely." William nodded.

Gilbert grinned. "I'm glad we see eye to eye. So where is this secret project of yours located? Or is that a secret as well?"

"It's on the Oregon Coast, and the location is serene and beautiful."

"That doesn't tell me much," Gilbert said. "If we are to let Kaia join your team, we need to see the place first and make sure that it's well-appointed, that she has her own room which she can lock, and that there are other women working on the project. I don't want her sleeping in army barracks or eating field rations, and most importantly, I need to make sure that she's safe." He looked at her and smiled. "You're not just a brain, Kaia. You are a beautiful young woman, and men are pigs."

She rolled her eyes. "I can take care of myself."

Gilbert had insisted on her attending a Krav Maga self-defense course for women, and surprisingly, she enjoyed it and became very good at kicking ass.

"I know. But let's be realistic. Unless you carry a gun and are willing to use it, you are not safe."

"You have nothing to worry about in that regard," William said. "No harm will come to Kaia on my watch, and I'm going to be there twenty-four-seven from start to finish."

17

WILLIAM

Kian would probably pop a vein when he heard about the compromises William was considering for Kaia, but to get her on his team, he was willing to incur the slightly increased risk along with the boss's wrath.

Safe Haven had been chosen for the research so the team members wouldn't feel like prisoners, but that didn't mean that they would be allowed to leave the compound or receive visitors. The idea was to keep them in a controlled environment, where they could be relatively free and interact with the small group of paranormals, but not with the outside world.

They would still be allowed to make phone calls, but those would be monitored by security, and given the compulsion they would be under, the risk of them blurting out something was minimal.

After the project was done, William would thrall them to forget what they'd been working on, and Emmett and Eleanor would add compulsion on top of that. The same would have to be done to everyone who had interacted with the scientists. Thralling them to forget that they had ever seen or talked to them could be performed by the Guardians assigned to the project, and for safe measure, Eleanor could add compulsion that would prevent them from talking about it.

Besides, the team would work on small sections taken from

different journals, and that would not provide them with the entire picture. William only needed them to decipher enough of the scientific language so he could take it from there.

But before he made any promises, he needed to verify that Kaia and everyone in her family, aside from the little ones, were susceptible to thralling. In his experience those who could be thralled could also be compelled, so his thralling tests should be enough. If any of them were immune to thralling, though, they might still be susceptible to compulsion, but he would have to put them on the phone with either Eleanor or Emmett to test it.

Compulsion was a strange ability, and it varied greatly in strength as well as in the susceptibility of the subject to compulsion by others. Kalugal was a powerful compeller, and so was Emmett, but both of them could be compelled by Annani. Eleanor was a weaker compeller, but she was immune even to the goddess's compulsion. Turner wasn't a compeller, but he was immune to both thralling and compulsion.

"William?" Kaia asked. "Are you still thinking about that flaw in your design?"

"I'm sorry." He smiled apologetically. "As I said, my mind tends to run off in different directions at the most inopportune moments. Did someone ask me a question?"

"I did," Gilbert said. "When can we see the place?"

"First, Kaia needs to agree to join my team. We can condition it on your approval of the accommodations, but I'm not going to lower my security standards just to satisfy your curiosity."

Gilbert nodded. "I understand. What else?"

"I will have to run a security check on everyone who wants to visit."

"We've already been vetted," Kaia's mother said. "I work for a defense software and hardware contractor, and I have a very high security clearance. They also checked Gilbert and the girls, and they all passed." She smiled. "We are a strange bunch, but we have no skeletons in our closets."

"Speak for yourself," Gilbert said. "I have a few fossils in mine that I need to get rid of."

"Yeah, your cutoff shorts need to go," Cheryl murmured. "You look ridiculous in them."

He affected an offended expression. "I only wear them in our backyard. No one can see me."

"I can." Cheryl grimaced. "And that's painful."

Kaia lifted her hand to stop the bickering. "We've kept William here long enough. He has eight more candidates to interview." She rose to her feet and turned to him. "I need to sleep on it, and I'll let you know my decision tomorrow. If you need to run background checks on us, go ahead, but I don't want to meet with security personnel and get interrogated, and I don't want to subject my family to that either. Once was more than enough."

William put his glass of water on the coffee table and got up as well. "There is no need for that. My guy will do some internet snooping, and that should suffice."

Andrew could probably pull the dossier that the government had compiled on the family, and if not, Roni could find out if there were any shadows hanging over Gilbert, who was the only one William considered a suspect, but not too seriously. The guy liked to stir things up, but he seemed harmless enough.

"Do you need to call a taxi?" Kaia asked.

"A colleague is picking me up. I should text him." William pulled out his phone and typed up a text to Max even though the guy had heard everything through the open earpiece in his pocket.

When he was done, he put the phone back in his pocket and smiled at Kaia's family. "It was nice meeting you all, and I hope we will have many more opportunities to meet in the future."

The surprising thing was that he meant it. He liked Karen with her no-nonsense attitude, and Gilbert with his penchant for drama, and he loved Cheryl with her sensible murmured comments.

But most of all, he loved Kaia with her brilliant brain and her lush lips and long legs—

Yeah, he needed to stop that train of thought. She was a kid, and if she joined his team, she would be a subordinate. Nothing could happen between them.

"I'll walk you outside," Kaia offered. "We can wait for your friend together."

He had a feeling that she wanted to talk to him in private, and even though he shouldn't, he was thrilled to be alone with her again.

"Thank you. That would be great."

18

KAIA

It was probably futile to ask William if he knew anything about Anthony, but if Kaia didn't do it now, she would regret it later, especially if she decided to decline his offer, and this was her last opportunity. As long as William still hoped she would accept it, he would be more motivated to help her.

Kaia waited to confess until they were standing outside the gate. "When I invited you to come over, I had no intention of accepting your offer." She gave him an apologetic smile. "I don't know what magic you used to make me consider it."

"My only magic is logic. But if you had no intention of accepting, why bother?"

She took a deep breath. "Because I hoped you would help me find my friend. He's also a bioinformatician, and a year ago, he accepted a similar offer to work on a secret project that was supposed to last a few months. No one has heard from him since. His parents and his sister think that he's dead, and they are obviously distraught, but there is nothing they can do. No one knows who recruited him or where he went. I refuse to accept that he's dead, and I want to find out what happened to him."

William frowned, his amiable expression turning hard. "Do you think that I had something to do with your friend's disappearance?"

She shrugged. "Now that I've met you, I don't think so. You are too nice of a guy to be involved in something shady." It never hurt to throw in a compliment to get in someone's good graces. "But maybe you can speculate about who might have taken him. Most of the big players in the bioinformatics field know each other."

William didn't seem appeased by her compliment, and his frown only deepened. "I come from a different field, so I'm not familiar with other players, but I can look into it."

"Thank you." Hope surged in her heart but then evaporated when she considered that he might be throwing empty promises her way to get her to accept his offer.

"I will need more information about your friend. His full name is a good start, and if you have a picture of him, that will save my people the effort of locating it. I also need to know when he left for the new job, and if you have an exact date and time, that would be helpful. Did he have social media accounts?"

William's very specific questions revived her hope that he at least intended to look into Tony's disappearance. "I can provide a picture, and I can find out what day he left, but his social media accounts would not be helpful. Tony is a geek and socially awkward. He might have browsed social media to look at pictures and videos of hot girls, but he never posted anything."

The creases in William's forehead smoothed out. "If you can talk about Anthony's browsing habits with such indifference, you are either very open-minded and don't have a single jealous bone in your body, or he wasn't your boyfriend."

So that was why William had seemed so bothered. It wasn't because she offended him by her suspicions, but because he had thought she'd manipulated him to help find her boyfriend. It was all true except for the boyfriend part, so if that was the only thing bothering him, he must be interested in her for more than her brain.

As excitement swirled in Kaia's chest, she felt guilty for thinking silly romantic thoughts while Tony was missing and might be dead.

She chuckled sadly. "Tony was my best friend, and at some point, he might have harbored hopes for being more, but I never felt that way about him."

When William looked doubtful, she added, "He's twenty-eight, which is way too old for me."

Kaia realized her mistake as soon as the words had left her mouth. William was thirty-two, and telling him that she didn't want to date Tony because of his age would make him think twice before initiating anything. And the worst part was that age had nothing to do with her not wanting Tony that way.

He smiled. "Thanks for making me feel old."

"I didn't mean it that way, and it wasn't only the age difference." Perhaps she could still save the situation. "I just wasn't attracted to him." She leaned closer to William. "Tony has a handsome face, but he is shorter than me. I know that it shouldn't matter, but it does. I want my boyfriend to be at least my height." Five feet and nine inches wasn't that tall, so it wasn't unreasonable of her to want a guy who was at least that.

Tony was also a bit of a condescending ass, not to her, but to others, and although he was fun to hang around with and smart enough to talk about everything, he wasn't boyfriend material.

Squaring his shoulders, William straightened to his full height, which was a good five to six inches taller than her, and she liked it a lot, but then he slouched back and let out a breath.

"I'll see what I can do. I know an excellent hacker, but he's extremely busy right now. The more information I can give him, the less work he would have to put into finding your friend's trail."

"You would really do that for me?"

"Of course, but I can't promise you that it will be done right away. It might take my hacker friend weeks to get to it."

Kaia wasn't surprised. She'd anticipated that William would use her request as leverage to sway her decision. Unless she joined his team, he wouldn't ask his friend to dig into Tony's disappearance.

She didn't mind.

As long as she had a shred of hope of finding what happened to Anthony and maybe rescuing him, she was willing to do whatever it took.

"I'll be forever grateful to you if you find Anthony for me." She wound her arms around William's neck and planted a quick kiss on his lips.

He didn't return the kiss, he didn't put his arms around her, he didn't even breathe.

The poor guy was stunned.

"It's okay." She laughed. "Gilbert is not going to kill you for kissing me."

"I didn't kiss you." He found his voice. "You kissed me."

"It was a small token of my appreciation." She lifted on her toes and kissed him again. "Goodnight, William, and thank you again."

19

WILLIAM

As Kaia rushed back into the house, William remained rooted in place, a stupid smile stretching his face.

She'd kissed him. On the lips.

Was it just gratitude?

Or was there more to it?

Was she attracted to him?

Had she felt the connection the way he had?

He hadn't sniffed arousal, but maybe she hadn't felt it until he'd promised to help her find her friend.

"Are you just going to stand there?" Max said through the open window.

William hadn't even noticed the car pull up to the curb. "Sorry." He opened the passenger door and got in.

"Judging by the smile on your face, I assume it was a success." Max pulled out into the street. "Keeping the earpiece in the pocket was a bad idea. I heard only every other word."

He suspected that Max had heard everything just fine. It was no coincidence that he'd pulled up to the curb a moment after Kaia had kissed him and had gone back into the house.

"Sorry about that. I don't know why the fabric of my pocket would cause interference."

"Maybe it was your phone?"

"That's possible. I should have put it in my other pocket." Usually, he wouldn't have overlooked a detail like that, but he'd been distracted by Kaia and his attraction to her.

"I heard that she was going to sleep on it, which is better than an outright no, but what's your sense? Was it just a brush-off, or is she considering it seriously?"

"I think she is serious."

He still wasn't sure how things had turned out the way they had, and what had been the turning point. Was it his promise to help find her friend?

"That's great news." Max cast him a sidelong smile. "I found a nice club where we can celebrate your success."

The last thing William wanted was to go hunting for a hookup. He was still reeling from the meeting, and what he needed was a stiff drink.

"I'd rather go to a bar if you don't mind. I'm not in the mood for female company."

Max frowned. "What's wrong?"

Like most immortal males, the Guardian was always in the mood, so he couldn't understand how and why William wasn't.

"Nothing is wrong. I need a drink to calm down after the meeting, and I need to figure out how to adjust our safety procedures to accommodate Kaia. She wants to go home at least every other weekend, and she wants her family to be able to visit her."

"I heard that part."

"Her mother and stepfather also want to see Safe Haven before giving their approval."

The Guardian shook his head. "That's too risky."

"Not necessarily. I can mitigate most of the risks. Her mother works for a defense contractor and has a high-security clearance. Her partner and older daughters have gone through briefings as well. Kaia is susceptible to thralling, but before allowing her family to visit, I still need to check whether they are susceptible as well."

The truth was that William wasn't sure about Kaia's susceptibility. He'd been able to peek into her mind, which suggested that she was, but he still needed to make sure that he could erase her memories and plant fake ones.

He also needed to find out why she thought of herself as a middle-aged man. He wasn't a psychologist, but it could be a coping mechanism, a way for a very young woman to deal with the world of academia where her peers were much older than her.

Or maybe it had to do with her missing friend?

He shifted to face Max. "Did you hear what Kaia told me about her missing friend?"

"I heard some of it, but first, tell me where you want me to take you. Are we going back to the hotel? Or am I looking for a pub?"

"The hotel has a bar. We can get a drink there, and if you find someone to hook up with, I won't have to call a taxi to take me back."

"True." Max let out a breath. "The hotel bar doesn't offer much of a selection, but it will do."

William chuckled. "I guess you are not referring to their selection of whiskeys."

"That too. So what do you think happened to Kaia's friend?"

"It's a long shot, but he could have been taken to the island. The guy has a PhD, and he's young and good-looking. He fits the profile of Navuh's currently preferred studs."

Max looked doubtful. "The Doomers are not the only bad guys out there, and if bioinformaticians are in such high demand, he could have been taken by the Chinese, the Russians, or one of the smaller players. It's not uncommon for scientists to be abducted and forced to work on secret projects, especially those that have to do with weapon development. It's also not uncommon for the kidnappers to get rid of them once the project is done."

"Then I hope he was taken to the island. Serving as a breeding stud might be humiliating, but it's better than being dead."

20

KAIA

As Kaia returned to the house, she could barely contain the excitement swirling in her belly. Schooling her features required a major effort, but she couldn't let her mother and Gilbert see her smiling like some silly girl with a crush on an older guy.

What had possessed her to kiss William?

Not that she regretted doing it, but usually she wasn't that impulsive. It was the gratitude, and Kaia was going to stick to that version even under torture. She would never admit that she'd been staring at William's lips throughout the interview and imagining how they would feel against hers.

They'd felt amazing, but William hadn't risen to the occasion. Well, one part of him had, but the rest had remained frozen. She'd hoped he would wrap his arms around her and take over the kiss, but he'd been either too stunned or afraid to touch her.

It definitely was the strangest interview she'd ever had. William hadn't asked her any questions about her qualifications, and he hadn't tested her knowledge. He'd just assumed that she was exactly the person he needed for his project. In fact, they had switched roles, with her being the interviewer and him being the interviewee.

Had he passed the examination?

Given Gilbert's frown, William hadn't passed his nose test, but given her mother's knowing smile, he'd passed hers. Cheryl was busy on her phone, no doubt checking her Instatock channel to see how many likes and shares she'd gotten in the past hour.

The girl was obsessed with social approval, and that wasn't healthy.

Kaia sat next to Gilbert and draped her arm over his shoulders. "So, what does your nose tell you? Is William a crook?"

Gilbert shook his head. "He seems like a good guy, but he has too many secrets, and he feels guilty about keeping them from us, which worries me. He might be an awesome fellow, but his business partners might be crooks."

"How does that work? Why would a straight shooter involve himself with bad guys?"

Smiling indulgently, Gilbert patted her knee. "People who find themselves in tight corners, or get pushed into them, sometimes have no choice but to compromise on their moral standing."

"True." She leaned against his side. "So, what should I do?"

"Do you want to go?" her mother asked.

"I do, and I don't. I've never left home, I've never lived in dorms, and I missed the whole college experience because I was the genius freak who started college at fourteen. The project will only take a few months, so it's not like I'll be away for all that long, and it might be fun."

Cheryl lifted her head from her phone and smirked. "Admit it. You want to go because you like William."

There was no point in denying that because it was the truth, just not in its entirety. She didn't want to tell them about William's promise to help find Tony. If they thought that was the reason she was considering going, they would never allow it.

Kaia was an adult, and she didn't need their permission, but that's not how their family worked. Her mother had asked Kaia and Cheryl's permission before she'd started dating Gilbert, even though they'd just been little girls and still missed their father. If they had said no, she wouldn't have gone out with him and would have missed out on the best second chance ever.

"Of course, I like William. He's smart, polite, and handsome. I don't have to dumb myself down to talk to him."

"He's too old for you," Cheryl said.

"A thirteen-year difference is not that bad." Kaia took her arm off Gilbert's shoulders and got up. "Especially for someone like me who has nothing to talk about with people her age."

Her mother winced. "That's why I wanted you to join that high IQ club, but you refused to go after attending the introductory meeting."

Kaia rolled her eyes. "What a bunch of freaks, myself included. One or two freaks in a room make things interesting, but a room full of freaks is just depressing." She sat next to her sister. "Am I right?"

"If you say so." Cheryl went back to scrolling through her Instatock account.

Her sister wasn't much of a talker, and engaging her in a conversation was like pulling teeth.

"A thirteen-year difference is huge," Gilbert said. "He's definitely too old for you."

She had to kill that subject before her family started obsessing about her wanting to date an older man. "I was just teasing. Even if I was interested, William is not because he thinks of me as a kid."

"Right." Cheryl snorted. "That's why he couldn't take his eyes off you."

"As if you would know. You were babysitting Idina." Kaia sighed. "Let's move on and focus on what's relevant. Let's say that we go there and it's just as beautiful and luxurious as William claims, and I accept the offer. I can't stand not seeing the little ones for more than a few days, and I will only be able to fly home every other weekend. We need to figure out how we can make it work. I will need you to come to visit me and bring Cheryl, Idina, and the twins with you."

"Did you hear that?" Gilbert looked at her mom. "She only cares about the babies. You and I are chopped liver."

"You're not chopped liver." Kaia laughed. "I want to see you too, but you are not going to change in two weeks or two months. Unlike you, Idina, Evan, and Ryan change from day to day, and I don't want to miss any of it. Besides, babies have short memories, and they might forget me."

"They are not going to forget you," her mother said. "Not even if you don't come home every other week." She looked at Gilbert. "But I don't think we would be able to visit you more than once or twice throughout the duration of the project. It's difficult to travel with the twins. Just the amount of stuff we need to take with us is staggering."

"What about Eric? He can fly you back and forth with all the things for the twins."

"My brother charters his planes to earn a living," Gilbert said. "He's not our private pilot."

"What if you pay him?" Cheryl asked. "Then we will be just like his other clients."

"He's not going to take money from us."

"Can you at least ask?" Kaia cast him a pleading look that was sure to break through his resistance.

"Don't look at me with those puppy eyes," he grumbled. "Fine. I'll talk to Eric."

"Thank you." She pushed to her feet and walked over to him. "You're the best." She leaned and kissed his cheek.

Gilbert grinned. "I know."

21

WILLIAM

It was after two o'clock in the afternoon when William was done with his last interview, and he hadn't heard from Kaia yet.

Should he call her?

Text her?

"Are there any more candidates on your list?" Max asked after dropping the silencing shroud he'd maintained throughout the interviews.

It had been the Guardian's idea to hold the interviews in a Starbucks but keep them private without the interviewees realizing that. Meeting in a public place made it feel less cloak-and-dagger and put the candidates at ease. After all, the project couldn't be about developing something nefarious if they were discussing it in a Starbucks.

"Corinne was the last." William leaned back in his chair. "Now, I'm ready for coffee."

"Me too." Max got to his feet and walked over to stand in line.

Sitting in a coffee shop all morning and sipping on water had been its own kind of torture, but William had heeded Darlene's advice to avoid caffeine during the interviews.

Even without stimulants, he talked too fast and had to remind himself to slow down, and Darlene had noticed that after drinking coffee, he got worse. William hadn't had any yesterday before the meeting with Kaia either, and he'd done well keeping his talking speed in check.

As his mind drifted back to her, he realized that he hadn't asked her even the most basic questions. He hadn't tested her knowledge because he wasn't qualified to do that, and after reading her published articles, he knew that she was exceptional. But he hadn't asked her any personal questions either, like whether she preferred coffee or tea, or whether caffeine made her jittery. He'd gotten to know her family, though, and how important they were to her. Her decision would largely depend on their approval and their willingness to come to visit her, and that would also depend on Kian and whether he would approve of the visits.

William hadn't called the boss yet, and if he didn't hear from Kaia, the only thing he would have to report was that he'd assembled a team of mediocre bioinformaticians who had no chance in hell of deciphering the journals.

Max returned with two grande cappuccinos and a stack of sandwiches and pastries. "That should do it for now." He handed William a paper cup.

"We could have gone to a proper restaurant for lunch." William took the lid off his cup.

"I'm too hungry to wait." Max pulled out one of the sandwiches and unwrapped it. "It would have taken at least an hour until we found a place to eat, sat down, ordered, and food was served. I wouldn't have lasted that long." He dug into his sandwich with gusto.

A couple of months ago, William would have attacked the food with the same fervor, but he'd taught himself to slow down and enjoy what he ate instead of gobbling it down.

When Max was done with his first sandwich, he wiped his mouth with a napkin and unwrapped the second one. "Any of them any good?"

"The sandwiches?"

"No, the candidates. Who did you decide to hire?"

William put his sandwich down. "Doctor Corinne Burke is an experienced bioinformatician, and she is eager to take the job. She's recently divorced, needs the money, and even more than that, she needs a break. She's taking a sabbatical, so it's not an issue for her to be gone for a few months. Owen Ferrel has just gotten his Master's, so he's a total greenhorn, but he's decent, and with proper guidance, he could function as an assistant. The same goes for Kylie Baldwin."

"So, you got two PhDs to do the deciphering work, one who is experienced and one who is not, and two donkeys to assist them with the tedious parts."

William chuckled. "More or less. I didn't hear from Kaia yet, and without her, I don't have a team. Corinne can lead the effort and organize the research, but she doesn't have Kaia's innate talent."

Glancing at the people sitting around them, Max leaned forward. "Then thrall her," he whispered. "Too much is at stake to leave it to the whims of a nineteen-year-old."

William smiled. "Shame on you, Max. You're supposed to uphold the law, not conspire to break it."

The Guardian shrugged. "The law is open to interpretation. You might claim that the research is vital to the clan's future, and therefore thralling a human to get it done is justified. Edna is not going to argue with you over that."

"I know." William let out a breath. "I'm just not comfortable with it."

"Do you want me to do it?"

He didn't want the Guardian anywhere near Kaia's brilliant mind, and not just because there was a second personality living inside of it. Her mind was like a fine-tuned instrument, and the slightest interference could be detrimental. In her case, compulsion would have to suffice, and if Kian had a problem with that, William would suggest dual compulsion by Emmett and Eleanor to make it iron clad.

Compulsion might be more intrusive than a thrall, but it caused no damage to the brain.

"I'll convince her to join my team the mundane way." He smiled. "With a bribe. She wants me to find her friend, and I'm going to use that as leverage. It's not honorable either, and I should help her regardless of her joining my team, but it's not as bad as thralling her to sign the contract."

Max shrugged. "Whatever works." He took a big bite of his second sandwich and washed it down with a gulp of cappuccino.

Sipping on his own coffee, William let his thoughts drift back to the strange duality inside Kaia's mind. She didn't behave or speak like an old man. She was mature for her age, but that was because she was smart. Sometimes, however, she acted her age, like when she'd suddenly kissed him on the lips.

Damn, that kiss still played havoc on his mind, not to mention other parts of his body that were not as astute.

He had to find out what the deal with the middle-aged guy was. Was it a memory? A play-pretend? A spirit like the one who used to live in Nathalie's head?

How could he find out more about it without invading Kaia's mind again? The less he messed with that precious brain of hers, the better.

Perhaps he could call Syssi and ask her advice. She would easily come up with a diplomatic way to pose the question to Kaia, but she was so busy these days, and he didn't want to bother her. Besides, everything he told her would go straight to Kian, and William hadn't figured out a strategy for dealing with the boss yet.

22

MIA

"I'm in love." Mia's grandmother kissed Okidu on the cheek. "If I ever leave my husband, it would be for you."

The butler grinned. "I am honored, mistress."

Kian had loaned them the cyborg to help with packing and loading their belongings into the clan's bus. It had made the entire process physically effortless, but it was still difficult emotionally.

Last night, Mia had cried when she said goodbye to Margo and Frankie, and they had shed a few tears as well, and then the three of them had laughed about how ridiculous they were being. They were going to see each other on the weekends and talk on the phone as many times a day as they wished. It was also only a temporary arrangement until Margo and Frankie could join her in the village, but that wasn't a sure thing yet.

Hopefully, the new developmental division of Perfect Match would be set up sooner rather than later, so her friends could quit their jobs, move into the village, and start working for Toven.

Margo and Frankie were ecstatic about dropping their dead-end jobs and becoming testers for Perfect Match adventures, and after she'd explained that the other partners were paranoid about leaks, they were even okay with moving into a secret compound. But she hadn't told them the rest of the fantastic story yet. That would have to wait for when it was time for them to move, and that was also when they would have the option to decline.

Although knowing those two as well as she did, they would be all for it. Neither had health problems, so transitioning would be a breeze for them, but there were downsides. Their families couldn't visit them in the village, and they would have to lie to them, which would be a big problem for Frankie, and to a lesser extent for Margo. It was also possible that they weren't Dormants after all, and if they didn't transition, the entire house of cards would come crashing down. They would have to leave the village after their memories of it were erased, and they would have to go back to their boring jobs. The clan could help them find better employment, but knowing that they were not guaranteed a happy ending might be a deterrent.

"Stop flirting with the cyborg, Rosy," her grandfather grumbled as he helped his wife climb the steep steps of the bus.

"Why? It's not like I mean it, dear. It's just a bit of fun, and unlike a man, Okidu is not going to take it seriously."

"Shh," he admonished. "We are in the middle of the street. Someone might hear you."

She waved a dismissive hand. "There is no one out here, and even if there was, they would just think that the old lady has dementia and is talking nonsense."

"God forbid." Her grandfather huffed out a breath.

Once her grandparents were seated in the bus, Toven lifted Mia off the wheelchair, carried her into the bus, and put her down. "Do you want me to bring the chair?"

"I have a new one waiting for me in the village. We can leave it here and have one less thing to schlep back and forth."

"True." He wheeled the chair back to the house.

"It's not going to be easy switching homes every week," her grandmother said. "But I have to admit that it's exciting. We will get to meet new people and go on virtual adventures."

Her grandfather groaned. "You can go if you want, but I'm not about to let these immortals strap me into a chair and attach electrodes to my head."

"You will." Her grandmother patted his knee. "Stop being such an old man."

After Toven had locked the house up and joined them in the bus, Okidu pulled into the street, and they were on their way.

"When are our cars arriving?" Mia asked.

Toven took her hand. "Last I checked, they were working on the modifications, so it should be done soon, but the shipping will take a couple of weeks."

Mia sighed. "I wish the delivery coincided with our move, but things seldom work out that seamlessly." When he frowned, she lifted her other hand. "I'm not complaining. I'm so full of gratitude that I could burst."

But that didn't mean that everything was perfect.

Orion, Alena, and Annani were not in the village, and it would be several more weeks until they returned from their trip. That meant that the reconciliation between father and son would have to wait, and so would Toven's reminiscing with Annani about the good old days of the gods.

He needed that to process the grief he'd bottled up for five thousand years, and once he finally let it all out, he might get his glow back and shine like the god he was.

"The good news is that your grandparents' cars are ready," Toven said.

"Awesome." She gave him a smile. "They would have hated being chauffeured everywhere."

Toven leaned to whisper in her ear, "I don't think your grandmother would have minded if the chauffeur was Okidu."

"She was just teasing." Mia leaned her head on Toven's arm. "I want that car to be here already."

It was her ticket to freedom. She couldn't bring her own modified car to the village because it didn't have the special windows that turned opaque or the self-driving capabilities. Toven could have gotten a car from Kian, but he wasn't happy with how basic the model was, so he'd ordered two SUVs for them, both with special modifications for her motorized wheelchair. Toven's SUV had a passenger side lift and no seat on that side, and hers had the same arrangement on the driver side, in addition to all the other modifications that made it possible for her to drive using only her hands. Once the vehicles arrived, she would no longer need to be carried around like a sack of potatoes and would get her independence back.

Mia couldn't wait.

Toven shifted in his seat to look at her grandparents. "I hope you remember that we are invited to dinner at Kalugal's tonight."

Her grandfather winced. "Can we be excused? People our age shouldn't eat that late. The heartburn will keep me awake all night, and I will be good for nothing tomorrow."

"You can eat a snack before," Mia suggested. "And not eat much at dinner."

"You know me." He sighed. "I'm on the see food diet. When I see it, I eat it. I have no self-control."

"I can help with that," Toven offered. "Do you want me to compel you not to touch anything during dinner?"

"And miss out on all the great food Kalugal's cook is making? No way. Besides, I don't want you taking over my will. It's enough that I can't say the word immortal in the company of other humans. My mouth just refuses to obey me, and that's disturbing."

Mia cast a sidelong glance at Toven, communicating with him wordlessly. How was he going to give her grandparents his blood without thralling them? To do so after her grandfather had explicitly said that he didn't want Toven in his head was just wrong.

She would have to come up with a story and lie to them about the benefits of Toven's thralls to get them to agree. But then if they told any of the other immortals about it, her lies would be exposed.

It was a conundrum, and at the moment, the solution eluded her.

Could the Fates give her a hint?

They had been so generous with what they'd bestowed on her so far that asking for more seemed like pushing her luck, but she needed help, and unless Toven came up with something clever, she would have to go against her grandfather's explicit wishes.

23

WILLIAM

It was after three o'clock in the afternoon, and Kaia hadn't called yet.

With a sigh, William sat down on his hotel bed and looked at his phone, willing it to ring. He also wanted to speak with Darlene before she went home for the day, but he didn't want to miss a call from Kaia.

It was odd that no one was calling him from the lab. He'd left Marcel in charge, expecting the guy to call him every five minutes with questions, but his phone had remained silent throughout the two days he'd been gone, and wasn't that sad.

He'd even checked to make sure that there was nothing wrong with the device, but everything worked like it was supposed to. He wasn't getting calls because no one missed him, and Marcel was doing just fine without him.

Evidently, he wasn't as irreplaceable as Kian had thought he was.

Maybe he should use Max's phone to call Darlene. That way his line wouldn't be busy when Kaia called.

The Guardian was in the adjacent room, watching a game on the television and cheering on his favorite human team, whatever the sport or the name of the team was.

William couldn't care less. Sports had never interested him, not as a participant and not as a spectator.

After long minutes passed and his phone remained silent, he let out a breath and called Darlene.

She answered right away. "How is it going, boss?"

"Good." He smiled, happy to hear her sounding so cheerful. "I have most of my team members lined up."

"You don't sound enthusiastic. What's the catch?"

She'd gotten to know him pretty well since her arrival at the village. More so since she'd started working at the lab.

"My best candidate, Doctor Kaia Locke, still hasn't given me her final answer, and that's why I'm calling you. I need your advice."

"Get her chocolates. That always works for me."

He chuckled. "I'm not asking her on a date."

"You're not?" She sounded genuinely surprised. "Why?"

"Why would I? She's nineteen, and I'm trying to recruit her. Can you think of a more inappropriate move than to ask her to go out on a date with me?"

"Yeah." She sighed. "You're probably right. Do you like her?"

William nodded. "I do."

"I mean as a woman, not just a brain."

"She's nineteen, Darlene."

"So what?"

He shook his head. "Just drop it. She's too young for me, and I'm about to become her employer."

"I thought that was what you needed advice on."

"It's not. I took a peek into Kaia's mind, and I saw something very strange. When she thinks of herself, she switches between thinking of herself as Kaia, a young woman, and a middle-aged man. I don't want to intrude on her thoughts, I don't want to thrall her unless it's absolutely necessary, and I don't know how to ask her about it without creeping her out."

"Don't ask her anything before she signs the contract, that's for sure. After she spends time with you at Safe Haven and gets to know you, you can tell her that she gives out a vibe of a much older person, and that it's slightly masculine. By then, she might trust you enough to tell you the truth, or she might tell you to mind your own business."

"What do you think it could be?"

"No clue, William. You should ask Vanessa."

"Right." He pushed his glasses up his nose. "As if she has time for that. You are the only one I can talk to about Kaia," he admitted. "I just hoped that as a woman you would have a clue about what's going on in her head. Does she have a split personality? Is it her way to cope with a chaotic world?

"I wish I could help you, but I can't."

It had been worth a try, and he hadn't really expected Darlene to have answers for him. "How are things going at the lab?"

She sighed. "It's boring here without you. Roni never talks while he works, and Marcel is kind of dull. I miss you telling me about this or that idea or how you're going to improve this or that gadget."

"I thought you were bored by my stories."

"Never. I just lost you when you talked at the speed of a machine gun. Are you following my advice and slowing down when you talk to the recruits, and especially Doctor Kaia?"

"I do when I remember."

"I should have come with you, and I should come to Safe Haven with you as well. You need someone to keep you organized. I don't want to even imagine what a mess you're going to make in that brand new office. Besides, you need someone to train with you, or you won't do it and you'll gain back all the weight you lost."

The more Darlene talked, the more he liked the idea of her coming to Safe Haven with him. He'd become so much more productive since she'd started working at the lab. He no longer misplaced things and had to waste time looking for them, because she knew where everything was, and he no longer forgot to order parts and then had to wait for them because she made sure he was on top of that.

"I like your idea."

"Which one?"

"Of you joining me at Safe Haven. I could use an administrator."

"Yay!" Darlene shrieked in his ear. "I can get out of here."

He chuckled. "You weren't a prisoner."

"I know. I like the safety of the clan, but going to Safe Haven is like branching out without actually leaving. I'll get to meet the paranormal talents, and maybe I'll find my one and only among them. But even if I don't, we are going to have fun out there."

"Sure thing. It was nice chatting with you."

"Same here. Good luck with your lady."

"Thanks." William ended the call, glanced at the time, and put the phone down on the bed.

He'd spent twenty minutes talking to Darlene, and no call had come in during that time. If Kaia didn't call soon, he needed to accept that her answer was a no and decide what his next move should be.

When his phone rang, he snatched it off the mattress, and his heart skipped a bit when he saw Kaia's name displayed on the screen.

"Hello," he said in the most nonchalant tone he could muster.

"Hi. I'm sorry for not calling earlier, but I was waiting for my uncle to get back to me and tell me when he could get here. Does eight in the evening work for you? By then the babies are going to be asleep for sure."

"It's perfect. Am I going to get grilled by another member of your family?"

"Yeah, sorry about that. Eric is Gilbert's brother, and he has two private planes that he charters. When Gilbert called him to ask if he'd be willing to fly us to Oregon, and Eric heard about you, he insisted on meeting you in person."

"I see. Are you waiting for him to form his opinion, or did you make up your mind?"

"Oh, I made up my mind yesterday after you promised me to look for Tony. Now I just need to convince my family that this is a good move for me, so do your best to impress Eric."

William let out a silent breath. "You don't know how relieved I am that your answer is a yes. Anything I should know about your uncle?"

"He's a younger, cockier version of Gilbert, but he's a great guy. You're going to like him."

"I don't know if I can handle an enhanced version of Gilbert. The original was tough enough."

Kaia laughed. "You'll do fine. Gilbert says that you're a good guy, and he has an infallible nose for people's characters. And if Gilbert thinks that you are okay, Eric is not going to give you a hard time."

24

DARLENE

After doing a victory dance in her tiny office in the lab, Darlene dropped into her rolling chair, lifted her legs up, and put them on the desk.

She could finally move out of Geraldine and Shai's house without her mother bursting into tears at the mere mention of her wanting a place of her own.

Maybe if she started calling her Mother, Geraldine would stop trying so hard to make up for all the years she'd missed from her life. After all, it hadn't been her fault, but it just felt weird to address a woman who looked young enough to be her daughter as Mother.

If she did that just to appease Geraldine, it would sound as fake as she imagined it would feel.

It was too early to call it a day, but since everyone in the lab made concessions for the fragile human, no one would bat an eyelid if she went home even earlier than usual. The others worked fourteen- and sixteen-hour days, and in the beginning, she had tried to keep up with their stamina and prove that she was just as strong despite being human, but it had taken only a few days for her to realize that she couldn't keep up.

Maybe if she were in her twenties she could, but at nearly fifty it was too taxing, especially since she also trained at the gym every day.

It was time to find an immortal male to induce her, so she could turn immortal and forget all about feeling dizzy after a run on the treadmill or needing a Motrin after lifting weights. Saying goodbye to wrinkles and saggy skin would be even nicer.

So what if she hadn't found the perfect guy yet? Any male that she could see herself getting naked with would do, and there were plenty of handsome bachelors in the village who didn't mind that she looked old enough to be their mother.

The problem was that she minded.

Maybe it was vanity, but she was a woman, and she wanted to look better than the guy she was having sex with. Or maybe it was just an excuse, and she was still not over her divorce even though it had been finalized.

Ugh. If only there was a store that sold courage. She would have spent her entire salary on that.

Pushing away from her desk, Darlene got up and walked out into the main lab.

"I'm going home." She stopped by Roni's chair and kissed the top of his head.

He frowned. "Are you feeling sick?"

"I'm feeling great." She grinned. "I'm going to celebrate. William invited me to come with him to Safe Haven to help keep everything organized."

Her son smiled. "That's awesome, but I hope that you will come to visit often. You've only just gotten here, and I enjoy having you around."

"Oh, sweetie." She leaned and kissed his cheek. "You don't know how much it means to me to hear you say that." She straightened up. "Maybe I shouldn't do it."

"Go." He waved a hand. "You need a change of pace after the divorce. Treat it as a vacation and take some of the classes they offer in the retreat. Most of it is New-Age nonsense, but it can be relaxing and reaffirming."

"That's not a bad idea. I'll do that, if I have any free time left, that is. Keeping William organized is a full-time job."

"Tell me about it." He reached for her hand. "Have fun, Mom. You deserve it."

"Thank you."

As she made her way back to the house, Darlene reflected on what Roni had told her and how good it had made her feel. She hadn't been the best of mothers, and yet he'd forgiven her, called her Mom, and told her that he loved her and liked spending time with her. Those were the kinds of goodies that all mothers lived for.

She shouldn't withhold that from Geraldine.

So what if it was awkward the first few times she called her Mom? She would get used to it, and it would mean the world to her mother.

Walking into the house, she knew that she would find Geraldine in the kitchen preparing dinner like she did every day.

"Hello, sweetheart. You're home early today. Is everything okay?"

"Hi, Mom." Darlene kissed her on the cheek. "Everything is perfect. What's for dinner?"

The spatula dropped from Geraldine's hand, and she stared at her as if she was an apparition. "You called me Mom."

"Does it bother you?"

"Bother me?" Tears started flowing down Geraldine's cheeks. "No, it doesn't bother me." She threw her arms around Darlene and squeezed hard. "I love you so much, and it means the world to me that you found it in your heart to call me Mother again. I'm so happy."

Great, now she didn't want to spoil Geraldine's mood by telling her that she was going with William to Safe Haven, but it was better to get it over with.

"I have great news, Mom." She unfolded herself from Geraldine's arms. "William invited me to join him at Safe Haven for the duration of the project. Both of us will probably come back for a visit every other weekend, so you are not going to miss me too badly."

Geraldine's chin quivered, but she smiled through the tears. "Does it mean that you two are getting together after all?"

"No, Mom." It was already easier to say that word. "We are just friends, but maybe one of the handsome Guardians Onegus assigned to the project will catch my eye."

25

ELEANOR

*E*leanor leaned back in her chair and looked out the window of her home office at the surf down below. Kian had chosen a great location for the paranormal division. The elevated plot meant that every bungalow had at least a partial ocean view, but hers was near the top of the hill, and had the best view of them all.

Emmett had wanted them to live in his cottage, or rather down in its luxurious underground quarters, but she didn't want the shadows of his past hanging over their relationship. He'd had orgies in those rooms, and even if she got new mattresses and new bedding, she wouldn't be able to get past the sleazy images lingering in those walls.

Poor Mey had no doubt encountered worse when she listened to the echoes embedded in walls. People were far less nice in private, and the stories the walls told her were probably mostly nasty.

What a dubious talent that was.

Eleanor, on the other hand, had been blessed with the best talent an immortal could have. Compulsion was a rare and incredibly useful ability. The only problem with it was the need to exercise restraint and not abuse it, and sometimes the line between necessary and abusive was blurry.

Before getting caught by the clan, Eleanor had used her talent often and not always out of necessity or for the greater good.

Hell, she'd abused her power, and the worst of it had been compelling a man she'd been in love with to act as if he loved her back, when he could barely stand her.

But that was in the past, and she was a different person now.

She had a man who loved her with the same intensity she loved him, and she had been put in charge of an important program, not by compelling her way through the ranks but by earning Kian's trust and respect.

Gazing out the window, Eleanor surveyed her little empire.

She could see all the other bungalows that comprised the paranormal enclave of Safe Haven, which was one more reason to work from her home office rather than the one in the main building, which also housed the program's two classrooms and another tiny office for its instructors. She used it only when she needed to confer with them or the damn doctor, who was a pain in her rear.

Thankfully, his clinic was in a separate bungalow.

She had the guy under such strong compulsion that he couldn't fart without her permission, but he was unpleasant to put it politely, and a sleaze bucket in a more colorful language.

Eleanor couldn't wait to get rid of him, but she still had a long way to go until that objective could be achieved.

First they needed to figure out who, if any, of the paranormals were Dormants, and that was a problem. Aside from Andy, who was still a kid, the rest had formed relationships with others in their group, so introducing them to immortals was not an option unless those relationships fell apart.

Lisa might be able to sniff out the Dormants among them, but Kian didn't trust her ability enough to rely on it exclusively.

When Eleanor had still been the program's recruiter, Mollie and James had already been an item, Jeremy had his eye on Naomi, and Abigail had been regularly hooking up with Dylan, but they hadn't been officially a couple. After she'd left, Spencer and Sofia had gotten together, Jeremy and Naomi had solidified their relationship, and so had Dylan and Abigail.

Compelling them to fall out of love was as impossible as

compelling them to fall in love in the first place, but she could compel them to do things that would sabotage their relationships.

Not that she was going to do that if there was any other way. Even if Kian would have approved, Eleanor wasn't callous enough to tear those couples apart.

The males could be tested without breaking up their relationship with their partners, but if they transitioned and their partners didn't, that would also be a problem.

Eleanor could see no easy solution for any of that.

The easier part of her job was dismantling the program. When the doctor continued to report insignificant findings, and the talents kept producing dismal results, the government would eventually lose interest and their contracts wouldn't get renewed. But that meant waiting until the current ones expired, which wasn't anytime soon.

Those who turned out to be Dormants could disappear to the village the same way Jin and her group had done, but those who didn't, would stay, and she would have to stay with them to keep up the charade.

It wasn't a hardship.

Eleanor loved her position of authority in Safe Haven, and not just because of the independence it afforded her and the prestige. Applications for the new paranormal retreats were exceeding expectations, and if even one potential Dormant was found in each group of guests, it would be a tremendous achievement.

Eleanor felt honored and privileged to be in charge of a program that could potentially breathe new life into the clan.

26

KAIA

"Eric." Kaia rushed over to her uncle and wound her arms around his neck. "Thanks for coming." She kissed him on both cheeks. "Ugh, you're prickly."

Laughing, he put his hands on her waist. "I came as soon as I could, and I didn't have time to shave for you. I need to check out that guy before I let him lure you to his lair."

"William is harmless." Kaia let go of him. "Even Gilbert says that, and he doesn't trust anyone."

"Yeah, I know all about his infallible nose." Eric bent to whisper in her ears. "His ability to sniff out crooks is just as inflated as the rest of his ego."

Kaia slapped his back playfully. "Look who's talking. You two can compete for the award of who has the bigger one." Her cheeks heated as she realized how that had sounded, but to clarify would make it even worse.

"I'd win." Eric winked. "Where are the little monsters?"

"Asleep, I hope. Mom and Gilbert are upstairs with them, and I don't hear crying. Can I get you something to drink?"

"I'm hungry." Eric beelined for the kitchen. "Are there any leftovers from dinner?"

"Always." Kaia opened the fridge and pulled out a glass container. "Berta doesn't know how to cook small portions."

"Why should she?" Eric took the container from her, grabbed a fork from the drawer, and walked over to the kitchen table. "You are a big family." He opened the container and dug in.

"Don't eat it cold. Let me warm it up for you."

"No need. It's good as it is."

"Bachelors." She pulled out a chair and sat next to him. "When are you going to find a girl and settle down?"

"Never." He collected another forkful. "I learned my lesson the first time around."

"Gilbert went through a nasty divorce as well and look how happy he is now."

"He got lucky. I'm very happy to remain a bachelor, thank you very much."

It was better to drop the subject before he got upset. Anytime anyone mentioned his ex-wife, Eric's good mood evaporated. Kaia didn't know the details of what had gone wrong in their marriage, but from what she'd heard, the woman was nuts. When she'd gotten mad at Eric, she slashed all the tires on his car and threw his big screen television outside. How she'd even managed to lift it was a mystery.

"Tell me about this job," Eric said. "It must be spectacular for you to give up Stanford for it."

"I'm not giving it up. The project should end before I need to start at Stanford. That position will only become available in October when the professor leading the research retires."

"Why didn't he retire at the end of the year?"

Kaia shrugged. "I don't know. I'm very lucky that he will, though. It doesn't happen often. I know the postdoc who's going to replace him, which is why I'm getting the job despite my lack of experience. I will take over the postdoc's position when he's appointed to head of the lab."

Eric dropped the fork inside the empty container, "Are you excited about working at the university?"

"Yeah, I am."

"You don't sound excited."

She shrugged. "I was very excited until William told me about his project. I can't wait to learn more details about it."

"Are you allowed to tell me what it is?"

"I'm not sure myself. It's about deciphering another scientist's work, which he'd written in code. William thinks once we crack it, we will find information that will revolutionize medicine, but that's all he's willing to tell me before I sign the nondisclosure agreement."

"Sounds mysterious." Eric leaned back in his chair and rubbed his flat stomach. "Gilbert tells me that the lab is somewhere on the Oregon Coast. Do you know where on the coast it is?"

Kaia shook her head. "How many private airports are there in that area?"

"Several. I need to know which one is the closest."

"So, you're going to fly us there?"

"Of course. I want to check the place out myself."

Kaia worried her lower lip. "I don't want you losing business because of us. We can fly commercial."

"With the little monsters? I don't think so. Besides, family comes first. Right?"

"Always."

Gilbert and Eric's parents were gone, and neither of them had children with their exes. The only family they had was a sister who lived in Ohio and was also divorced and didn't keep in touch, so when Gilbert had started dating her mother, both brothers had adopted them as their own.

They'd started as family by choice, and after Idina and then the twins had been born, they had also become a family by blood.

27

WILLIAM

By the time Gilbert and his brother had finished grilling William, his shirt was sticking to his back, and he was craving a stiff glass of whiskey. Those two could work for Turner.

Luckily, he'd prepared well for the meeting. Max had thrown questions at him at a rapid rate, and he'd come up with the answers on the spot.

With how fast William's brain worked neither Max nor the brothers had a chance to trip him up, but it had been an intense experience, especially since he'd been distracted by how good Kaia looked today.

Instead of the librarian's blouse she'd worn yesterday, she had a simple T-shirt on, and the light pink fabric and low neckline did little to hide the sumptuous curves underneath.

"I'm sorry for the third degree," Eric said. "But we had to make sure that Kaia was in good hands. I intend to visit frequently to ensure that she's doing okay. I don't need to know what you're working on, but I need to know that she's well."

That would be a problem, but William would cross that bridge when the time came. Right now, he needed to close the deal. "You don't need to apologize. I'm glad that Kaia has such dedicated protectors."

Eric smiled. "No hard feelings then?"

"None."

Kaia let out a breath. "Can I talk now?"

"Of course." Her mother turned a warning look at the brothers. "You guys are done, right?"

"For now." Gilbert crossed his arms over his chest and directed a look at William that was meant to be intimidating.

Kaia turned to him with an apologetic smile. "How did the interviews with the other candidates go? Did you manage to recruit anyone else?"

"I hired Corinne Burke, Owen Ferrel, and Kylie Baldwin. Do you know any of them?"

"I know them mostly by reputation, and they are all good. Owen is not the brightest of the bunch, but he's hard-working. You won't be disappointed. Corinne is average, but she's more experienced, and Kylie is probably the best of the three."

"Will you be comfortable working with them?"

"I haven't heard anything bad about any of them, so I hope they are easy to work with." She flicked her long hair behind her shoulder. "The only difficulty I can foresee is them bristling about a kid leading the team." She trained her big blue eyes at him. "Not everyone can see past that."

Had that comment been directed at him?

William wasn't sure. "I'm putting Corinne in charge of organizing the findings, but I'll make it clear that they all answer to you. Anyone who has a problem with that can leave."

His answer seemed to satisfy Kaia. "Thank you. If they are professionals, they will stay."

"So, do we have a deal?" He looked at her and then her mother, Gilbert, and lastly at Eric.

"We do," Kaia said. "I'll sign the nondisclosure agreement whenever you want, but I will sign the contract only after my family approves of the location." She gave him an apologetic smile. "I feel like a prima donna for making such unreasonable demands."

"That's okay. You have a right to be demanding. I feel privileged to have you on my team."

"When can we see the place?" Gilbert asked.

"The other team members are arriving next Sunday, and we start working on the project on Monday. If you want, you can come on Saturday and stay for the weekend. The research lab is located in a high-end resort that serves as a spiritual retreat."

"Are you talking about Safe Haven?" Eric asked.

"How did you know?"

"A woman I dated participated in one of those. She wanted me to come with her, but I'm not a very spiritual guy. She said that the location was beautiful and that the accommodations were simple but comfortable."

"It's under new ownership, and it's much more luxurious than it used to be when your friend was there." William took off his glasses and looked into Eric's eyes. "Please don't mention where Kaia is working to anyone." He used a shallow thrall that was directed not just at Gilbert's brother. "I also need you all to sign a nondisclosure agreement. To ensure the safety of everyone working on this project, it's very important to keep the location a secret."

A thrall wasn't as strong as a compulsion, especially the kind William had just used on the brothers and on Kaia's mother, but if they were so concerned with Kaia's safety, they wouldn't volunteer the information anyway.

Gilbert frowned. "Who are you afraid of and why?"

"Scientific espionage is rampant, and everyone wants a leg up in the game. I'm protecting my people from every conceivable risk."

The guy didn't look satisfied by the vague answer, but he must have understood that William couldn't disclose more than he already had, and he didn't ask him to clarify.

"Let's sign those agreements," Kaia said. "Do you have them prepared?"

"I do." William rose to his feet and took his satchel from the back of the chair. "Since Cheryl is a minor, I will need her legal guardian to sign the agreement for her." He pulled the stack of papers out and handed a copy to each one of them. "It's pretty straightforward but go ahead and take your time reading through it."

Edna had written the agreement in her uncompromising style, so it sounded draconian, but he didn't expect anyone to object. With

Karen working on sensitive defense technology, they were all familiar with the need for secrecy.

Once everyone was done reading and the documents were signed, William collected them and put them back in his satchel.

"Thank you."

"We can't stay for the weekend," Karen said. "We will come on Saturday and fly home the same day. If we find the place agreeable, Kaia will sign the contract and stay. If we don't, we will take her back with us."

"I'm sure that you will find the accommodations more than adequate, and the resort is beautiful."

"How come you are doing it there?" Kaia asked. "Is it safe with all the guests of the resort and the people maintaining it?"

"It's safe. The lab and the team's accommodations are located in a separate restricted area that has every security measure conceivable. We will be sharing it with another group that's engaged in unrelated research, but they are bound by the same nondisclosure agreements as the ones you've just signed. I'm confident that the research will remain confidential."

The compulsion they would be under would ensure that.

"Is the other group using the same research facilities we will be using?"

He shook his head. "They have their own, but you'll be sharing the dining hall and the gym with them. I didn't want my team to spend months in isolation. It's not good for morale."

"I bet." She rubbed her hands on her jeans. "I'm nervous. I've never been away from home for more than a few days."

"You'll be fine," her mother said.

"Yeah, I will."

William pushed to his feet. "Thank you all for hearing me out and for supporting Kaia's decision."

"You're welcome," Karen said.

Gilbert got to his feet and walked over to him. "Nothing is finalized yet."

"I'm aware of that, but I have no doubt that you will love the place."

"That remains to be seen."

Kaia patted Gilbert's arm before threading hers through William's. "I'll walk you out."

"Thank you," he said again. "I will see you all next Saturday. Let me know if you change your mind about staying for the weekend, and I'll have rooms prepared for you."

"I would like you to stay." Kaia turned a pair of pleading eyes to her mother. "It will make it a little easier for me."

Karen released a breath and looked at Eric. "Is it okay with you?"

"I need to check my schedule. I might not be able to fly you back, but I'll try to move things around."

28

KAIA

Kaia was impressed. William had not only survived Gilbert and Eric's interrogation, but he'd done it while she'd been purposely distracting him.

The T-shirt had been a strategic choice designed to draw his attention to her ample cleavage. After the nun-style blouse she'd worn yesterday, that was a big improvement, but its success had been partial. She'd confirmed that he was attracted to her, which after his stunned reaction to her kiss last night she hadn't been sure about, and she'd also discovered that despite his healthy male appetite, William was a gentleman.

She'd caught him glancing at her cleavage several times and then quickly shifting his gaze back to her eyes with a guilty expression on his handsome face.

Other girls might have been offended, but she found it adorable.

Regrettably, he hadn't been distracted enough to reveal more than he'd intended.

He'd let slip a few details that had helped Eric figure out the location, and later she was going to google Safe Haven and find out more about it, but he hadn't revealed anything about the people who were financing the project. Were they big pharma? The military? A secret government organization?

Judging by his simple clothes and affable attitude, William wasn't wealthy, so he was just an employee of the organization. Heck, he hadn't even rented a car. He had a friend dropping him off and picking him up.

"I should text Max." William pulled out his phone and typed up a message.

"How long before he gets here?" she asked as they walked out the gate.

"About ten minutes."

"Good, so we have time to talk about Anthony. Did you have a chance to check whether your hacker friend could look into his disappearance?"

Looking guilty, William shook his head. "Yesterday it was too late to call him, and today was very busy. I'll call him tomorrow."

Kaia knew he wasn't going to do that. He was using it as a bargaining chip until she signed the contract, and she could understand that, but she would have preferred if he were just honest about it.

"You're not going to do anything until I officially join your team, are you?"

He swallowed. "I really didn't have time, and even if I did, I don't know when Roni will be able to look into it. He's swamped with work."

"If you find out anything before next Saturday, call me or text me. Any little bit of information would be appreciated. I hate not knowing what happened to him, and I feel terrible for his parents who think that he's dead."

"I promise to call Roni tomorrow, and I'll plead with him to make time for this."

"Thank you." She rewarded him with a big smile.

He nodded, and as his eyes shifted to her lips, Kaia wondered if he expected her to kiss him again, but after the strange way he'd reacted last night, she wasn't sure.

"I'm sorry for kissing you yesterday. I was so grateful for your help that I acted on impulse."

"Nothing to be sorry about."

She tilted her head. "You looked shocked."

He swallowed again. "I was taken by surprise, but I would be lying if I said that I didn't like it."

"You were frozen."

He closed his eyes for a brief moment. "What else could I have done? You are beautiful and brilliant, and I can't help my attraction to you, but it would have been inappropriate for me to respond the way I wanted to. Even if you were not about to start working for me, the age difference alone is enough for me to keep my distance."

That was a very good answer that explained his reaction without offending her, but it also nipped in the bud any ideas she might have harbored about stealing another kiss.

"Thirteen years difference is not a lot, and I'm not working for you yet."

He chuckled. "I'm sure your mother and Gilbert have a different opinion, and rightfully so."

Tucking her hands into her back pockets, Kaia shrugged. "My family's opinion is important to me, but they don't get to decide who I can date. Besides, on the inside, I'm even older than you."

It was true, but she didn't expect him to agree with her. Surprisingly, he nodded.

"You are very mature, and you are smarter than most people I know, but it still doesn't make it right." He lifted his hand and waved at the approaching car. "My friend is here."

"It's goodnight then." She offered him her hand. "But regrettably, without a kiss."

Taking her offered hand, William moved faster than a big man like him should have been able to. Wrapping his arm around her waist, he pulled her against his chest and planted a quick kiss on her lips. "Goodnight, Kaia."

Talk about a surprise.

What had made him do that?

"Goodnight," she remembered to say as he ducked into the idling car.

He opened the passenger-side window. "Until next Saturday."

Lifting her fingers to her lips, she smiled. "I can't wait."

29

KALUGAL

"Welcome to my home." Kalugal held the door open for Mia, Toven, and Mia's grandparents. "My name is Kalugal." He offered Mia's grandmother his hand.

He had a bit of a snob reputation that he needed to overcome, especially this evening, which was why he hadn't sent one of his men to open the door and lead his guests to the dining room.

"I'm Rosalyn." She shook his hand with a warm smile on her kind face.

"Curtis." The grandfather offered him his hand. "Your home is much bigger on the inside than it appears to be on the outside."

"It's like Doctor Who's Tardis," Mia said.

Kalugal had heard about the British television show, but he hadn't watched it and had no idea what a Tardis was. Did it have anything to do with being tardy?

Probably not, and he wasn't going to ask. He wasn't in the mood to delve into a discussion about British television.

"The magic was performed by the clan's very talented architect." He motioned for them to follow him into the elevator. "Most of the structure is located underground, but the skylights bring in plenty of natural light and fresh air. At night, the automatic shutters go up, so the artificial lighting is not visible from above."

"That's a shame," Mia said. "You can't see the stars."

"I wondered about that." Curtis waited for Toven to wheel Mia into the elevator before taking his wife's hand and following. "When we stayed in the village during Mia's initial stages of transition, the shutters closed each evening as soon as the sun came down, and when we opened the front door at night, the light in the living room turned off. It was so dark that I was afraid Rosy would stumble on the steps. I thought that it was about saving on electricity or about preventing bugs from getting into the house. Now I know the real reason why it was necessary."

"The lights turning off as soon as you open a door or a window is a new security measure." As the elevator stopped at the lower level, Kalugal held the door open until his guests got out. "As the village grows, it becomes more important to control its visibility at night."

"Why do you have an elevator in the house?" Mia asked. "I'm glad that you do, but immortals don't need it."

"True, but my wife is expecting, and once our son is born, the stairs will become problematic."

He intended to put gates on both ends of the stairs and have everyone in the household use the elevator exclusively. Boys were fragile until they reached puberty and could transition, and he was going to make sure that no harm came to his son.

As they entered the sprawling dining room, Mia's grandmother gasped. "This is like a banquet table in a fairytale. It's huge."

"Who else is coming?" Toven asked. "I thought that you were just inviting the close family."

Kalugal smiled. "That's a lot of people, and I also invited Syssi and Kian, Amanda and Dalhu, and Andrew and Nathalie." He leaned closer to the god. "I had to invite Kian, or he would have suspected me of trying to plot something with you."

Not that he would have been wrong, but at this stage in the game, Kalugal was only sending out feelers to assess how potentially useful his newfound uncle could be to him.

He'd invited the usual gang for the simple reason that Kian and Amanda included him and Jacki in all of their family's gatherings, and he could do no less. Besides, he liked having them over.

The good-natured rivalry he and Kian routinely engaged in was fun, and so was sharing a cigar and a glass of whiskey with his cousin. They were more like brothers than he and Lokan were, perhaps because they had more in common. He and Kian were both leaders of their communities and shouldered many responsibilities, but that was where the similarities ended.

Kalugal was one of a kind and proud of it.

Lokan was too uptight, and Kian wasn't exactly an island of tranquility either. Both his brother and his cousin were overly serious and somber. Perhaps he would find more in common with Toven, although given his initial impression of the god, that wasn't likely.

"Hello, everyone." Jacki walked into the dining room wearing a very fetching outfit of a pair of white maternity trousers and a loose, yellow silk blouse. "Please, sit down. We can have some wine before the others get here."

"Are they bringing the little ones with them?" Mia asked hopefully.

"Not tonight." Jacki smiled. "The moms wanted to enjoy a quiet dinner with adults, so the girls are having their first sleepover at Nathalie and Andrew's home. Ella and Wonder are babysitting."

"That's a shame." Mia pouted. "I hoped to see them."

"You'll have plenty of opportunities." Toven moved a chair away from the table, making room for Mia's wheelchair. "Now that we are living in the village, you can probably see them every day."

"You can catch Phoenix and Ethan at the playground most afternoons," Jacki said. "And sometimes Syssi and Amanda take their little ones for a stroll and stop by to chat with Eva and Nathalie. During the day, Phoenix attends a preschool, while Allegra and Evie are with their mothers at the university. Amanda converted her office to a nursery, and they hired a human nanny to look after the babies while they work."

"Isn't that dangerous?" Toven asked. "Kian told me about the attack at Amanda's lab four and a half years ago. If her location was compromised before, it can happen again."

"That's not likely." Kalugal uncorked a wine bottle. "The one who discovered the lab's location was Dalhu, and he's no longer a threat."

"Oh my." Rosalyn put a hand over her chest. "From enemies to lovers to fated mates. Now, that's a story I would love to hear."

30

TOVEN

By the time Kalugal had finished his abbreviated version of Dalhu's story, starting with his past in Navuh's camp and up to his capture by the clan, the rest of the guests had arrived, and Amanda had added all the spicy details that Kalugal either hadn't known or deemed inappropriate to share in polite company.

Kian glared at his sister, either for what she had done back then or for telling the story shamelessly, and Dalhu looked like he wanted the floor to swallow him whole.

What had surprised Toven the most, though, was not that Amanda had fought tooth and nail for her right to keep the mate the Fates had chosen for her, but that Annani had helped her against her son. She could've ended the feud between the siblings by simply decreeing it, but she'd gone about it in a roundabout way, letting Kian slowly realize that Dalhu was worthy of Amanda, and that he was the right mate for her.

"I wonder," Nathalie said. "How did Annani's probe of Aliya go? No one told Andrew and me anything."

"That's because there was nothing to tell," Kian said. "Aliya's childhood memories were all scrambled, probably because of the trauma she'd suffered. What she remembered were parables that Jade had liked telling the children, and there had been nothing useful we could learn from that. But Annani said that Jade was a talented storyteller, which surprised me given what her tribespeople had said about her."

"That actually makes sense," Syssi said. "Aliya said that she learned English from the movies Jade brought back from her travels abroad. That means that she enjoyed watching fictional stories and that she appreciated what the children could learn from them."

Amanda waved a hand. "Don't spoil it for me. I've gotten used to thinking of her as a monster. I don't want to hear that she did nice things for her people."

"The only one who describes Jade as a monster is Emmett," Kian said. "Vrog waited for her return for over two decades, and he still talks about her with respect. So does Aliya." He grimaced. "I bet some clan members think of me as a monster as well."

"No one thinks that." Syssi slapped his arm playfully. "And they never did, even when you were much grumpier."

Kalugal chuckled. "He was even worse than he is now?"

Shai nodded. "I can attest to that. Married life agrees with him."

"Traitor." Kian cast a mock glare at his assistant.

Onegus, who had been Kian's chief Guardian many years before Kian had met Syssi, kept an impassive expression and didn't comment, which was probably wise.

Next to Toven, Curtis shifted in his chair. "When is dinner going to be served?" he whispered, forgetting that all the immortals could hear him just fine. "It's nearly nine o'clock."

Kalugal lifted his hand, and a moment later several men entered the dining room carrying trays.

"Is everyone hungry?" asked a guy in a white apron who looked more like a drill sergeant than a cook.

"Yes, we are," Amanda grinned at him. "What have you made for us today, Atzil?"

"A feast worthy of a king." His eyes darted around the table until they landed on Toven and widened to the size of saucers. "Or a god." He bowed deeply. "I'm honored to serve you today, Master Toven."

"It's just Toven. I let Okidu address me as master because I know it's futile to argue with him, but we live in an era where no one should be considered another's master. Not that demanding obeisance was ever okay. It took thousands of years for the gods' teachings to finally have an effect, and for humans to embrace the ideas of democracy and equal rights, in no small part thanks to Annani."

From across the table, Kalugal eyed him curiously. "As far as I know, the gods enjoyed their grand status very much. I doubt they considered humans or even immortals as equal."

"They didn't," Toven admitted. "And at the time, they were entitled to that elevated status. But they led by example. The gods governed themselves in a democratic way, with all the advantages and pitfalls that democracy entails, and they wished for humans and immortals to emulate them."

Kalugal didn't look impressed. "They didn't practice democracy on their home planet. They had a king."

Evidently, Mortdh hadn't been as tight-lipped with his son as Ahn had been with Annani, but given that Kalugal hadn't been close to Navuh, or at least that was the impression Toven had gotten, he wondered how his nephew had learned that.

"There was a king, but his rule was similar to Ahn's. He couldn't make any major decisions without his council's approval, and he had to politic the same way Ahn did."

"What else can you tell us about the gods' home planet?" Syssi asked.

"That's more or less it. I know that at some point, there was a war that had started as a rebellion, but my father refused to elaborate on it."

31

KIAN

Kian had a feeling that Toven knew more than he was willing to reveal, and he wondered why he saw fit to keep it to himself. Then again, he had nothing to base that feeling on. The god had a poker face to rival that of the best professional players, schooling his expression and tone to perfectly align with his words. Given that he was the oldest being on Earth, he'd had plenty of time to perfect it.

He waited until dinner was over to spring the question that had been nagging him ever since Okidu had gifted him with the journals. "You are seven thousand years old." Kian leveled his gaze at Toven. "You must know things about the gods' origins that my mother doesn't. Do you know why the Odus were used in the gods' war?"

Toven's lips lifted in a sad smile. "I wasn't told, if that's what you're suggesting, but the answer to that is simple. They are an incredible weapon. Whoever designed them limited their capacity to learn, and by doing so avoided the danger that artificial intelligence poses to all organic beings. The moment AI becomes self-aware, the first thing it will do is eliminate the competition. And since its capacity to learn is limitless, no biologically limited beings could stand in its way."

Talking in generalities was a great way to avoid answering the question, but Kian wasn't about to give up that easily. "I'm aware of the dangers of AI, but we are not there yet. I'm more interested in the why and how the Odus, who had been created as domestic servants, had been turned into soldiers."

Toven shrugged. "Someone figured out that an indestructible servant who is programmed to obey its master could be used as a weapon. If someone attacked you when you were with Okidu, wouldn't he destroy them?"

"He would shield me, and he would do his best to protect me, but he would not attack unless I commanded him to do so."

"There you go." Toven waved a hand. "Maybe the Odus were used to defend their masters. My father clammed up anytime I asked him about it. The only thing he told me was that the technology had been banned, the instructions for building them destroyed, and the Odus had been decommissioned. He said it was a great tragedy, and he didn't want to talk about it." Toven smiled. "Ekin always championed the underdog."

"You mean humans," Syssi said.

"And Odus." Toven leaned back in his chair. "I have a theory, but it's only speculation."

"Let's hear it." Kalugal uncorked another wine bottle and started refilling everyone's glasses.

"I think that Ahn, Ekin, and their sister Athor were rebels and that they were involved in what happened to the Odus in some way. The king couldn't execute his own children because it would have looked bad for him, given that he needed to maintain the illusion of democracy, so he sent them on an expedition to Earth, probably to mine for gold, and when everyone back home had forgotten about them, he severed contact with them. Our advanced technological devices were falling apart, and there was no way to fix them because the supply chain had winked out, and there were no replacement parts. My father tried to find solutions using materials that were readily available on Earth, but it was akin to being stranded on an island and trying to make do with what was there. He was a brilliant scientist, but no single person can encompass the knowledge of an entire civilization to recreate its technology from scratch."

Kalugal nodded. "I came to a similar conclusion, but it's also possible that something happened on their home planet. Perhaps it was conquered by other space-faring people, or perhaps its sun exploded, or some other disaster brought an end to their planet or just their ability to communicate with their satellites."

"That scenario is too sad to consider." Jacki put her hand on her husband's arm. "Let's talk about a more pleasant subject." She smiled. "Kalugal is finally taking me on a proper archeological dig in Egypt. We are leaving on Sunday." She put her hand on her substantial belly. "I want to do that before Junior gets here."

"You can't be serious," Amanda gaped at her. "You only have two weeks to go. What if your labor starts in Egypt? Do you want to deliver your baby in a Third-World country?"

Jacki shrugged. "I'm immortal. I can deliver Junior in a field, and I'll be fine."

"Yeah, but Junior might not be." Amanda turned to glare at Kalugal. "I can't believe that you agreed to this insanity. I thought that you had more sense than that."

"We are only going for three days, and Bridget says that Jacki's belly hasn't descended yet, so there is still time."

"Don't tell me that Bridget green-lighted your trip. If Jacki gives birth in an Egyptian hospital and immediately heals right in front of their eyes, you will have to thrall everyone in there."

"I can do that easily, so that's not a problem." Kalugal sighed. "But perhaps you are right, and we should wait until after Junior is born. We can go a month later and hire a bunch of nannies to take with us on the trip."

Jacki pouted, but Amanda's impassioned speech seemed to have achieved its intended result.

"Fine. So Egypt is out. But I want to go somewhere fun. We haven't been anywhere since we returned from China."

"How about Catalina Island?" Amanda suggested. "It's not far, and you can charter a luxury yacht to get there. If your labor starts, we can pick you up with the helicopter and bring you straight to the clinic."

"I guess that could be fun as well." Jacki rubbed her belly. "I had my heart set on Egypt, though."

Kalugal took her hand and covered it with his other one. "We will go as soon as you are up to it, and Junior is okay to travel."

"Six weeks," Amanda said. "That's the absolute minimum. I would wait until he is at least one year old before taking him to a place like that, but that's me."

"What about you?" Jacki asked Syssi. "How long are you going to wait before traveling with Allegra?"

"I haven't given it much thought, but I don't think I need to wait until she's one year old to take her with us on a short trip."

They hadn't been anywhere in the longest time, and even though it terrified Kian to take Allegra out of the village, Syssi had already taken the first step by taking her to work with her.

"Allegra is five months old. Where would you like to take her?"

"Not Egypt, but Hawaii could be fun."

"When?"

"In a couple of months."

Kian turned to Shai. "Put it on my schedule."

"Yes, boss."

32

KAIA

Idina climbed onto Kaia's lap. "Where is Uncle Eric taking us?" She bounced up and down on Kaia's knees.

The advantage of flying on a private jet was that there was no need to shush the little ones, and they could make as much noise as they pleased. Although so far, the twins had been relatively quiet, and Idina was just asking questions and not mutilating Barbies or pinching anyone, so all was good.

"I've told you already. We are going to a nice resort on the beach, and we are going to meet William. Do you remember him?"

"Yeah. The guy with the glasses and the brown shirt with the creases."

Chuckling, Kaia ruffled her sister's curly hair.

Idina remembered the oddest things about people, and she noticed things that a three-year-old shouldn't. Maybe they were raising another prodigy. Although in Idina's case, she would grow up to be an evil dictator. The girl could be the sweetest thing one moment and a mean monkey the next.

Cheryl lifted her head. "He must have bought a new shirt for the interview and didn't wash it before wearing it. That's why it still had creases from when it was folded in the packaging."

"You noticed that too? How come I didn't?" Kaia didn't even

remember the color of William's shirt. All she'd seen were his incredible blue eyes.

Well, she'd stared at his lips as well.

Cheryl snorted. "You were too busy looking into his pretty blue eyes and kissable lips."

"Hey." Gilbert shook his finger at her. "You are too young to notice a guy's lips, and especially one who is old enough to be your father."

"I'm fifteen, Gilbert, not five, and William is only thirty-two, so maybe he could have made a baby when he was seventeen, but he didn't. Besides, I was talking about Kaia noticing his lips, not me." She cradled her phone in her hands, looking at it with sad eyes. "I need a satellite plan. I hate being in cyber limbo. Do they even have internet in that place?"

Kaia winced. "I don't think so. It's supposed to be a spiritual retreat, and I read that the guests have to leave their phones in a safe until the retreat is over. If there is an emergency, they can use the phone in the office."

Looking like she was about to pop a vein, Cheryl clutched the phone to her chest. "That's barbaric. I'm not letting anyone touch my phone."

With a sigh, their mother shifted Evan to her other thigh. "You need an intervention. You are addicted to that device, and it's not healthy."

As the two started arguing about Cheryl's obsession with her phone, or rather her Instatock channel, Kaia adjusted Idina on her lap and closed her eyes.

Eleven days had passed since she'd last seen William, and she hadn't stopped thinking about him and the two kisses they'd shared. Not that they qualified as proper kisses. Neither had involved tongues and both had lasted less than a second.

After she'd texted him that Eric couldn't make it on Saturday and they could only arrive on Sunday, William had called to give her the name of the airport Eric should use and to coordinate the time for picking them up. He'd also apologized for his hacker friend's busy schedule and had asked for more information about Tony, but since

Kaia hadn't heard back from him, Roni the hacker had probably still been too busy to look into it.

Either that or William was dragging it out on purpose to make sure that she signed the contract.

"Are you sleeping?" Idina asked.

"I'm napping. You should nap too."

"Okay." She cuddled closer, pulling her legs up and tucking them under her.

Kaia leaned down and kissed her sister's curly mop of hair and sniffed the sweet baby smell she somehow still had. She was going to miss her and the twins so much. Heck, she was even going to miss Cheryl and her grumpy comments.

As tears prickled the back of her eyes, she closed them again and visualized William to distract herself.

Would he come to greet her? Or would he just send a driver to pick them up?

She hoped he would come. If he'd been thinking about her even half as much as she'd been thinking about him, he would be there.

"I don't want you to go," Idina said with her eyes still closed. "I'm going to miss you."

"I'm going to miss you too." Kaia kissed her head again. "But we can talk on the phone and do video calls. It's not like you're not going to see me."

"You said they will take away your phone."

"I'm not going to let them do that. I'll tell them that I need to call my little sister every day."

"Good. And if they say no, pinch them really hard." Idina demonstrated while twisting her little face into an evil expression.

Kaia chuckled. "You shouldn't pinch people. It's not nice."

Idina huffed. "It's not nice to take people's phones either."

"This project is going to be good for you," her mother said. "You need to stretch the umbilical cord a little farther, flap your wings, and live a little."

"Children should stay close to their parents," Gilbert grumbled quietly, so as not to wake up Ryan, who was asleep in his arms. "People are meant to live in tribes. All those blue zones where people live to be over a hundred have one thing in common. They live in small villages and are actively social."

"They also eat healthily," Cheryl said.

He stifled a snort. "I bet that's not as important as their emotional health."

"We are going to grow up and get married one day." Cheryl put her phone in her backpack. "What are you going to do? Build a gated community just for your kids and their spouses so they stay close to you?"

"You bet your sweet pickles that's precisely what I will do. I will commission a big billboard with a picture of all of us smiling and waving, and it will say—if it's good enough for my family, it's good enough for yours."

It was so like Gilbert to find a profitable angle in everything.

"You're weird." Cheryl's lips twitched with a suppressed smile. "That's a horrible idea for a billboard. No one will buy your houses."

"They will buy. They always do. I build nice homes."

"That you do," her sister conceded.

"Does it mean that you will come live in my gated community?"

She gave him one of those penetrating looks that made people uncomfortable. "Maybe I will, and maybe I won't."

33

WILLIAM

William sat at the front of the bus, just behind the driver, and checked his emails, forwarding most of them to Darlene to take care of.

It had been such a smart decision to bring her along. She was taking care of everything.

She'd arranged the flights for his three other recruits, made sure that their rooms were ready, and arranged for a car to pick them up at the airport. She'd also met them when they'd arrived at Safe Haven and had shown them to their rooms. The only thing William had done was introduce them to Eleanor and Emmett, and he'd left them with those two to get compelled.

It was so easy to delegate things to someone who was smart and capable and didn't need things explained to her twice.

It was a shame that there was no spark between them.

Darlene was a good woman, precisely the type William usually went for, but even before he'd met Kaia and had gotten infatuated with the sexy nineteen-year-old, he and Darlene just hadn't clicked.

"How many people are we picking up?" The bus driver pulled into the airport's parking lot.

"Four adults, a teenager, a toddler, and twin babies."

"Do I need to get a porter to bring their things?"

"They are not going to have a lot of baggage because they are not staying the night. They are going back later today."

Hopefully, minus Kaia, and he didn't expect her to arrive with loads of suitcases. She wasn't the type who cared about clothing and shoes. Her suitcase would probably be full of books just like his was.

"You can wait here," he told the driver. "I'll get them."

The private airport's small terminal was nearly deserted, and there were plenty of seats to choose from. William selected one next to the glass wall overlooking the runways.

Kaia's uncle was scheduled to land his jet in about ten minutes, so William had plenty of time to mentally prepare for seeing her again. He needed to keep himself in check and stifle the attraction he felt for her. Perhaps if he appeared uninterested, Kaia would stop flirting with him, and he could retain his sanity.

Fates, the girl was a blessing and a curse at the same time.

She was the key to deciphering the journals, he had no doubt of that, but it was difficult enough to stay away from her when she wasn't looking at his lips with hungry eyes or just flat out kissing him.

He needed to keep his distance as much as was possible under the circumstances, which was going to be impossible since they would be working together for the next three to four months.

Out of the three bungalows that were assigned to the lab, he'd chosen the one that was the farthest from Kaia's. Each bungalow had two bedrooms, a small living room, and a kitchenette, and the rooms were more or less the same, but there were small differences, mainly in which direction the windows were facing and whether there was an ocean view or not.

Since the others had arrived earlier, he'd made sure to reserve the nicest room for Kaia ahead of time so no one else would snatch it, and he assigned the other room in that bungalow to Kylie.

Corinne and Owen were sharing the other, and he had one to himself. He'd offered the other room in his bungalow to Darlene, but she'd asked to get a place all to herself, so he'd gotten her one in the paranormals' section.

After spending months in Geraldine and Shai's home, Darlene

craved privacy, and he could totally empathize with that. Besides, she needed to find an immortal male to induce her, and if one of the Guardians assigned to the compound caught her eye, she would be more comfortable bringing him to her place if she didn't have a roommate.

William was rooting for Max, but so far, it didn't look like she liked him any more than she liked the others.

When the private jet touched down, William swallowed the ball of stress that had lodged in his throat, pushed to his feet, and walked out to meet Kaia and her family.

34

KAIA

"How long is the drive?" Cheryl asked a few minutes into it.

William turned around. "About an hour and a half."

Kaia pretended to be absorbed in Idina's picture book to avoid his eyes.

Their meeting at the airport had been awkward. William had been polite, courteous, and full of smiles for everyone, but he'd seemed detached.

He'd shaken her hand, but despite the form-fitting T-shirt she had on, his eyes hadn't roamed over her body like they had outside her house while he'd waited for his friend to pick him up.

It looked like from now on, William would be all business. This would be her place of employment, and he would be her boss, so he was probably afraid of breathing the wrong way and getting sued for sexual harassment, which would be catastrophic not only on the personal level but also given the secret nature of the project.

How could she convince him that he had nothing to fear from her?

It didn't matter if she was the one who initiated, that would still expose him to potential trouble, so the only way would be to earn his trust. Once he realized that she would never do anything to harm him unless he really deserved it, he might become less guarded around her.

Besides, even if he ended up hurting her and deserved retribution, she wouldn't go through the court system to get it. If he was right and she was indeed the only one who could decipher those writings, sabotaging that would be the best payback.

Maybe that was what William was afraid of?

Damn. She didn't like that dynamic one bit. Perhaps someone else would have thrived on the rush of power she had over him, but Kaia hated being feared, and she didn't want to spend the next three to four months of her life in an awkward situation with a guy who was attracted to her but was fighting it with all his might.

"That's one hell of a schlep." Gilbert leaned down and picked up the toy Evan had dropped on the floor. "Between the flight and the drive to and from the airport, a whole day is wasted."

"Thanks for stating the obvious." Cheryl went back to her phone. "But if I have cellular reception the entire way, I have no problem with this part of the trip." She snapped her head back up. "William, are you going to take our phones away once we get there?"

He looked at her over his shoulder and smiled reassuringly. "You must have read old information. It used to be that guests were required to give up their phones for the entire duration of their stay, but now only those who participate in the spiritual retreat have to surrender theirs, and only during classes. They get them back at the end of the day."

Cheryl let out a relieved breath. "What about cellular reception? Is it any good there?"

"It's decent, and there is also Wi-Fi. Before we bought the resort, only the offices were connected to the internet. Now there is access everywhere except for the lab." He turned to look at Kaia. "Things are little stricter with the research team members. I'll explain later during the briefing."

Kaia nodded, despite the alarm bells that had gone up in her mind. She still hadn't signed the contract, and if William sprang some draconian restrictions on her, she was going to bail.

Being able to talk with her family every day was a hard line she wasn't willing to cross. If he wouldn't allow her that, she was going back home despite her attraction to him, her curiosity about the project, and the satisfaction she expected from solving a mystery no one else could solve.

There was no guarantee that she would actually be able to do that, but William was confident that she would, and since he'd read all of her published papers, he might have a good reason to be so sure. Perhaps he'd found something in them that led him to believe she had what it took to decipher the writings.

What about Tony, though?

Roni the hacker was her only hope of finding out what had happened to him. If she bailed, he wouldn't bother helping her.

Could she survive weeks at a time without talking to her family?

She had no choice.

No one else was looking for Anthony, and she was his only hope. Even if he was dead, his family deserved to know how and where he died and to bring his body home for burial.

35

WILLIAM

William had never been happier to see Darlene than when the bus stopped at Safe Haven's parking lot.

She would take over and engage everyone in conversation, giving him a few minutes to recuperate from the stress of spending the last two hours with Kaia and trying his best not to look at her beautiful face or ogle her young supple body.

He'd purposely sat at the front of the bus while she'd sat a few rows behind him, but he hadn't expected to feel her eyes burning holes in his back throughout the drive.

It had been torture to keep from turning to look at her.

She had one of those tight-fitting low-necked T-shirts on that didn't leave much to the imagination, and her faded jeans hugged her legs and her backside perfectly.

Kaia didn't wear any makeup or jewelry, but her nails and toenails were painted pink, and she had flip-flops on her pretty feet. She looked beautiful and sexy and ready for a day at the beach, but the outfit was totally inappropriate for meeting her co-workers and signing contracts.

Evidently, Doctor Kaia Locke was not one to follow conventions, and that made him like her even more.

As soon as everyone was out of the bus and the twins had been put in their double stroller, William introduced Darlene. "This is my administrative assistant, Darlene." He turned to Kaia. "Doctor Kaia Locke, her mother Karen Locke, her stepfather Gilbert Emerson, her uncle Eric Emerson, her sisters Cheryl and Idina, and in the stroller are her brothers—Evan and Ryan.

Eric was the first one to offer Darlene his hand. "A pleasure to meet you."

The look she gave him was one that William hadn't seen her giving anyone before, and the fact that he'd noticed it despite his own turmoil meant that it was blatant enough for everyone to see.

"The pleasure is all mine," she purred. "Thank you for bringing the entire family to check out Safe Haven."

"I'm glad that I did." He held on to her hand a moment longer than necessary. "My niece is very important to me, and I need to make sure that she's treated as the precious, unique diamond that she is."

Kaia rolled her eyes. "Stop it, Eric. You're embarrassing me." She offered Darlene her hand. "I'm Kaia, and you can drop the doctor part. Each time someone calls me that I have the urge to look over my shoulder and search for the person they are referring to."

Shaking her hand, Darlene laughed. "That's how I felt when I first got married and people addressed me as Mrs." She shifted her eyes to Eric. "But now that I'm single again, I can go back to being Miss."

What had gotten into her?

This wasn't the Darlene William knew, the one who was reserved, rarely smiled, and was all work and no play.

Evidently, it took the right guy to bring that part out of her, but Eric was human, several years younger than her, and he looked like a player.

Maybe that was precisely what she wanted? A short fling with an attractive guy who she was confident wouldn't stick around?

If so, good for her. She deserved some fun after spending decades with that shitty husband of hers.

After all the handshaking was done and Darlene introduced herself to the little ones, they headed into the lodge.

Kaia had brought only one suitcase, and she refused to let anyone take it from her. Rolling it behind her, she fell in step with him. "Have you and Darlene been working together long?"

The others followed Darlene, who led them to the coffee station.

"Not at all. She started working for me less than a couple of months ago, organizing my mess."

"That's surprising." Kaia slung the strap of her little purse over her body, so it rested on her other hip. "You seem very comfortable with each other."

Detecting a slight sarcastic tone, William tilted his head to look at her. "What are you trying to say?"

She shrugged. "Nothing. I just wonder whether you went out with Darlene before she started working for you or during."

Hadn't she noticed the way Darlene had reacted to Eric? Maybe she had and thought that Darlene was doing that in retaliation for something?

"Darlene and I never dated." He smiled. "We were introduced by mutual friends who hoped something would come out of it, but we just never clicked that way. We became friends when we both joined another friend on her mission to get healthier. If not for Darlene, I doubt I would have gotten back in shape and lost thirty-some pounds. She just didn't let me quit, and if I didn't show up for our morning runs or evening workouts, she would come to my lab and drag me out."

"This lab?"

He shook his head. "This one is reserved just for special projects. It's not where I usually work."

"And where is that?"

He winced. "I can't tell you that. It's another secret location."

Kaia tsked. "You are full of secrets, aren't you?"

"I like to be mysterious." He waggled his brows, hoping to make her laugh.

36

DARLENE

It had been years since Darlene had flirted with a guy, but Eric somehow brought out the naughty side of her that had lain dormant during her marriage.

His irreverent charm combined with his bad-boy good looks made him the perfect specimen for a fling, someone to celebrate her newfound freedom with. He looked to be in his late thirties or early forties, which was a little too young, and he was also a little too handsome for her, but he seemed interested, and that was good enough for her.

Darlene wasn't looking for a long-term relationship. She still had to find an immortal to hook up with, but the hunky immortal Guardians were too intimidating. Thinking of getting in bed with one of those perfect bodies should have been arousing, but it had the opposite effect on her.

Perhaps it was stupid vanity, but she wanted to look at least as good as the guy she was with, and despite the weight loss and the better shape she was in after all the training she'd done, her breasts were still droopy, and the cellulite on her thighs was still there.

Never again would she allow herself to be someone's compromise, and that was precisely what she would be for one of those perfect male specimens.

They wanted her because she was a Dormant, the granddaughter of a god, so they vied for her attention as if she were a Venus.

Perhaps after she lost those last fifteen stubborn pounds and got a boob job, she would be ready to take on one of them as a lover. Until then, though, she could start the journey of rediscovering her sexuality with a human man who looked just a little younger than her and not like he could be her son.

When Kaia's family was done touring the lodge with all of its new entertainment options, she led them outside. "Do you want to see the new gym? It has two heated lap pools, and you can reserve a time slot for swimming." She smiled at Kaia. "You'd better be there on time or they will give your slots to someone else. They only allow one person at a time in the pools."

"I'm not a fan of swimming." Kaia cast a sidelong glance at William. "Do you like to swim?"

His eyes momentarily roamed over her young body, but then he forced them away from her and grimaced. "I don't like any kind of exercise, but swimming and running are not as bad as weight training because I can think of other things while doing that, so it's not a total waste of time."

The poor guy had it bad for the girl. What a shame that she was too young and was about to start working for him.

"I want to go to the pool." Kaia's little sister tugged on her hand. "Let's go."

"We didn't bring swimming suits, Idina," her mother said.

"I swim in my underwear in our pool at home."

Kaia tugged on her hand. "But we are not home, are we?"

The child pouted. "Can I see it?"

Idina was very articulate for a three-year-old, and she was adorable.

"Yes, you can." Her father lifted her and placed her on his shoulders.

"Do you swim?" Eric fell in step with Darlene.

She nodded. "Every morning since I got here. I reserve the five o'clock time slot."

"Ouch." He grimaced. "That's an ungodly hour. I'm not willing to wake up so early even to see you in a swimming suit. I haven't gotten out of bed before seven since I finished my last tour of duty."

It seemed that he was definitely interested.

"And when was that?"

"A long time ago." He chuckled. "If you are trying to guess how old I am, I'll save you the trouble. I'm forty-two."

That was what she'd guessed, and even though he was a few years younger than her, it wasn't a no-no. "Don't expect me to return the favor. I'm not going to tell you how old I am."

"Then I'll have to guess. Thirty-five?"

Darlene laughed. "You are such a charmer, Eric. You can't possibly think that I'm that young."

"Are you coming in?" Kaia's sister held the doors to the gym open. "Or do you prefer to stay outside and flirt?"

Eric pointed at her with a mock stern look. "Watch it, sprite. Being my favorite niece doesn't mean that you can be disrespectful to me."

She chuckled. "You tell each of us that we are your favorite, and besides, I was just stating the facts."

"You and your sisters are my favorite nieces." He rubbed the top of her head as he and Darlene stepped through the door.

"We are your only nieces, and Kaia and I are not even officially yours because Mom and Gilbert don't want to get married."

"Paperwork doesn't mean anything." Eric put his hand over his heart. "You are my nieces in here, and that's the only thing that counts."

As tears prickled the corner of her eyes, Darlene got angry at herself for being such a sap.

Eric was a player, and he'd known that she would love hearing him say that.

Perhaps she should tell him that he didn't need to work that hard. She was more than ready to say yes, please.

37

ERIC

*D*arlene obviously wasn't thirty-five, and she hadn't bought the line, but women loved that crap, and it never failed to work.

She was about his age, maybe a year older or younger, and given that his typical hookups were in their early and mid-twenties, that was much older than what he usually went for, but there was something about Darlene that drew him to her.

She was pretty and had nice curves in all the right places, but she wasn't a great beauty. It was something in her expression, or maybe her eyes that were a little sad, a little introspective, but also smart, welcoming, and warm.

Perhaps he was getting too old for girls who were nearly half his age, or maybe seeing Kaia blossom into a young woman forced him to realize that all too soon, she would be in her twenties as well, and it would be gross to have sex with women who were his niece's age.

He still remembered her as a seven-year-old girl, still traumatized by her father's sudden death and putting a brave face on for the sake of her mother and baby sister. Kaia was one of the strongest people he knew, and he was proud to be called her uncle, even if it was only an honorary title.

Fourteen years was long enough for Gilbert to get over the nastiness with which his first marriage had ended, and he should marry the mother of his children and officially adopt Kaia and Cheryl.

But maybe it was Karen who didn't want to make it official?

She'd loved her first husband and had been devastated by his loss, so perhaps this was her way to remain loyal to his memory. It wasn't logical, but affairs of the heart rarely were.

"That's my lane." William pointed to the pool on the left. "And that's Darlene's." He pointed to the one on the right. "She drags me out here at five o'clock every morning. I'm just grateful that the pools are heated, or it would be even less pleasant than it is."

"That's a strange arrangement." Gilbert walked down the aisle separating the two rows of gym equipment and the two lap pools. "It would have been more economical to build one pool with two lanes than two separate ones."

As William went into a long explanation of why it had been more expeditious to use single-lane pre-fabricated lap pools, Darlene gazed at him as if he were the brightest star in the sky. To be tasked with leading the genetic research project, he was probably brilliant, but a woman looked at a guy with such admiration in her eyes and a smile on her lips only if she had the hots for him, and Eric didn't like it one bit.

Why had Darlene flirted with him if she was in love with William?

The guy was way too young for her, but then he couldn't fault her for wanting a handsome, smart dude. She was a free agent and could hook up with whomever she wanted.

"You really like him," he said quietly next to her ear.

She turned to look at him with puzzlement in her eyes. "Who, William?"

"No, Gilbert," he said sarcastically. "Of course, William. You looked at him as if you were in love with the guy."

A smirk lifted one corner of her lips. "What if I were?"

"He's too young for you."

"Oh, I don't think so. A three-year difference isn't that much."

"Three?" He arched a brow.

"Yeah. Do the math." Amusement danced in her eyes. "William is thirty-two, and I'm supposedly thirty-five."

When William finished his explanation, he turned to Darlene. "Are you ready to show Kaia and her family the bungalow she'll be staying in?"

Casting a quick smile at Eric, she waved a dismissive hand at William. "You can do that. After all, you chose the room for her."

As William glared at his assistant, his cheeks turned red. "I just wanted to make sure that Kaia roomed with Kylie, who is closer to her age."

"That's what I meant." Darlene smiled at him sweetly. "If you want me to come, I will," she said with enough reluctance to make it clear that she didn't want to tag along.

Perhaps he'd been wrong, and she wasn't in love with William?

Threading his arm through hers, he said, "I'm parched. So, if you don't need Darlene, she can show me where to get a Coke."

"We don't have Coke at the lodge." William looked at his assistant. "The directors insist on only healthy soft drinks."

"We have great-tasting cucumber-infused water." Darlene tugged on Eric's arm. "When you are done inspecting the bungalow, you can join us at the cafeteria. I'm sure everyone is hungry."

"I am." Idina started wiggling on Gilbert's shoulders. "Can I come with you?"

"Don't you want to see my room?" Kaia asked

For a moment Idina looked unsure, but then she sighed dramatically. "I want to see it, but I also want to go to the cafeteria after that."

"No problem, munchkin. Let's do that quickly because I'm hungry too."

"Phew." Eric wiped pretend sweat off his brow. "That was a close call."

"She's adorable and speaks so well for a three-year-old."

"Idina is three and a half, and she's been talking like a teenager since before she was two."

As they walked back to the lodge, he wrapped his arm around Darlene's shoulders, and she didn't even bat an eyelid at it.

"You didn't answer me about William. Is he or was he your boyfriend?"

She laughed. "Nope, never was, and never will be."

"Why? Because he's too young, or because he's your boss?"

"It's not an age issue. I like William a lot, but we are not each other's types. But even if we were, I work for him. It's bad to mix business with pleasure."

"So you're single?"

She lifted her face to him and smiled. "I am. How about you?"

"Very single and have no intention of changing my status." He pulled the lodge's door open for her.

"Is that supposed to scare me off?"

"No, I just don't like to lead anyone on."

She chuckled. "You're painfully blunt, but I like it, and I will be as blunt with you. I've just finalized my divorce, and I haven't been with anyone other than my ex for many years. I'm not looking for Mr. Forever. I'm looking for Mr. Right Now, and you seem like the perfect guy to celebrate my new single status with."

It was music to his ears.

Eric grinned. "You have a good eye, missy. I am the perfect choice to celebrate with."

38

KAIA

"It's a beautiful room." Kaia sat on the bed and pulled Idina onto her lap. "The mattress is very comfortable."

So far, the boys had behaved splendidly. Curious about all the new people and sights, they hadn't cried or protested even once about being strapped in their stroller.

"Let me see." Cheryl sat down beside her and smoothed her hands over the coverlet. "Everything is so luxurious. It really is like a high-end resort."

At the doorway, Gilbert grudgingly nodded. "I have to admit that it's much nicer than what I expected. Good job, William." He clapped him on the back. "You really care about your team."

"I want them to feel pampered. It's not easy to leave their friends and family, and I didn't want them to feel as if they were living in a boot camp on top of that. I want it to be a pleasant experience for everyone involved."

"Hi." Kylie Baldwin squeezed by Gilbert's bulk. "Welcome aboard, Kaia." She walked over to her and extended her hand. "I feel privileged to be working with you on this project."

She hadn't given her final okay yet, but after seeing the accommodations Kaia had run out of objections, so she was most likely in.

"The feeling is mutual." She shook Kylie's hand. "Let me introduce you to my family. They came to check out the place."

"It's beautiful, isn't it? I didn't expect to be working in a resort."

"Neither did I." She proceeded to introduce her family, and when all the handshaking was done, she asked, "Where are the other team members?"

"Corinne and Owen are in their bungalow. We just came back from lunch."

"I'm hungry." Idina looked up at Kaia. "Are we going to eat now?"

"Yes, sweetie." She lifted her off her lap and set her down on her feet. "Let's go."

"It was nice meeting you all," Kylie smiled before heading to her room.

"I can't believe that I'm actually doing this." Kaia shook her head as she took Idina's hand.

"You brought a suitcase," William said. "You must have expected to stay."

She smiled nervously. "I kept thinking that something would come up and I would decide to go back home." She looked at her baby brothers. "It's going to be tough to be away from them."

"You're going to be okay." Her mother wrapped her arm around her waist. "You will come home every two weeks, and we will try to visit at least once a month." She shifted her gaze to William. "Now that we've seen how lovely it is here, we might stay for the entire weekend the next time we come, provided that Eric will be able to fly us."

"Darlene can book seats for you on commercial flights, and I'll gladly cover the cost."

Gilbert cast him a glare and puffed out his chest. "I can afford to fly my family to Oregon. When is the contract signing going to take place?"

"It can wait for after you leave." William rubbed the back of his neck. "With how difficult it is for Kaia to part from her family, I don't want her to miss any time with you."

"We want to go over the contract with her," her mother said in a tone that brooked no argument.

William shook his head. "I'm sorry, but that won't be possible.

The contract contains sensitive information, and it's for Kaia's eyes only."

"I don't like it," Gilbert said. "Kaia is young and inexperienced. She wouldn't know what to look out for and might miss some of the catches and pitfalls."

Kaia wanted to roll her eyes, but she stifled the impulse out of respect for Gilbert. Her ability to process new information outpaced his by a wide margin, and she was trained to pay attention to the small print, but he still saw her as the little girl he'd taken under his wing twelve years ago, and he wanted to take care of her.

She patted his arm. "It's okay, Gilbert. I can read a contract just as well as you can. After lunch, William and I will go to his office, and you'll wait for me in the cafeteria. If I have any questions, I will give you and Mom a call."

That seemed to appease him, but he still cast William a suspicious glance from under hooded eyes. "I hope for your sake that you will deal honestly with Kaia." He turned to her. "Take a pen, and if anything seems vague or can be interpreted in more ways than one, underline it, and when you are done, call us before signing anything."

"Yes, sir." She saluted.

"Can we go now?" Idina tugged on her hand.

"Let's find Uncle Eric." Gilbert lifted her onto his shoulders. "I hope he's still in the cafeteria with William's assistant trying to charm the sweet-smelling petunias off her."

"What's petunias?" Idina asked.

Kaia wanted to ask what the hell he'd meant by that, but not in front of William. Were petunias a code name for panties? And why were they sweet-smelling?

"Petunias are flowers." Her mother glared at Gilbert. "You really need to pay attention to what you say in front of her. She's much smarter than you think."

"Oh, I know." He patted Idina's back. "She's Daddy's brilliant little girl. Right, Idina?"

"Yes." She planted a kiss on the bald spot at the top of his head.

Kaia glanced at William, curious to see if he was bothered by Eric moving in on Darlene, but he seemed no more and no less stressed than he'd been since he'd first greeted them at the airport.

Was he still worried that she would decline his offer? Or was he worried about working with a girl he was attracted to but thought of as forbidden fruit?

39

WILLIAM

As William entered the code lock of the door leading to the office wing of the lodge, Kaia patted her belly. "I ate too much, and now my brain is foggy from all the food. I won't be able to concentrate on the contract."

"I doubt it." William led her down the corridor to Emmett's office. "Your brain is a fine-tuned machine that keeps churning no matter what. It probably solves problems for you while you sleep."

She laughed nervously. "How did you know?"

"Because mine does the same."

"Is your office located here in the lodge?"

He pushed his glasses up his nose. "My office is at the lab. We are going to use Emmett Haderech's for the contract signing. He's the founder of Safe Haven, and he and his partner are going to be there to witness it."

She frowned. "How are they connected to the project? I thought that you were only sharing the facilities with them."

"I'll explain when we are inside, but I can give you a hint. Emmett's presence is needed to ensure the project's secrecy."

Her eyes widened, and she leaned closer to him. "Is he the hypnotist?"

Putting a finger to his lips, William nodded.

"I didn't expect to meet him today." Kaia looked worried. "What if that doesn't work on me?"

He took her hand and gave it a gentle squeeze. "Without you, the team is worthless, so let's hope that it does."

"It didn't occur to me that I could still be turned down." She let out a breath. "I don't know whether I should hope that it will work or hope that it won't."

He stopped in front of Emmet's office and turned to her. "Do you still have doubts?"

Given how fast her pulse was racing, Kaia was either concerned about meeting Emmett, getting hypnotized, joining the project, or all of the above.

"I haven't seen the lab yet, and that's where I will be spending most of my time. Can I see it before I sign the contract?"

"Is it really that important for you to see the lab, or are you just stalling?"

She smiled sheepishly. "You caught me. I want to see the lab, but it's not going to influence my decision unless it's horrible. Though after seeing how much effort has gone into the bungalows we will be staying in, I have no doubt that the lab will be at least adequate. Besides, if I don't like working there, I won't put in as many hours, so you should hope that I'll love it."

"I think you will. It's underground for security reasons, and it has a thick door that can withstand one hell of a blast, but it's spacious, well-lit, and nicely furnished. We have two couches down there, a kitchenette, a bar, and even a ping-pong table for when we need to let off steam."

William had never played ping-pong, but he'd gotten the idea from an article he'd read about keeping employees happy. The couches and the break room had been inspired by the same article, and he even asked Ingrid to figure out a way to incorporate some of those ideas into the village lab.

"I don't know how to play ping-pong," Kaia said. "But the setup sounds lovely. Are there any desks and chairs in there as well? After all, we are supposed to put in some work, not just lounge around and play ping-pong all day."

"Of course, there are. The other stuff is there for when we need to take a break or to brainstorm." He gave her a reassuring smile before knocking on Emmett's office door. "I'm looking forward to brainstorming with you. I'm sure it's going to be delightful."

Her demeanor changing in an instant, she gave him a look full of promise. "I'm looking forward to that as well."

Damn, the girl wasn't subtle, and she'd gotten him to respond precisely as she'd intended.

Stifling a groan, William depressed the handle and opened the door.

"Hello, sweet child." Emmett rose from behind the desk and walked over to Kaia. "How lovely you are." He enfolded her in his arms, the long sleeves of his white robe hanging down the back of her thighs.

Kaia cleared her throat. "It's nice to meet you, Mr. Haderech."

"Call me Emmett." He released her from his embrace and motioned for her to take a seat on one of the chairs in front of his desk.

"Where's Eleanor?" William asked as he sat down on the other chair.

"She had to step out for a few moments, but we don't really need her here." Emmett put his finger on the folder with Kaia's contract and pushed it toward her. "Before you open the folder, I need you to listen carefully to what I'm going to say."

Swallowing, she nodded.

"You will never discuss, write down, mime, or use any form of communication to reveal the details of this contract with anyone other than William. Is that clear?"

His words had been laced with a heavy dose of compulsion, and even though it hadn't been directed at William, he could feel its effect. Hopefully, Kaia had felt it as well.

"What if something is not clear and I need to ask my mother or Gilbert for advice?"

"William will explain everything in detail, and a smart girl like you will have no trouble understanding it. It's not written in legal jargon, and it's straightforward." Emmett grinned. "Basically, it says that if you tell anyone outside your team or William any details about the research, we will have to kill you."

She gasped, her eyes darting to William.

Emmett's attempt at humor was a big mistake given what had happened to Kaia's friend, but he didn't know about the missing scientist.

"Bad joke, Emmett." William shook his head. "Really bad."

"My apologies." Emmett reached for Kaia's hand across the table. "I just couldn't help myself. Although to be frank, the monetary consequences of breaching the confidentiality are so bad that you might wish we killed you instead of taking away all of your money."

"I don't have any." She pulled her hand out of his grasp. "I'm nineteen."

"Right. But after this job is done, you will have plenty of it." Emmett leaned back. "Now put your hand over your heart and repeat after me. I, Doctor Kaia Locke, will never reveal any details about the research conducted in this facility to anyone other than those working directly with me on it."

She put her hand over her heart as he'd instructed, but instead of repeating his words, she tilted her head and put her hand down. "What about you and Darlene? Are you involved in the research? I need to know precisely who I'm allowed to talk to about it and who I'm not."

A cold shiver ran down William's spine. Kaia should have repeated Emmett's instructions like a robot. The fact that she'd stopped to ask more questions suggested that she was immune to compulsion, which wasn't possible. He'd tested her susceptibility to thralling, and he'd had no problem entering her mind.

Emmett looked at her with the same concern in his eyes. "Eleanor, Darlene, and I are not directly involved in the project, so you shouldn't discuss it with us collectively or individually. You can only discuss it with William, Doctor Corinne Burke, Kylie Baldwin, and Owen Ferrel. Is that clear enough?"

"You should have said so from the start." Kaia put her hand over her heart. "I, Doctor Kaia Locke, will never reveal any details about the research conducted in this facility to anyone other than those working directly with me on it."

"Very good." Emmett smiled. "I need you to do one more thing for me before you open that folder." He pointed at William. "Tell him what you were thinking about just now."

"I was thinking that you are trying hard to appear indifferent to me, but you are failing." Her eyes widened in alarm, but she continued. "I know that you're attracted to me, and no matter how hard you try, you can't deny it, so just stop fighting it."

William swallowed. "Am I that transparent?"

"Yeah, you are." She turned to Emmett. "Did you hypnotize me to do that? I didn't want to tell him what I was thinking."

Emmett grinned. "I did. I had to test you to make sure that it worked."

She frowned. "I didn't feel anything, and I was sure that it hadn't worked. I would have known if you hypnotized me, and besides, I'm not hypnotizable."

"Evidently, you are. I'm very good at what I do."

Shaking her head, she turned back to William. "Are you okay? You look a little frazzled."

"I thought I was doing a better job of hiding my very inappropriate attraction to a girl who is much too young for me to even notice that way."

"Don't sweat it." She opened the folder and pulled out the contract. "It is what it is, and we can't control how we feel about people. We can only control what we do about it." She sighed. "I just don't want it to be awkward between us."

Kaia sounded so mature, but the fact remained that she was nineteen and probably still a virgin, though given how forward she was, maybe she wasn't. It made no difference.

She was off limits.

40

DARLENE

"I need to change the boys' diapers." Karen rose to her feet. "Can you point me in the direction of a changing station?"

"We don't have one." Darlene followed Karen up. "If you haven't noticed, there are no kids here." She leaned closer. "The community members who run this place believe in free love and no children, if you know what I mean, and no kids are allowed in the spiritual retreats."

"That's just sad." Karen slung the strap of her enormous baby bag over the stroller's handle. "I'll just take them outside and find a bench. I have a changing pad."

"I'll come with you." Gilbert rose to his feet. "Come, munchkin." He ruffled Idina's hair. "Help Mommy and Daddy change your brothers' diapers."

"Okay." The girl looked at her uncle. "Do you want to come change poopie diapers?"

"No, thank you. I smelled their poops before, and I'm not getting anywhere near that."

"I'll come too." Cheryl smirked under her breath. "We've been here half a day and didn't get to walk on the beach yet."

"We can take a walk," Karen offered. "But we don't want to be gone for too long. Kaia should be back any minute now, right?" She looked at Darlene. "How long does it take to read the contract?"

"Not that long. The other team members were done in less than half an hour. I don't know what is taking Kaia so long."

"She's reading it with a magnifying glass." Gilbert took Idina's hand. "Let's change those diapers."

As the family headed out, Darlene sat back down next to Eric. "I admire your brother and Karen for having three little kids at their age. I have only one son, and even though I was much younger when I had him, I still remember how difficult it was."

"How old is he?" Eric pulled his chair a little closer to hers.

Darlene smiled. "I'm not going to tell you because that will reveal my age. Do you have kids?"

"Nope, and even though I adore my nephews and nieces, I'm glad that I don't. My ex is a piece of work, and the only smart thing I did when I married her was to refuse to have kids with her."

"Is that why she divorced you?"

He looked at her down his nose. "Who said that she divorced me? Perhaps I divorced her?"

"You wouldn't be as bitter. You would feel guilty. Ask me how I know."

"How?"

"My ex was a piece of work as well, and I was the one who filed for divorce. But despite all the crap he had done to me, I still feel guilty about ending my marriage."

Eric's face darkened. "What did he do?"

"I'd rather not talk about it." She put a hand on his thigh. "Am I going to see you again?"

"Do you want to?"

"I wouldn't have asked if I didn't, and you are leaving soon."

He leaned so close to her that his breath tickled her ear. "I would have loved to stay, but I have to fly my brother and his family home. I'll come back here as soon as I can."

Darlene wasn't sure she believed him. He'd just met her, and she wasn't a great catch worthy of flying over for, but as the saying went —hope springs eternal.

"You didn't ask for my phone number, but I'll give it to you anyway. If you manage to work out a visit, let me know." She pulled out her phone, anxious to see if he would give her his number.

He regarded her with hooded eyes. "I might get back here tomorrow. I had a client scheduled to charter the jet for the next two days, but he didn't put down a deposit, which was due today, and since I haven't heard from him, I assume that he has changed his mind. But until I hear from him, I can't just take him off the schedule. He's been chartering my jets for years."

Eric's explanation had been too long and too detailed for it to be a brush-off, but she still couldn't believe that he was so eager to hook up with her. Had he been going through a dry spell?

That was doubtful.

He was handsome and charming, and he was a pilot who owned two private jets. That made him irresistible to 99.9 percent of the single ladies' population, and probably fifty percent of the not-so-single one as well.

"Call me as soon as you hear from your client, and I'll arrange for a driver to pick you up at the airport."

"Nah." He leaned back. "That would spoil the surprise. I'll get a rental and drive myself over here."

"Sounds romantic, but that's not a good idea." She leaned closer to him. "Because of the research, the security around the resort is insane, and any unrecognized vehicle is stopped and inspected."

Eric didn't look concerned. "I'll risk that. What are they going to do, shoot at me?"

"No, but they are going to stop you and search the car, and it won't be pleasant."

She was probably exaggerating, but Darlene didn't want him to surprise her. If she was going to hook up with a guy for the first time in twenty-three years, she wanted to be mentally and physically prepared.

He leaned closer and brushed his lips over her cheek, sending shivers through her body. "I want you to wait for me with bated breath, but I don't want you to be prepared for my arrival. When I get here, I'll sweep you off your feet and take you straight to bed."

"Oh my," she said breathlessly. "I won't be able to sleep tonight."

"Good." He leaned back. "Then you won't mind if I call you in the middle of the night to talk dirty to you."

She looked around her in alarm, but no one seemed to have heard him. Leaning toward him, she whispered, "Is that your thing? You like dirty talk?"

Eric smirked. "Among other things."

41

WILLIAM

Darlene stood next to William as they both watched Kaia say a tearful goodbye to her family. "Poor girl. She seems so confident, so strong. I didn't expect her to fall apart like that." She chuckled. "Roni couldn't wait to get out of the house. The moment he turned eighteen, he moved out even though he was just exchanging one prison for another."

It broke William's heart to see Kaia cry her eyes out as she hugged her baby brothers and kissed their cheeks.

"She's very attached to her younger siblings. I don't think it would have been as difficult for her if it was just the adults and Cheryl. She must have strong maternal instincts."

"That reminds me." Darlene looked up at him. "Did you ask her about the old guy inside her head?"

"He was middle-aged, not old, and no, I didn't." Grimacing, he whispered, "I had a hard enough time just controlling my libido."

"I don't know why you are fighting it so hard. So she's young, but she's very mature, smart, and she's into you. So, what's the problem?"

"She's practically a kid. I feel like a pedophile for even thinking about her as a woman."

Darlene shook her head. "She is a woman, William, legally and otherwise, and you two are a match made in heaven. Where are you going to find another lady who is smart enough to actually challenge you? Besides, wasn't Wonder only nineteen when she and Anandur first met?"

"That was different. Wonder is ancient. She's older than Annani by a year or two."

Huffing out a breath, Darlene put a hand on his bicep. "Wonder had spent all those thousands of years in stasis, and she'd only accumulated nineteen years of experiences. I bet that Kaia is more mature than Wonder was when she fell in love with Anandur. In fact, Kaia's soul is so old that she might as well be my age."

He cast her a small smile. "How did it go with the uncle? Are you two going to see each other again?"

"I hope so. We've exchanged phone numbers, and he said that he would try to return as early as tomorrow, but I'm not holding my breath. Eric is a player, and frankly, I don't know what he sees in me when he can get women half my age."

"Maybe he likes more mature ladies? I for one prefer older women who know what they want, and who don't play games."

"You just described Kaia. She knows what she wants, and she's not bashful about it."

Perhaps that explained why he was so attracted to her. It wasn't just about her incredible brain and her sexy, young body. It was also about her assertive attitude and her directness.

"She kissed me," he admitted. "It was to thank me for agreeing to help find her friend, but she kissed me on the lips, so it couldn't have been just about gratitude."

"Good for her!" Darlene said a little too loudly. "Sorry," she whispered. "I got excited. Was it a real kiss, or just a peck?"

William felt his face getting warm. "It was more of a peck, but she did it with gusto."

"I see. So no tongue."

"Fates, you sound like a teenager, but then in immortal terms, you are."

"Really?" Darlene tossed her hair back. "That makes me feel so much better about my age."

"You are a beautiful woman." He patted her arm. "I don't know why you are so self-conscious."

She sighed. "Twenty-seven years with a man who loved pointing out all my flaws have done a number on me. I know now that I was beautiful back then, but I'm no longer young, so no matter how hard I work on my body, it's not going to look like it did in my twenties."

"It will when you transition." He didn't want to butt his nose into her private affairs, but they were friends, and he felt like he needed to remind her of what should have been obvious. "I get it that Eric is charming and handsome, and he seems less intimidating than the immortal males available to you, but you will be wasting your time and his if you pursue a relationship with him." He rubbed the back of his neck. "Max is a nice guy, and he's interested. Why won't you give him a chance?"

She shifted her gaze to Eric, who was hugging Kaia and murmuring encouragement to her. "I haven't been with anyone other than Leo in over two decades, and I need to re-enter the dating scene gradually. Eric is not relationship material, and I don't have any expectations from him other than a few tumbles between the sheets. If that goes well, I'll take the next step and look for a suitable immortal male."

"There was no one in the village who appealed to you?"

She shook her head. "Maybe I should visit your clan in Scotland and check out the selection there."

"And leave Roni? And what about your mother and sister?"

She shrugged. "If I find someone there, I'll just drag him to the village with me. I'm a Dormant, which makes me worth any sacrifice, right?"

William didn't know whether she meant it or was just being sarcastic, but it was a good opportunity to show his friend his support. "You are definitely worth it, Darlene. And not just because you are a Dormant. You are smart, beautiful, and capable. Any man, whether human or immortal, would be lucky to have you as his mate."

42

KAIA

Kaia waved at the bus as it drove away with her family. The torrent of tears refused to abate no matter how much she tried to staunch it, and now, in addition to that, a choking sensation in her throat was adding to her distress.

She kept waving until the bus left the parking lot, and she couldn't see it anymore unless she ran after it, which she was tempted to do.

It was irrational to get so emotional over a short two-week separation, but she couldn't help it, and she hated the feeling of being alone. Her family was her fortress, her source of strength, and without them, she felt like a leaf that had fallen off a tree and drifted away, carried on the wind.

"Let me show you the lab." William put a gentle hand on her shoulder but stayed behind her, giving her a moment to regain her composure. "You can get a sneak peek at the journals."

Wiping the tears off her cheeks with the back of her hands, she heaved a sigh. "Is Darlene coming with us?"

"I can't," Darlene said. "I don't have the security clearance. I don't even know what you will be working on."

"Right. I forgot." Kaia finally turned around.

Given the pitying look in William's eyes, she must look as dreadful as she felt. Her eyes were probably red and puffy, and she needed to blow her nose, but she didn't have tissues in her tiny purse.

"Can we stop by the lodge first? I need to visit the ladies' room."

"Of course." William lowered his hand to the small of her back.

She appreciated that. The cold seeping throughout her body had nothing to do with the weather, and only the warm human contact he offered could remedy it.

Darlene followed them into the lodge. "Do you want me to come with you to the bathroom?"

"I'm okay." Kaia gave her a small smile. "Thanks for everything."

"Anytime." Darlene enfolded her in her arms. "If you need anything, and I mean even if you just feel lonely and want to talk, call me. I left my number on a sticky note stuck to the toaster in your bungalow."

"Thank you." Kaia moved out of the woman's embrace and ducked into the ladies' room.

Thankfully, there was no one there, and she released a shuddering breath before reaching for a paper towel to blow her nose into.

A look in the mirror confirmed her suspicions. Her eyes were red and puffy, and her cheeks looked blotchy. Some girls looked pretty when they cried, but Kaia wasn't one of them.

It was good that she didn't cry often. Cheryl, who was a little sarcastic and liked to make snarky comments about everything and everyone, cried like a baby when watching a sad scene in a movie. But Kaia didn't cry, not even when she was just as moved by the story.

Maybe it was because of the memories she carried with her from a life as a man who hadn't been allowed to show emotions as freely.

After splashing her face with cold water, Kaia felt a little better, but after she'd dried it with a couple of paper towels and looked in the mirror again, she groaned. Her appearance hadn't improved much, but maybe it wasn't all bad. William would be relieved, not because she was sad—he'd seemed genuinely disturbed by her tears—but because it would be easier for him to resist his attraction to her.

He'd offered to show her the manuscripts to cheer her up or to distract her, and it had been a good move. She was curious to see them, and if she started working right away, she wouldn't be thinking about her family and how much she was going to miss them.

When she walked out of the bathroom, William pushed away from the wall he'd been leaning against and walked up to her. "Are you feeling better? Do you want something to drink? Tea, perhaps?"

"I want a Coke, but you don't have any, so I'll settle for tea."

"If you want a Coke, you'll get it." He pulled out his phone and typed up a message so fast that his fingers blurred. "Not immediately, but it will get here in about three hours." He put the phone back in his pocket. "The bus driver will buy a crate of it on the way back."

"That's so nice of you. Thank you."

"Don't hesitate to ask for anything you need or want." He put his hand on the small of her back again, the warmth of it again chasing the cold away. "My job is to make you happy."

She smiled up at him. "What if I want to go to Paris? Will you take me there to make me happy?"

"Of course. Right after the project is done."

"What if I want to go into space? Will you pay a million dollars to get me a spot on the shuttle?"

He laughed. "I'm not that rich. You are a dangerous young lady, and I shouldn't make open-ended promises to you."

"I was just teasing. I don't want to go to space."

What she wanted was a handsome, smart, and adorable nerdy guy with a heart of gold, and getting him wouldn't be nearly as difficult as getting a seat on the space shuttle.

43

WILLIAM

Kaia sat in front of the computer, leaning so close to the screen that her nose was nearly touching it. "Whoever wrote this had very neat handwriting. It almost looks like print." She rolled the chair back and looked at William. "I need to see the originals or at least a printout of the screenshots you took. I can't decipher anything if I have to look at snippets. I need to go back and forth and compare sections."

William had been afraid of that, but he'd hoped that with her genius, Kaia could start deciphering Okidu's journals page by page.

"I can print out the first journal for you, but it can't leave the lab, and I don't want you sharing it with the others unless there is no other choice. My idea was for you to give them limited tasks that would prevent them from putting the puzzle pieces together."

Frowning, she slid the chair closer to his. "What do you think is in those journals? And where did you find them?"

He'd expected that question, and he had prepared a fictional story that he hated to tell Kaia, but the less she knew, the better.

"The journals were found in an archeological dig, and we don't know who the author was."

She glanced at the screen and adjusted her glasses. "What's your theory?"

He smiled. "I have several, but as a scientist, you will roll your eyes at all of them."

"Try me." Her blue eyes shone with curiosity. "You'll find me very open-minded to the supernatural, the alien, and even to conspiracy theories if they are well thought out."

That was good to hear, but his so-called theories were fabrications loosely based on the truth.

"My first thought was that the journals had been written by alien scientists who had somehow gotten stranded on Earth. Their technology didn't survive the trip, and they wanted to preserve their knowledge because they didn't want to forget it, or maybe they were dying and didn't want it to die with them. They recorded everything using the tools available to them and buried the treasure for future generations of humans to find and make use of."

Kaia leaned even closer to him, her knees almost touching his. "When were they written? Did you have the journals dated? That would give you a good estimate of when those aliens arrived on Earth."

"It wasn't a very long time ago. They were written in journals that were manufactured in this century."

Her eyes widened. "When? In the fifties? Were they found near Area 51?"

The leather-bound journals that Okidu had used had been manufactured in China since the early 2000s, but he needed to preserve the air of mystery around them to keep Kaia misinformed.

"I'm sorry, but I can't tell you that. The information is classified."

She pouted but then shrugged. "I'll probably figure it out when I decipher the writings." She slid the rolling chair back to her station and put her nose to the screen again. "It really looks like an alien language. What are your other theories?"

"It could have been written by humans who used some sort of code that my most advanced software couldn't crack because I didn't have the key. It's possible that it's hidden within the manuscripts, and only a worthy scientist will be able to uncover it."

"Like Excalibur." Kaia pretended to pull a sword out of the rock. "Am I the worthy scientist?"

He smiled. "Evidently, I wasn't, but then I'm not a bioinformatician, and after many hours of poring over the symbols, I had the brilliant realization that the code is genetic and that I would need to assemble a team of people who are experts in that sort of code."

She nodded. "That was a smart move. Any other theories?"

"Yeah. That the crate full of journals contains the ramblings of a lunatic, and I'm wasting incredible resources and valuable time on nonsense that just appears scientific."

"You don't really believe in that one, do you? You wouldn't have gone to all the trouble of building this super-secure lab and equipping it with computing power that could rival Stanford's."

"No, I don't. My favorite is the first one. Aliens." He smiled and waggled his brows.

She laughed as if he'd done the funniest thing. "You look ridiculous when you do that thing with your brows, but it's adorable." She leaned forward and poked his cheek with her finger. "You have such cute dimples when you smile. You should smile more."

William could barely breathe.

Kaia was leaning over him, her ample breasts nearly spilling out of her low-necked T-shirt, and her feminine scent filling his nostrils.

Sensing his distress, she leaned away and looked at him with those eyes that looked too old on such a young face. "I'm sorry for invading your personal space." She chuckled. "I tend to do that when I get excited, and I'm with people who I like and trust."

He didn't want her to feel guilty about something that wasn't her fault.

"I'm glad that you like and trust me, and if I weren't so damn attracted to you, I wouldn't have even noticed that you were in my personal space, because I tend to do the same with people who I like."

Kaia grinned. "We are so much alike, you and me. Maybe too much."

"What do you mean?"

She shook her head. "Never mind."

"Now that you've blurted that out, you can't leave me hanging. Why are we too much alike? In what way?"

44

KAIA

Sometimes Kaia's mouth ran away from her, saying things she shouldn't have. What was she going to tell William? That she often switched to thinking from a man's perspective? That she knew precisely what was going through his head when he got a peek at the tops of her breasts because she remembered having those feelings as Edgar?

Men were visual creatures, and they went from zero arousal to a hundred in a millisecond. William was probably sporting one hell of a hard-on right now, and he was desperate to adjust his painful erection in his pants but didn't want her to see that.

"We both have blue eyes and wear glasses." She turned back to the screen, giving him the opportunity to get more comfortable.

"Why is that a problem?"

Because she sometimes looked at her own body in the mirror and got excited, not as Kaia, but as Edgar, and that was not only confusing but also disturbing.

"It's hard to kiss when the two people kissing both have glasses on." She leaned as if to get a better look at the strange symbols while seeing nothing but a blur.

"Do you have a lot of experience kissing someone with glasses?"

"Other than you? Yeah, I do." She didn't turn to look at him.

Let him stew on that for a while.

She squeaked in surprise when he pulled her chair toward him, and when he wheeled it around, so she was facing him, Kaia got an even bigger surprise.

It must have been a trick of the light, but his eyes were glowing, and since he was wearing glasses, it couldn't be light reflecting from contact lenses.

"Was it Anthony?" he growled.

"Not that it's any of your business, but I've already told you that there was nothing romantic between us. I never kissed Tony."

"Did he kiss you?"

She narrowed her eyes at him. "What is it to you?"

"I don't like being manipulated, and I don't appreciate you thinking so little of me. I suspect that you told me that Anthony was just a friend because you assumed that I wouldn't help you look for him if I thought that he was your boyfriend."

"Would you have helped me if he was?"

"Yes, I would."

Perhaps, but he wasn't entitled to play the saint when he was dragging his feet about helping her until she signed the contract and came to work for him.

"So why didn't you? Because you were waiting for the contract to be signed before you helped me?"

"That was true in the beginning, but for your information, I forwarded everything you gave me to Roni. He hasn't gotten back to me yet, and that's because he has his hands full at the moment." William pulled out his phone. "I'll text him right now and ask if he's had a chance to look into it."

"It's Sunday."

"Right." William put his phone down on the desk. "Roni's mate doesn't allow him to work on Sundays. I'll text him first thing tomorrow morning.

Looking at the device, Kaia frowned. "How come you can have your phone in here and I can't?"

He smiled. "Because I'm the boss. Besides, yours won't work down here. Mine is special."

"I bet."

"You still didn't answer my question. Who was the guy with glasses you kissed? Was he a fellow student?"

"Why are you so interested in my love life?"

"You didn't mention past boyfriends in the security briefing."

Ah, so that was what bothered him.

Kaia was willing to bet that William had assumed she was still a virgin and had never had a boyfriend. When she'd mentioned kissing a guy, he'd gotten angry because he was jealous, and not because of the potential security breach caused by the omission of a former boyfriend from the list of friends and acquaintances she'd provided.

He was lucky that she knew how a male's brain worked and how influenced it was by testosterone. Otherwise, she would have been offended.

"It was close to two years ago, didn't last long, and we didn't stay in touch. There was no reason to mention him in the briefing."

Kaia had been seventeen at the time and desperate to explore her sexuality, but since she'd gone through puberty surrounded by people twice her age, there hadn't been anyone she could have explored it with. They'd still regarded her as a kid when she'd turned into a woman. Besides, she hadn't wanted an older guy either. The problem was that when boys closer to her age had heard that she was on her way to earning her PhD, they'd thought she was either a liar or a freak and had hoofed it away.

She was a liar, and a very good one at that, but her lies ran in the opposite direction.

Her only option was to lie about her academic achievements and claim that she was a regular girl who was homeschooled.

When she'd met the cutest boy at a Starbucks, that was what she'd told him, and they'd started dating.

It had been fun.

He was eighteen, a little older than her, and he'd already had sex, or so he'd claimed. If he had, he hadn't been very experienced, and it had been a little awkward at first, but after a few times, it had gotten better, and she'd started to enjoy it. But then he'd gotten into a good college in Ohio, and that had been the end of it.

He'd promised to call and come to visit her during vacations, but he'd stopped calling after a couple of weeks, and she'd gotten the message.

It hadn't been a great loss, and Kaia hadn't been heartbroken over it, but she hadn't had time to pursue another relationship while working on her thesis and publishing papers in scientific journals.

45

WILLIAM

Was Kaia telling the truth?

William wasn't great at detecting lies, but he sensed that she was evading his inquiries with half-truths. Then again, unless whatever she was hiding was connected to the journals or could sabotage the safety of the research, it was Kaia's right to tell him as much or as little as she pleased.

Theoretically, she could have had a boyfriend at seventeen, but practically, it was unlikely. She'd been working on her doctoral thesis at the time and had no contact with people her age, and she'd told him that older guys didn't interest her.

But that had been a lie as well. If she was showing interest in him, a pudgy, dorky guy that was as charming as a physics textbook, then he probably wasn't the first older man she'd pursued.

It was none of his business, especially when he was trying to keep a professional distance from her and shouldn't get too close to her. But he couldn't deny the burning need to unravel the mystery of Doctor Kaia Locke. He had to know what she was about, what was the truth and what was a fabrication, and why she had a male persona hiding behind her delicate, feminine features.

Perhaps he could goad her into revealing the truth.

"I find it hard to believe that you had only one boyfriend at seventeen and no one since. Or was he just the only one with glasses?"

Kaia threw her hands in the air. "What do you want from me, William? First, you don't believe that I've ever had a boyfriend, and then you don't believe that I've had only one? Make up your mind."

He let out a breath. "I'm sorry. It's just that you baffle me. On the one hand, you are a young woman who is still strongly attached to her family, but on the other hand, you have the maturity and insight of a much older person, and to be frank, I sense something masculine in you, and I don't know where it's coming from."

That was probably the worst way to ask Kaia about her other persona, but it was too late to take it back.

She huffed with her big eyes full of indignation. "Figures. When a woman is successful and assertive, she gets accused of being masculine. I didn't peg you for a chauvinist, William McLean."

"I'm not a chauvinist." He took his glasses off and wiped them with the corner of his shirt, but he'd forgotten that it wasn't one of his Hawaiian silk ones, and the fabric of the new shirt he was wearing was the wrong kind for cleaning glasses. "I'm sorry if my ill-phrased comment offended you, but I'm just very intuitive, and that's the vibe I get from you. Perhaps I'm mistaken."

Hopefully, the line Darlene had suggested would work better than his previous fumbling attempt.

"Ugh." Letting out a breath, Kaia closed her eyes and slumped in her chair, looking defeated or pretending to be. "You think that I'm into women."

"I didn't say that, and I didn't think that. It was just an observation, and it was obviously wrong. Can we forget that I even mentioned it?"

"Nope." She opened her eyes and looked at him with a naughty smile lifting one corner of her lush lips. "You challenged my femininity, and now I have to prove to you that I'm all woman." She rose to her feet, took a step toward him, and put her hands on the armrests of his rolling chair. "Can I kiss you? Or are you going to freeze up on me again?"

He wanted to grab her, plunk her on his lap, and do much more than just kiss her, but he wasn't going to do any of that.

"Don't. You're thirteen years younger than me, and you're my subordinate. It would be criminal of me to succumb to the temptation."

She didn't back up. Instead, her smile widened. "For it to be criminal, I would need to be underage, which I'm not, and you would have to be in a position to take advantage of me, which you're not. You need me for this research much more than I need this job, so if either of us could be accused of using their advantageous position to coerce the other, it would be me, not you. So, I'll ask you again. May I kiss you?"

46

KAIA

Could William hear her heart pounding?

Kaia heard it loud and clear, but maybe it was the sound of her blood pulsing in her veins?

Would he call her bluff and laugh in her face?

She didn't lack confidence, but she'd never been so daring. Something about William had awakened a naughty side of her that she hadn't been aware she had until he'd shown up in her life. It spurred her to goad him and torment him until he broke down and surrendered to that wild thing pulsing between them.

A pained groan was her only warning before his hands landed on her waist, and she was hoisted up and plunked onto his lap, the evidence of his desire a hard ridge under her bottom.

"You have half a second to say no," he gritted as he whipped his glasses off.

Was he kidding her?

"Yes."

As his palm closed around her nape, he commanded, "Close your eyes."

"So bossy," she teased but found herself wanting to obey.

Bossy William was sexy, and if he thought that his assertiveness would scare her, he couldn't be more wrong. Kaia had absolutely no doubt that if she wanted him to stop, all she had to do was say the word.

As if to prove she was right about that, his lips hovered over hers for a long moment, giving her the opportunity to retreat if she so pleased, but she had no intention of doing that. Instead, she closed the distance between them and fused their mouths.

When his tongue swiped over the seam of her lips, she opened for him with no hesitation, and when it found hers, the deep growl reverberating in his chest made her want to purr in satisfaction.

Winding her arms around his neck, she ground her bottom against his hard length, eliciting another sexy growl from him that went straight to her breasts, stiffening her nipples.

Then his hand tangled in her hair, tugging on it gently, and heat flooded her core. She'd never felt desire so all-consuming. William was a man and compared to the inferno of fire he was igniting in her, her one and only boyfriend had been a tiny candle, no pun intended.

His hand trailed under her T-shirt, finding the bare skin of her stomach and making her heart thunder in her chest, but he never moved it up as she hoped he would.

All she could do to quench her thirst was to grind herself over his straining erection.

When he pulled his hand out from under her T-shirt and released her mouth, she groaned in frustration, but she knew better than to press her luck by pushing him to go further.

Her lips still tingling from his kiss, Kaia was afraid to open her eyes, not because she was waiting for him to tell her that she could, but because she was afraid of what she would see.

Would he look guilty, disappointed, or angry?

Would he tell her that it could never happen again?

She wouldn't be able to bear it if he did. Not today, not when she still felt fragile after saying goodbye to her family.

"Kaia," he said her name as if it was a prayer. "Look at me."

Given his pained tone, she knew what he was about to say.

Resting her forehead against his, she whispered, "Give me one more moment to enjoy this before you tell me it can never happen again."

"That's not what I was going to say."

"It wasn't?" She lifted her head and looked into his intense blue eyes that were still shining with that strange inner glow.

Brushing his fingers over her cheek, he drew a line down to her jaw. "It's been an emotional day for you, and I should have realized that you felt vulnerable and needed to do something, anything, to make you feel better. I hope that you won't hate me tomorrow for taking advantage of that."

Ugh, the man was infuriating. Lifting her hands, she cupped his cheeks and glared right into his glowing eyes. "Don't you dare turn this into something ugly. It was the best kiss I ever had, with the best man I ever met, and it was beautiful."

A small smile bloomed on his handsome face and then turned into a big grin. "This really was your best kiss ever?"

"Hands down, no competition. You are an amazing kisser." Tucking her head under his chin, she smirked. "I hope that you are not going to hate me tomorrow for taking advantage of you."

He chuckled. "If you are stealing my lines, I'm going to steal yours. This was the best kiss I ever had as well."

"But? I can practically hear the but in your tone."

"But this is as far as I'm willing to go while we are working together."

"What about after the project is done?"

"By then, we will know each other better, and if the attraction is still there, we will take it to the next step."

William thought that he was so smart, but she knew what he was trying to do. By offering her a small carrot, he hoped that she would back off and give him a break.

If there was any merit to why he was resisting, or if he wasn't into her as much as she was into him, she would have respected his wishes, but since his reasons were nonsensical, she would keep pushing until he caved in and gave her what she wanted, and that was all of him.

"I guarantee that it will be there, even stronger than it is now, because we will be fighting it for months. You are just sentencing us to unnecessary torment."

He chuckled. "I'm a big believer in the merits of delayed gratification. All good things come to those who wait."

47

WILLIAM

What a liar he was, feeding Kaia that line about delayed gratification. Perhaps it had been true in the past when he'd been too busy to even think about female company, but she was bringing out all of his suppressed male immortal urges, including a dominant bent that William had never felt before.

Well, that wasn't true.

He was running a lab that had grown from a solo endeavor to an enterprise with dozens of people working for him, and he couldn't have done a good job of heading it if he didn't have leadership qualities, which required at least some degree of dominant tendencies.

Sexually, however, he'd never been assertive, and he had been more than happy to follow the female's lead.

Then again, he had never been pursued with such determination by a nineteen-year-old who thought that she was the boss.

Not that she was necessarily wrong. Kaia had him by the balls in more ways than one.

"Let's get out of here." He lifted her off his lap and set her down on the floor. "It's almost dinner time, and you should say hello to the rest of your teammates before we go to the dining hall."

"Are we going to dine in the lodge cafeteria?"

"No, we share a separate, smaller dining room with another program."

From now on, they wouldn't be using the lodge. Their bungalows and the lab were in a separate fenced-off area, but they would make use of the gym and the dining hall in the paranormals' section of the resort.

William wasn't happy about sharing the facilities with the paranormal program, but it didn't make sense to build a separate kitchen and dining hall for his team. Each one of the nine paranormals was under Eleanor's control, so in the event that one of his four team members let something slip despite the strong compulsion they were under, it would be easily contained.

The only one he was worried about was the doctor, but Eleanor had him so firmly under her control that the guy was nearly catatonic.

Kaia ran her fingers through her tangled hair. "I need to stop by my room and freshen up, if you know what I mean." She winked at him.

He had no idea what she meant, other than perhaps wanting to brush her hair. Maybe she wanted to wait until her lips were no longer swollen from their kiss, and her cheeks were no longer rosy with excitement, and her eyes were no longer glossy from desire…

Damn. He needed a breather before he could let anyone see him as well. His new jeans were uncomfortably tight, and not because he'd overeaten at lunch, and his eyes were probably still emitting light.

Kaia hadn't commented on that, so maybe she hadn't noticed, but that was doubtful. She watched him like a hawk, deciphering and learning him just as she did with every complicated project she'd ever tackled. If he wasn't super careful around her, she might figure out that he wasn't human.

"We can take a walk on the beach," he suggested. "It's not too windy today, and the ocean is calm."

"I would love that." Kaia lifted her ridiculously small purse off the desk and slung the thin strap across her body. "What's the protocol for locking the lab?" She took his hand.

"It locks itself." William led her out the door. "There are cameras everywhere, and the moment the door closes behind us, the locks and alarms engage. Only I can open the lab, and it requires the scanning of my iris."

As they reached the top of the stairs, he lifted his eyes to the scanner to open the second out of the three doors.

Kaia eyed him from under lowered lashes. "Aren't you worried that the people in security saw us kiss?"

The Guardians would have a field day teasing him about it, especially Max, but he wasn't too worried about that. What bothered him was them seeing Kaia in his arms, looking aroused and flushed. No one other than him was allowed to see her like that.

Hell, he shouldn't have seen her like that either.

Thankfully, they hadn't done anything more than kiss, so no harm was done to Kaia's reputation or his.

"We've done nothing wrong, and given the circumstances, I was the perfect gentleman. If I refused to kiss you, I would have offended you and hurt your feelings, which wouldn't have been very gentlemanly of me. So I kissed you, but I gave you every opportunity to change your mind, and I didn't put my hands anywhere I shouldn't have."

"I see." She looked a little put out. "So that's why you succumbed to my charms. You knew that if I wanted to cause you trouble, you would have proof of your good behavior."

He stopped and turned to her. "It was definitely your irresistible charm. I forgot all about the cameras, and it didn't occur to me that we were performing for an audience until you mentioned locking up the lab. I would have never willingly given the guys in security a show."

That seemed to appease her, but she still looked like a kid who had lost her favorite new toy.

When they went through the third door, she looked up at the camera together with him, watching it scan his iris. "This place is so 007. If someone wanted to infiltrate the lab, they would need to knock you out, haul you down here, and shove your eye under the scanner. Or they could just cut out your eyeball."

"That's so gruesome. Where did you come up with that idea?"

She smiled. "Movies. To mitigate the risk, you should have

scanned another person's eyeball. Then there would be two, cutting your risk in half."

"Are you volunteering yours?"

Kaia pursed her lips. "To be entrusted with such a treasure, I'm willing to take the risk."

48

KAIA

Dinner had gone by with Kaia replaying the kiss in her mind and stealing glances at William while trying to keep up the conversation with her teammates. She'd been so absent-minded that the others probably doubted she was as smart as William had claimed. She could barely remember what they'd talked about.

As they all headed back to the bungalows, William stopped in front of hers and Kylie's. "I'll see you all bright and early tomorrow morning."

"Do you want to come in for a cup of coffee?" She looked at Kylie. "Do we even have coffee? I haven't had the chance to check yet."

"We do, and we also have a pod coffee and cappuccino maker, and surprisingly, I found a box full of Coke, which given Safe Haven's healthy nutrition dictum, is akin to finding pot in a church. You are all invited." She waved her hand to include Corinne and Owen.

"Thank you." Kaia cast William a grateful smile. "I forgot that you asked the bus driver to get Coke for us."

He nodded and smiled back. "Thank you for the invitation, but I still have a lot of work to do tonight, and I'd better get on it, or I will be working until morning."

Bummer. Kaia had hoped they wouldn't have to say goodbye yet.

"It's Sunday," Corinne said. "You should allow yourself some time off, or you'll burn out."

"I happen to love what I do, so I doubt I'll burn out anytime soon, but I agree that balancing work and leisure is important." He cast a quick glance at Kaia. "I'm not very good at that."

It was her fault. She'd kept him from doing his work.

William hadn't left her side since she'd arrived in the morning. Well, not all of it had been her fault. He had to eat, so lunch and dinner didn't count, and it was also his job to introduce the team members to each other, so that didn't count either. Her culpability had been limited to three or four hours, and some of it had been work-related, so Kaia didn't feel too guilty for keeping William occupied with other things.

Despite the separation anxiety she'd suffered earlier when her family had left, it had been one of the best days she could remember in a long while.

Nothing could rival the elation she'd felt when her siblings had been born, but time spent with William was a close second, especially when it involved kissing.

"Does anyone have any questions before we part for the evening?" William's eyes darted to Kaia.

"What time are we supposed to get to the lab tomorrow?" she asked.

"Breakfast starts at six in the morning and lasts until seven-thirty. I'll meet you all at the dining hall at quarter to eight, and we will head to the lab together."

"What about our phones?" Owen asked. "You said that we couldn't bring them into the lab. Should we leave them in our rooms?"

"You can do that, or you can bring them with you and hand them over to me before we enter the lab's building. I'll put them in a secure locker."

When they all nodded, William's eyes shifted to Kaia again. "Well, goodnight, everyone." He smiled.

"Goodnight, William." She forced a smile back.

Why was it so difficult to part ways with him? She'd spent most of the day with him, and she was going to see him tomorrow morning. She shouldn't feel anxious because she was going to spend the night without him.

Perhaps she was still experiencing the lingering effects of her earlier anxiety attack?

It didn't make sense for her to feel such a strong pull toward him.

If she combined all the hours she'd spent with William so far, it would be less than one day, and she couldn't even think of him as her boyfriend. He was just a guy who she'd kissed a couple of times.

Nevertheless, as she watched him enter his bungalow and close the door behind him, she fantasized about sneaking inside in the middle of the night and curling up next to him in bed.

She wasn't going to do that, but knowing that the possibility existed eased the anxious feeling pressing on her chest.

"Do you want to hang out in our bungalow?" Kylie offered to Corinne and Owen.

Corinne shook her head. "Thanks, but I'm tired, and I want to veg in front of the television."

Owen looked like he was debating whether to accept Kylie's invitation or keep Corinne company. "I'll call it a night as well." He smiled at Corinne. "We can veg in front of the television together. What do you like to watch?"

As the two continued to their bungalow, Kaia followed Kylie into theirs. "Have you tried that coffee maker already?"

"I did, and it's great. Do you want me to make you a cappuccino?"

"Yes, please." Kaia plopped down on the couch and reached for the remote. "I like Corinne's idea. Do you want to watch a movie?"

"What do you have in mind?"

"William said that they have all the latest movies on their server, even those that are still playing in theaters." She started scrolling through the selection. "How about *One Morning in Barcelona*?"

Cheryl had seen it in the theater with her friends and had said that it was silly but sweet and funny. It was the perfect combination to lift her mood before she called home and talked with her mom.

Kaia had made such a scene when her family said goodbye that her mother was probably worried about her. She'd texted her and

Cheryl during dinner to tell them that she was feeling better and would call them after the twins were asleep, and she needed to sound cheerful and upbeat to convince her mother that it was true.

"Isn't that a chick flick?" Kylie finished frothing the milk and poured it into two cups.

"It is." Kaia was in the mood for something light and romantic, but maybe Kylie was a movie snob and liked to watch only foreign drama. "Do you want to watch something else?"

"No, a chick flick sounds awesome. It was a stressful day, and I want to relax with something silly." She handed Kaia a mug. "I didn't put any sugar in because the vanilla soy milk is already sweetened."

Kaia grimaced. "The one thing I really don't like about this place is their so-called healthy nutrition. If we can't get some snacks in here, I'm going to lose weight."

"You shouldn't let that happen." Kylie sat next to her on the couch. "You have a killer figure. What's your secret?"

Good genes and being nineteen, but she wasn't going to say that because it sounded condescending.

Kylie was in her late twenties, which was still young, but she hadn't been taking good care of herself. Most postdocs didn't. They worked too hard and got paid too little.

"I walk a lot while pushing a double stroller with my twin baby brothers in it. Surprisingly, it's a great workout and burns a lot of calories." Kaia kicked her flip-flops off and tucked her legs under her.

Kylie pursed her lips. "Interesting. Perhaps once this project is over, I'll look for a second job babysitting twins and get workouts as a bonus. Does your mom need help?"

"We have a nanny, but I can ask."

Kylie sipped on her cappuccino for a few moments and then put the cup down on the coffee table. "It's probably none of my business, but is there something going on between you and William?"

Was she asking because she was interested in him?

Kaia had the urge to bare her teeth at Kylie and tell her to stay away from him, but instead, she shrugged. "Maybe. I like him a lot, but he thinks that I'm too young for him."

Kylie snorted. "Of course, you are. You're practically a kid."

Shrugging again, Kaia pressed play on the remote. "Let's watch the movie."

The body she was occupying might be young, but her soul wasn't. She was, however, inexperienced, and it wasn't limited to sex. Edgar Rosu had been a bachelor and a loner, and if he had any relationships with women, Kaia didn't remember them. She had vague memories of him looking at women and lusting after them, but no actual sexual or amorous encounters.

What she remembered most vividly was the mathematics that had fascinated Edgar so thoroughly that he'd forgotten there was more to life than academia.

49

JADE

"I need access to the computer." Jade hated to ask Igor for anything, but the internet was the only connection she had to the outside world, and she needed his permission to use it.

He lifted his head and pinned her with his hard eyes. "What for?"

He didn't tell her to sit down, so she remained standing and schooled her facial features to hide her hatred for him. "I ran out of ideas for stories to tell the children. I need inspiration."

It was a Kra-ell tradition to teach the young through stories and parables, but since the old tales about the struggles of Kra-ell heroines, the tribal wars that had decimated the number of males, and the queen who had altered their future held no meaning under Igor's rule, she relied on human fairytales to teach them the basic tenets of what it meant to be honorable and to strive to become the best versions of themselves.

"Go ahead." He waved at the small desk in the corner of his office.

"Thank you."

Jade hated that she had to do it under his watchful eye as well, but what choice did she have?

Igor had told her time and again that she should be thankful that he was so generous with her, and that the privilege of using the internet would remain hers only as long as she was his prime female.

Jade would have gladly passed that dubious honor to another, but the privileges that came with it were worth the sacrifices. As the prime, she had some maneuvering room to ease the lives of the other females and their young.

Besides, she still would have been forced into his bed whether she was prime or not, so the only thing she would have accomplished by acting up would have been to lose the little freedoms she'd fought so hard for.

She was too smart to let that happen just to satisfy her need to lash out.

Sitting at the small desk with her back to Igor, she flipped the laptop open and typed the subject of her search into the browser—becoming the best version of yourself. There were many Kra-ell parables that examined the subject and inspired youngsters to push harder for excellence, but they didn't fit the circumstances of the children living in the compound. She needed new stories that would speak to them and inspire them.

Scrolling through a long list of articles and blog posts, she clicked on one that looked promising, read a few paragraphs, and then continued to the next. After about an hour, she had two articles printed out and a list of topics she could develop further. That was more than enough, but she wasn't ready to leave the internet yet.

Hopefully, someone would come into Igor's office and distract him long enough for her to find out what was going on in the world. It would be even better if he left while letting her stay.

Jade had done that so many times before that she no longer feared discovery. Igor had never caught her or called her out on that, so either no one was checking, or he didn't mind her little forays into forbidden websites.

After all, there was nothing she could do with that information aside from satisfying her curiosity. No one knew that she even existed, and even if there was someone searching for her and the other females, she couldn't ask for their help because of Igor's compulsion.

An hour later, she was still scrolling and pretending to read more articles about reaching one's full potential, but no one had come into the office, and Igor hadn't left even once. She was about to give up and end her search when she clicked on the last article on the sixth page, and a picture of a man in a white ceremonial robe came up.

He looked ridiculous, like one of the prophets from human scriptures, but there was something familiar about his dark eyes. Leaning closer to the screen, Jade enlarged the picture, and barely contained her gasp. Those were Kra-ell eyes, a hybrid's eyes to be more precise, and she knew who they belonged to. The one who'd run off years ago, the hybrid compeller who had been able to throw off her hold on him.

Veskar, who according to the virtual brochure was calling himself Emmett Haderech these days, ran a spiritual retreat that taught, among other things, how to achieve one's full potential.

It was such a fundamental Kra-ell concept that it had to be him.

Finally, she had found a member of her tribe who was free. Except, Veskar hadn't been a member of her tribe for many years. He'd always been smart, so she wasn't surprised that he'd used his compulsion ability to make money, and since he'd been doing that for decades, he was also smart enough to avoid discovery.

Good for him.

Should she contact him?

There wasn't much he could do to help her, unless he'd found another Kra-ell tribe after leaving hers. His compulsion ability was no match for Igor's, so on his own, Veskar was useless to her. Besides, even if he could, she doubted that he would be inclined to help her. There had been no love lost between them. But he might be willing to help the other females of their tribe.

Did he even know what had happened to their compound? Did he know that his father was dead?

But even if he could do nothing to help them, just knowing that someone on the outside knew that they were alive and that they were being held against their will would bring Jade more hope than she'd had in twenty-two years.

It wasn't likely that the queen would send new settlers after so many years, but if she did, Veskar could tell them about his tribe's fate.

The problem was figuring out a way to contact him without alerting Igor.

50

DARLENE

"Good morning." Darlene stopped next to Mollie and James's table. "Can I join you?"

Of the nine paranormals, they were the only two in her age group. Mollie was a year or two younger and had post-cognition ability, and James, who was a remote viewer and a weak telepath. He was in his mid-fifties but didn't look it.

Mollie smiled. "Of course."

"Good morning." James leaned over and pulled out a chair for her. "How are things going on the other side of the fence?"

Darlene put her plate down on the table and sat down. "Can't you just read my mind?" she teased.

Eleanor had told her that James's newfound telepathic ability was limited to feelings and impressions. If he could read her actual thoughts, Darlene wouldn't have been sitting with him and his girlfriend at breakfast.

"Let me see." He closed his eyes. "You feel disappointment, and I can tell that it has to do with a man." He opened his eyes. "Am I right?"

"You are. Good guess." She took a sip of her coffee to hide her grimace.

A message from Eric had waited on her phone this morning, letting her know that he couldn't make it after all.

It shouldn't have surprised her.

A guy like him wouldn't put so much effort into hooking up with a woman who was older than him and looked it.

The fact that he'd left the message at three o'clock in the morning probably meant that he'd done it at the end of a date, no doubt with some twenty-something hottie who had still been in his bed when he typed up the text.

Except, the message also said that he was flying Kaia's family for a visit on Saturday, and they would all stay for the weekend, so there was that.

Darlene had no right to feel jealous, and she should be glad that he was coming at all, but she would believe it when she saw him.

"It's not a guess," James said. "I can read your aura, and it seems muted, which indicates either depression or disappointment, but since you don't seem depressed, I assume that it's the latter."

She gave him a tight smile. "I thought that Spencer was the aura reader."

"I am," the guy said from the next table over. "And I agree with James. Your aura is dimmed compared to how it was yesterday, so you must have gotten some bad news today."

His girlfriend just smiled. Sofia's claim to fame was the ability to affect the flip of a coin or dice, but according to Eleanor, her talent was negligible.

Darlene shook her head. "You people are freaky."

Mollie laughed. "We will try to behave when your scientists get here." She glanced at her watch. "Are they joining us for breakfast?"

"It's still early, but they'll be here." Darlene put a tiny bit of jam on her toast. "William is meeting them here."

As the dining hall door opened, she hoped it was William with members of his team, but it was just Eleanor, who walked in with Abigail, Dylan, and Andy.

"You are up early." She regarded her flock. "Did you join Darlene and William in the gym this morning?"

Darlene snorted. "I had the place to myself. William didn't show up, and when I called him, he grumbled something about sleeping only two hours and hung up on me."

"He and Kaia make a cute couple." Dylan pulled out a chair for Abigail at the table next to Spencer and Sofia.

Was he suggesting that William had spent the night with Kaia and that was why he hadn't shown up for their swimming session?

Evidently, the guy wasn't a good judge of character despite his paranormal talent. It was something called claircognizance, which was supposedly the ability to acquire psychic knowledge without knowing how or why he knew it.

"They are not together," Darlene said.

Dylan arched a brow. "Are you sure? I had a strong feeling that they were."

Breakfast with the paranormals was turning into an episode of *The Twilight Zone*, and Darlene was starting to doubt the wisdom of mixing the two groups together. If the scientists had heard that conversation, they would have laughed their butts off.

On the other hand, maybe it wasn't such a bad idea to introduce them to phenomena they couldn't explain. It might get them thinking, and it might teach some humility to those know-it-alls who believed that science had all the answers.

Perhaps they were right, and one day the paranormal would acquire a scientific explanation, but for that to happen, they first needed to acknowledge that the phenomena were real.

51

WILLIAM

As a loud ringing woke William up, he groaned and reached for his phone, intending to turn the alarm off and go back to sleep, but it wasn't the alarm. It was a phone call, probably Darlene calling him again to get him to the gym.

"I'm not swimming today," he barked without even opening his eyes. "I got in bed less than two hours ago." He ended the call, dropped the phone on the nightstand, and when the ringing started again, he covered his head with a pillow.

If anyone needed him urgently, they could get ahold of one of the Guardians and send them over to knock on his door.

When the ringing stopped, he sighed in relief, but a moment later it started again. He was going to fire Darlene and send her back to the village.

With a groan, he tossed the pillow aside and grabbed the phone, opening his eyes this time to check that it was really her and he wasn't about to bark at Kian.

It was indeed Darlene, but as he glanced at the time, his anger flew out the window. It was quarter to eight, and he was late collecting his team from the dining hall.

"Hi," he answered as he threw the blanket off. "I'm sorry about before. I thought it was still early in the morning."

She chuckled. "As long as you get here in the next fifteen minutes, you're forgiven. I told everyone to grab another cup of coffee, and I asked the kitchen staff to keep it open. Do you want me to prepare a plate for you?"

"Maybe something to go."

"No problem."

"You're the best, Darlene. See you soon."

And to think that a moment ago he wanted to fire her. The woman deserved a raise.

When he was dressed and ready to go out the door, his phone rang again, but this time it was Roni.

That was odd. The guy never started his workday before nine in the morning.

"Good morning," William answered as he closed the door behind him. "You're calling early. What's the emergency?"

"After your text message from last night, I figured it was urgent and came in an hour earlier to check on Kaia's friend."

William had sent it before going to sleep, and he hadn't expected Roni to do anything about it right away.

"Thank you. What did you find?"

"He booked a flight to the Maldives. Coincidence?"

A shiver ran down William's spine. "Perhaps. The Maldives is not just a hub for the Brotherhood. Anything else?"

"That's it. After that, he disappeared from the face of the net. His emails remained unopened, and he didn't send any. Not from his main address, anyway. He might have one of those throwaway emails. His bank account shows a fifty-thousand-dollar deposit right before his trip, but there was no activity beyond automatic payments that kept going. The same is true for his credit cards. There were a couple of charges from airports on the day of the flight, and nothing since."

Fifty thousand dollars wasn't a big enough amount to pay a scientist for participating in a secret project that was supposed to last several months, but it could have been just the deposit. Was that a new mode of operation for the Brotherhood?

According to Lokan, brainiacs were lured to the island by promises of free, unlimited sex and then returned to their homes at the end of their sex vacation. But maybe the Brotherhood had started using an additional tactic and was luring them with a promise of a job?

Traffickers had been employing that method for ages, promising young girls and their families a modeling job, or even something more mundane like a nanny position with a rich family. The Brotherhood might have decided to expand their recruiting net and implemented a method they were all too familiar with from their trafficking operations.

After the men got to the island and realized that there was no project, they could be blackmailed into silence by compromising pictures taken of them with the ladies. Either that or something more nefarious, like offing them once they'd done their job and impregnated a Dormant.

"So, what's our next step?"

"I would suggest asking Lokan for help. You have the guy's picture, so if he's on the island, he shouldn't be too hard to find."

"If he's in the Dormants' enclosure, which is what the brainiacs are brought to the island for, then Lokan can't help us. He doesn't have access to them."

Roni chuckled.

"It's Lokan we are talking about. The compeller who can walk into people's dreams and who plotted to kidnap Ella and Vivian. He will find a way."

"I don't want him to take unnecessary risks to help a human."

"Of course not. But he might be able to help without exposing himself to risk. It doesn't hurt to ask."

"You're right. What time is it in China?"

"It's eleven at night. He should be awake."

"I'll send him a text. Thanks, Roni. I really appreciate you coming into the lab early to do this for me."

"Hey, that's what friends are for. Good luck with Kaia."

How the hell could Roni know that there was something going

on between them? William hadn't even talked with him since Kaia's arrival.

"What do you mean?"

"I spoke with my mother. She says that you are smitten and that Kaia is lovely."

William was going to have words with Darlene. She was supposed to keep everything going on in Safe Haven a secret, but apparently, she didn't think that included his private affairs.

"Kaia is nineteen."

"So what? I was eighteen when I met Sylvia. She was twenty-six at the time, and look at us now. We are living our happily ever after. The heart doesn't care about age, and as long as the lady is not a minor, it's not a crime to fall in love with her."

"I'm not in love."

"I wasn't either, but then I was. Keep an open mind. That's all I'm saying."

"I will. Thanks again, Roni." William ended the call and checked the time.

He was beyond late, but Darlene was keeping the team occupied, and they could wait a few minutes longer.

Walking at a brisk pace, he typed up a text to Lokan, asking him to call back.

Lokan's call came in a couple seconds later. "What can I do for you, William?"

After he explained the situation, Lokan heaved a sigh. "I can ask my servant to snoop around. He's human, so he can get in almost everywhere, and my compulsion keeps him from telling anyone what he is doing for me. I'll call him tomorrow."

"Thank you, Lokan. I appreciate your help."

"Is this guy important to the research you're conducting? Or is it just a favor for your lady friend?"

Evidently, the rumor about his infatuation with Kaia had spread so quickly that it managed to reach as far as China.

"It's a favor for my friend, who is crucial to the project. The other people on my team are just good enough to be her helpers. Without her, we don't have a chance."

"I understand. You need to keep her happy to get her to do her best."

"Precisely."

"I'll do what I can."

52

KAIA

Kaia nibbled on a piece of toast and watched Corinne and Owen exchange smiles when they thought no one was looking. The two had obviously hooked up last night, and she was envious.

Corinne was older than Owen by at least eight years, and it didn't seem to bother either of them. Why did William have to be such a prude?

Yesterday, she'd finally managed to break through his resistance, and for a few glorious moments she'd basked in her success, but he'd put a damper on that with his insistence that other than kissing, there would be nothing more between them until the project was done.

What century was he living in?

Talk about frustrating.

Kaia had no problem with taking it slow, but by slow she meant a couple of weeks, maybe a month, but not more than that. She had waited long enough for the right guy to come along, and now that she'd found him, she was antsy and impatient to explore this thing between them.

She'd never met a guy who'd made her feel like this before, and not all of it was good. She loved how awakened her body felt, how aware, but her brain was functioning in a diminished capacity because most of its bandwidth was taken up by William.

If she wanted to shorten the wait time by breaking the code faster, she needed to get her head back in the game. But she needed to be realistic. She'd seen those alien scribbles, and although she could discern a pattern right away, she had no database to compare them to and no software to run them through. It would be like translating a foreign language with no key. It wasn't impossible, but it wasn't something that could be done quickly either.

On the other side of the dining hall, Kylie laughed, drawing Kaia's attention. She was chatting with the older couple, James and Mollie, if Kaia remembered their names correctly, the only two who lingered after the other paranormals had left along with their boss. Even Darlene had excused herself, saying that she had an urgent matter to attend to and couldn't wait for William.

There were nine paranormals in Eleanor's team, and Kaia had tried to memorize their names when they had been introduced, but she remembered only some of them. Their fascinating talents, though, she remembered vividly.

Perhaps she should talk with Eleanor about her own paranormal thing? Were memories of a past life considered a paranormal talent?

Probably not.

Besides, Kaia had learned early on not to talk about that. People reacted with either dismissal or amusement when she talked about her strange memories, and no one other than Cheryl had ever believed that they were real, not even her own mother.

When Kaia had told her that she remembered being a man in her past life, her mother suggested visiting a therapist. She'd thought that Kaia was making up a male persona as a result of the trauma of losing her father, and that she was coping with grief by clinging to the belief that a person didn't end when their bodies quit.

It made sense, and it was a comforting thought, but her memories were real.

Kaia had found references to Edgar Rosu in a couple of books dealing with the history of mathematics and the different mathematicians who had contributed to the field throughout recorded history. Rosu, a mathematician who'd lived through both World Wars, hadn't been famous enough to be featured in a documentary she might have seen as a kid, so she couldn't have heard about him and somehow assimilated his persona. Besides, she'd had those strange memories even before her father had died, and she even remembered telling him about them.

He'd laughed, ruffled her hair, and said that he would always love her, even if she turned out to be a grumpy old man.

Kaia had been three or four at the time, but the memory of that exchange was so vivid in her mind that it still brought tears to her eyes every time she thought about it.

Her father would have never suggested a shrink.

Not that she'd ever gone to see one. She'd wiggled out of it by lying and saying that she'd made it up. Her mom had figured that it had been a phase, and there had been no more talk of visiting a psychologist.

The only one who she'd confided in was Cheryl, but the secret was safe with her sister. The girl was like a vault, and no secret she'd been entrusted with ever got out.

"Good morning, team." William strode over to their table. "I apologize for being late. I had an important phone call I had to take."

He seemed a little frazzled.

"Did you work all night?" Kaia asked.

"Most of it," he admitted. "Is everyone done and ready for their first day of puzzling out a mystery?"

"I am," Kaia said. "Darlene left a bag for you." She handed it to him. "She asked me to remind you to drink water."

He glanced longingly at the coffee dispenser and then nodded. "I'd better stick to water for now." He opened the dining room's door and held it open until they all stepped out.

"What's wrong with coffee?" Kaia asked. "I saw you drinking it yesterday."

"I need to limit my consumption of caffeine." He chuckled. "People say that I talk at the speed of a machine gun, and Darlene noticed that it gets worse after I drink coffee."

Kaia hadn't noticed that. Had he been trying to slow down for her sake?

He shouldn't have bothered. She had no problem with fast talkers. She had a problem with people who talked too slowly.

Patience was not one of Kaia's virtues.

53

WILLIAM

William had been debating all morning whether to tell Kaia about what he had learned from Roni. It was nothing earth-shattering, and suspecting that Anthony was on the Doomers' island was pure speculation on their part, so it wasn't worth mentioning even if he could tell her about it. All he had for her was Anthony's last known location, and that could wait for later. He didn't want to raise her hopes and distract her from her work.

In only a few hours, she was making tremendous progress and pulling the entire team behind her.

Following her advice, he'd printed several pages for her and her three helpers, and he'd let them brainstorm ideas and jot down notes. Naturally, Kaia was the one leading the effort, and to distract her was to slow down their progress.

As a knock sounded on his open door, William lifted his head. "Do you need me?"

Standing in the doorway to his office with a yellow pad clutched in her hand, Kaia gave him a suggestive smile. "Always. May I come in?"

Swallowing, he motioned for the chair in front of his desk. "Please." He was already hard just from that one sultry look and grateful for the desk hiding his reaction.

She closed the door behind her, walked over, and pulled out a chair. "Do you want to see what I have so far?"

"Of course."

"It's not much, but I think that these symbols represent the four bases. I just don't know which one is which yet, and to figure it out, I need to see a larger sample. You said that you would prepare one for me."

"I did, but I don't want you working on it in front of the others. You will have to do it in here."

It would be torturous to have her sitting in front of him all day, but he would leave the door open so that neither of them would succumb to temptation, and so the others wouldn't think they were doing anything inappropriate.

"Okay." She seemed all too happy to comply, and William had a feeling her reasons had nothing to do with the genetic code she was eager to translate.

"I didn't mean now. It's your first day, and I think it should be spent on bonding and learning to work as a team. You can start tomorrow."

Looking disappointed, she nodded but remained seated. "I hate to be a nag, but did you call your hacker friend?"

"Roni called me this morning. He found out that Anthony booked a flight to the Maldives around the time you said he'd accepted the job. But since it's a popular tourist destination, he might have gone there to relax before starting the project. Did he tell you anything about where he was going?"

She shook her head. "Tony couldn't afford a vacation in a place like that unless he got a big advance or a signing bonus, and he didn't mention either. But that could have been confidential as well, so he couldn't tell me about it. When I nagged him to give me some details, he said that it was located on the other side of the world. So maybe he was referring to the Maldives."

"The islands are also a hub, so he could have continued to Indonesia, Australia, New Zealand, and even Japan, but Roni didn't find any connecting flights booked under Anthony's name."

She frowned. "So that's it? That's all Roni, the great hacker, has been able to find?"

"He's not done yet. He just wanted to let us know that he found something." William smiled. "Don't underestimate what he has done. Roni is swamped with work, and he came to the lab an hour earlier than usual to do this for you."

When she still didn't look impressed, William added, "Just so you can fully appreciate what a sacrifice that was, you should know that Roni is not a morning person, and he's never volunteered to come in early for any of the other projects he's working on, some of which are much more important to us than your missing friend."

"I appreciate that, I really do." She let out a breath. "It's just that I was hoping for a clue, and unless Roni can find out where Tony went after arriving at the Maldives, that's a dead end."

There was another possibility that had occurred to William that Kaia wasn't going to like.

Leaning over the desk, he took her hand. "The Maldives are also a popular transshipment destination in the illicit drug trade. Do you know if Anthony dealt in drugs?"

She snorted. "Tony didn't even smoke pot. He was just your average nerdy postdoc, looking for a job that paid more than minimum wage."

"Are you sure? Maybe he didn't use drugs but dealt in them? Did he ever flaunt money he shouldn't have had?"

Kaia shook her head. "He drove an ancient yellow Toyota hatchback that was worth less than a hundred bucks, and his mom bought his clothes at Costco. That's the opposite of flaunting."

William frowned. "He was twenty-eight, and his mother still bought his clothes for him?"

"He lived at home and worked sixteen-hour days. Tony wanted to head a lab someday and to teach, but the competition for professorial positions is brutal, and he isn't the brightest of the bunch. He was struggling to publish a paper in a decent scientific magazine, and I think that was what eventually broke him and the reason he took on the secret project. He was starting to realize that he would never get the publications he needed to move his academic career forward, and that he would have to settle for work in the private sector."

"Is that so bad?"

"It was for Tony. His dream has always been to become a professor."

54

KAIA

Kaia left William's office disappointed, and not just because the information the hacker had found about Tony wasn't much.

Except for the brief moment when William had taken her hand, he'd been all business, acting as if what they'd shared in the lab yesterday had never happened.

Perhaps she should visit the security office and ask to see the recording to prove to herself that she hadn't dreamt the kiss up.

It wouldn't be the first time Kaia had had dreams so vivid that she confused them with real memories. But she'd told Cheryl about it when she'd called her last night, so unless the call had been part of the dream, the kiss must have been real.

As Kaia sat at the team's round conference table, Corinne eyed her with a smirk on her face. "I thought that you abandoned us in favor of our handsome boss."

Kaia didn't feel like explaining herself, but she had to say something. "I showed him our progress."

"Right," Owen murmured without lifting his head off the page he was scribbling notes on.

Ignoring his comment, Kaia peeked at what he'd written. "What do you have there?"

"Nothing mind-bending. I'm just translating a couple of lines assuming that this one is the G, this one is the A, and so on. Then I'll try a different combination to see which one looks like something I recognize."

It was a good idea, but the problem with that was that there were many more symbols than just the four representing the familiar nitrogenous bases.

"You should ask William to write a software for us to feed the symbols into," Corinne said. "Doing this by hand will take forever. Darlene told me that he's a genius with software development, but he's also a hardware man. He's an inventor."

Pride for William swelled in Kaia's chest. "We have to figure out what we need first."

William had never bragged about his accomplishments, but Kaia had figured that out from his comments about lying awake at night and thinking about new ideas and solutions to problems he was having with what he was working on.

"He's handsome for a brainiac," Kylie said. "If he lost some weight, he would be a hunk."

The comment angered Kaia much more than it should have. "Watch it, Kylie. The people in security hear and see everything that happens here. You don't want to offend the boss. Besides, William is perfect the way he is. A guy like him doesn't have time to spend hours in the gym just so he can look pretty for the ladies. He has much more important things to do."

Owen, who was skinny as a twig, pretended not to be part of the girly conversation, but she saw him smiling under his breath as if he had some advantage over William because of that. He couldn't hold a candle to her guy, not in looks, and certainly not in brains.

Looking up at the cameras that weren't even trying to be hidden, Kylie winced and lifted her hand to hide her lips, dipped her head, and whispered, "I didn't say anything bad. I said that he was handsome for a brainiac. He just needs to get rid of the little padding he carries around the middle."

Kaia shrugged, not bothering to speak quietly or hide her mouth. "I like it that he doesn't have washboard abs. What's more pleasant to hug, a plush teddy bear or a Barbie doll Ken?"

Laughing, Corinne followed Kylie's example and lifted her hand to hide her lips from the camera, whispering "That depends on the purpose of the hug and who you're hugging." She cast Owen a lascivious glance. "I like my boyfriends thin."

"To each her own." Kaia tried to keep the irritation out of her tone and rose to her feet. "Anyone want coffee before we go back to what we are „paid to do?"

"I can use a cup," Kylie said.

Corinne and Owen were too busy eye-screwing each other to respond.

Anger still pulsing through her, Kaia filled the coffeemaker's tank with water, and pushed a pod into the slot with too much force, so it dropped into the trash compartment.

Cursing under her breath, she pulled it out and tried again, pushing gently until it snapped into the slot.

She loved everything about William, and she didn't want to change a thing about him. The problem was that he didn't feel the same. He thought that she was too young for him, and technically he was correct, but he didn't have the whole story and wasn't going to get it either.

55

WILLIAM

Kaia had left the door slightly open, so William couldn't help but hear the entire discussion regarding his hunkiness or lack thereof, including the whispered parts.

He loved that Kaia had gotten offended on his behalf when Kylie had suggested that he needed to lose weight, and he loved even more that she had no issue with his padding. If that was what she liked, he had no problem being her cuddly teddy bear. Hell, it was the perfect excuse to stop swimming every morning.

But what had put a big grin on his face was that she'd defended him.

The girl was a fighter, and she took no prisoners.

He wondered who she'd gotten that from. Karen Locke seemed like a delicate, soft-spoken woman, but he'd seen the steel determination in her dark-brown eyes, not to mention the way Gilbert had silently deferred to her despite the alpha-male show he'd put on.

The guy was an extrovert who loved making waves, but his partner was no less formidable and probably more dangerous. If either of them had an issue with him not treating Kaia right, he would have been much more afraid of her mother's retaliation than Gilbert's.

When his phone rang, William knew it was Max before looking at the screen.

"Did you hear that?" Max asked. "Because if you didn't, you can come up here, and I'll replay it for you. I can even make you a copy for safe keeping."

"Yeah, I did, and thanks for the offer, but don't make a copy. That's not what the surveillance is for. We are not supposed to spy on their private conversations."

"Yeah, yeah. They are also supposed to be working instead of gossiping about their hunky employer. Way to go for your girlfriend, though. The way she defended your honor made me all tingly on the inside and seriously jealous. I want one just like her."

William groaned. He wasn't going to hear the end of it from Max and the other Guardians. As he'd suspected, they'd all seen the recording of his and Kaia's kiss by now, and he regretted not erasing it last night. Although, it probably would have been too late anyway. He had no doubt that the Guardians on duty watching the kiss live had made a copy to show the others. They were bored, and they had nothing better to do than gossip.

"Kaia is not my girlfriend. She's a young human who's infatuated with me for some inexplicable reason. She'll get over it."

Liar. He didn't believe that she would, and neither would he, so why had he said that?

Max chuckled. "I'd say that the epic kiss proves otherwise but I digress. I also called to tell you that lunch is on its way and to open the door for Paul."

"Thanks. The breakfast Darlene packed for me is long gone, and I'm hungry." He rose to his feet. "I'll see you later." He ended the call before the Guardian came up with more comments about Kaia.

That was the problem with living and working with family. Nothing was sacred, and everyone felt as if they had the right to meddle in everyone else's business.

One would think that centuries-old immortals would act more mature than that, but as he'd realized a long time ago, characters didn't change with age, especially when the bodies housing them didn't reflect that and were still working perfectly. Calamities and happy times had a short-term effect, either dampening or raising moods, but after a while, a person's character returned to its base state.

"Lunch is here," he said as he walked through the lab. "I need another set of hands to help me carry the delivery to the break room."

"I'm on it." Kaia got up to her feet and followed him to the door. "Are we getting Safe Haven's standard fare or can we place orders next time?"

"I wish we could, but we get whatever they make in the kitchen on a given day." He lifted his head, so his eyes aligned with the scanner and then took a step back as the door started to swing in.

"It leaves a lot to be desired," Kaia said.

As the door swung all the way, the Guardian delivering the food nodded at William and smiled knowingly at Kaia. "Here you go." He handed William the tray piled high with covered dishes and Kaia the two paper bags that he'd carried hanging from his forearms. "Someone should have thought to build an elevator in here. I could have wheeled a cart instead of carrying all that."

"There were schedule and budget constraints." William gave him a smile. "Thanks for bringing it in."

As Paul saluted and pivoted on his heel, William moved away from the door, and it started closing.

"How did you get away with not installing an elevator in here?" Kaia asked as she followed him to the break room. "Isn't it required to make all new public places accessible?"

"I wasn't in charge of the building project, so I don't know, but this lab is supposed to be the opposite of a public place. The idea was to make it as inaccessible as possible, not the other way around."

56

KAIA

Kaia went through the notes her team had collected, including the ones she'd written, and when she was done, she looked up at the cameras and moved the pages so they weren't in direct view of it.

William was so concerned with security, and yet the people in the security office could see everything that was going on in the lab, and what was worse, they were recording it. It would be child's play to zoom in and read not only the notes but also the photocopies of the originals that William had given them.

Her stomach was rumbling, reminding her that it was time to call it a day and go get dinner, but she sensed that she was starting to get a whiff of an idea, and she wanted to stay and run with it before it dissipated.

The others had left more than an hour ago, but William had returned after escorting them out, and he was probably hungry as well. The lunch they'd eaten in the break room was more of Safe Haven's healthy fare, which was more suitable for rabbits than people, and it had left her unsatisfied.

It seemed like that was the story of her life lately.

"Ugh, don't be so dramatic." She lifted the stack of papers and strode to William's office.

He lifted his head and smiled. "Done?"

"For today. I'm hungry, and there are a few things I want to talk with you about." She glanced at the camera. "But not in here."

He blushed, probably assuming that she wanted to play, which she did, but it wasn't about that.

"It has to do with a security concern I have."

"You do?" He took his glasses off, looking at her with his incredibly blue eyes. "I assure you that it's top-notch."

"Yeah, you've told me that." She motioned for him to get up. "Let's talk on the way to the dining hall."

"Okay." He gave her an indulgent smile.

She didn't say a word until they were out of the building. "You must be aware that the people in security can see everything we are working on. On top of that, everything gets recorded. How hard would it be for them to make a copy and sell the info?"

"Very hard." He took her hand. "First of all, I know each one of the guys working there, and I trust them implicitly, and secondly, no one can make a copy of the recording or send it out. It's a closed circuit, and it erases every twenty-four hours."

Kaia shook her head. "Even I know how to circumvent that. I could just whip out my phone and record whatever is on the monitor screen. It might come out blurry, but that's easy to fix with the right equipment."

He chuckled. "That's precisely what those idiots did with the recording of our kiss. But as I said, I trust these people. I've known them and worked with them for many years."

"You are too trusting." She followed him inside the dining hall. "We need to continue this talk later."

Her teammates were already gone, and the paranormals must have eaten early as well. A single red-headed guy whose name she'd forgotten was sitting a couple of tables over. He was the aura reader who was about her age. Spencer? Was that his name?

When he lifted his head and smiled, she waved. "Hi. How was dinner?"

"Terrible," he mouthed. "I say we fire the cook."

She gave him the thumbs up. "I'm adding my name to that petition."

After they loaded their plates with mushy stuff that was barely recognizable, they walked over to one of the tables and William pulled out a chair for her. "Why the sudden concern with security?"

"Thank you." She sat down. "Given that I just started working today, I wouldn't call it sudden." She leaned closer to him. "I was going over what we've done today, and it occurred to me that one of the cameras was pointing directly at the table where I was sitting." She collected some of the mush onto her fork. "The stuff we are working on might be dangerous and worth a lot of money to someone with dastardly plans."

"What makes you think that?"

"I have a hunch." She put the fork in her mouth.

Surprisingly, the mush was not as bad as it looked. She tasted zucchini, eggplant, and peas.

For the next several minutes they ate in silence, until the red-headed guy stopped by their table on his way out.

"You have a very strange aura," he told Kaia. "I've been watching you for a while to make sure I wasn't seeing things."

Kaia tensed. Could he sense her previous self? Wasn't she the same person, the same soul, just in a different body?

Hopefully, he wouldn't say that she had a masculine aura.

"What do you mean by strange?"

"You have two auras, and I've never seen anyone who has two. One is so bright that it's almost blinding, and in comparison, the other one is dimmed, but if it was on its own, it would have been just like any other aura. The other thing that's strange about the secondary one is that it flickers on and off. One moment it's there, and the next it's gone."

"What does that mean?" William asked. "Does Kaia have a split personality?"

"That's what I thought." The guy threaded his fingers through his curls. "Do you?" he asked.

"Not as far as I know." She forced a smile. "One aura probably belongs to my big ego, and the other one to its ugly twin. Sometimes I think that I'm the most advanced human in the world, and other times I think that I'm a big fraud."

Both statements were exaggerations meant to throw the guy off, but there was a kernel of truth in them.

Kaia had a big ego, which she tried to wrestle down so she wouldn't appear condescending, but she also owed her so-called genius to things she'd learned in a previous life, so she was a bit of a fraud.

The guy gave her a tight smile. "I just hope that you don't have a parasitic spirit latching onto your bright aura."

Goosebumps rose over her arms. "Is that a thing? Have you encountered a spirit like that before?"

"No, but when I was thinking about a possible explanation for what I was seeing, that was one of the things that popped into my mind."

Rubbing her arms, she let out a relieved breath. "You scared me."

"Sorry. I didn't mean to." He raked his fingers through his red curls. "Well, goodnight. I'll see you tomorrow at breakfast."

"Goodnight, Spencer," William said.

When the door closed behind the guy, he smiled. "Well, that was odd."

"Tell me about it." Kaia rubbed her arms again. "He shouldn't be going around and creeping people out with his so-called aura readings."

William lifted one shoulder in half a shrug. "I bet he doesn't do that outside of this place. He knows that it's safe to give voice to his unique talents here."

"I guess."

Life must be difficult for those paranormals. They had an extrasensory perception that they hadn't asked for, and when they shared what they knew, they were regarded as freaks or lunatics. Still, Spencer should have exercised more discretion before blurting out things like parasitic spirits.

Kaia pushed her plate away. "Are we done? I feel like taking a shower to scrub that other aura off."

"We are." William rose to his feet and collected their plates. "Is the need to scrub urgent? Or are you up for a walk on the beach? You can share the rest of your concerns with me while we get some fresh air."

"That sounds even better than soap and water. Let's go."

57

WILLIAM

The second aura Spencer had seen was no doubt the middle-aged man living inside Kaia's head, but the way she'd reacted made William think that she didn't know what he was or where he'd come from. Otherwise, she wouldn't have been so freaked out by Spencer's comment.

When she rubbed her arms for the third time, he wrapped his arm around her. "It's windy." It was only a gentle breeze, but it was chilly, and it gave him a great excuse to do that. "Do you want to get a jacket?"

It had been on the tip of his tongue to tell her that her teddy bear could keep her warm, but then he would reveal that he'd overheard what she'd said to Kylie and Corinne.

"I'm fine." Kaia leaned closer to him. "It's so beautiful out here, and it will get dark soon. I don't want to miss any of it."

A dense marine layer hung low over the beach, coloring everything a monochromatic gray and making the ocean look ominous as the waves forcefully splashed against the rocks. The sound was so loud that it was making conversation difficult.

Nevertheless, William loved the coast's harsh beauty, the salty smell of the water, and most of all, the feel of Kaia's back under his arm.

She had on one of her flimsy T-shirts, and he could almost feel the texture of her skin under the fabric. It was perfectly smooth, and although she was wearing a bra, she probably didn't need it to hold up her generous breasts.

He had to admit that there were certain advantages to youth, and those fleeting gifts of human beauty shouldn't be squandered. Then again, they were meant to please human males who were also young and in their physical prime, so healthy babies could be born.

The survival of the species was a delicate and beautiful dance, just not always. Sometimes, things got ugly, especially for young females.

At the thought, his fangs started elongating and his venom glands filled up. His aggression was spurred by the need to protect her from anyone who wished her harm, but since there were no potential threats lurking at Safe Haven, it was entirely uncalled for, and so atypical of him that he scared himself.

What was it about Kaia that brought out those primitive male urges?

Did it have anything to do with her double aura?

He moved his hand to rub her arm up and down. "Do you have any idea what Spencer was talking about?"

"No clue," she answered immediately as if she'd been waiting for him to ask. "I think that auras are bullshit. Our bodies emit an electrical charge, and sensitives might be able to sense it, or maybe even see it, but I most definitely do not emit more electricity than the next person."

He widened his eyes in mock surprise. "You don't? I think that you are the brightest star in the sky. Are my eyes playing tricks on me?"

She tilted her head and looked up at him with a smile tugging on her lips. "We both need to get our prescriptions checked, and maybe Spencer needs glasses as well. I thought that I saw your eyes glowing on several occasions, but it must have been a reflection from either your or my lenses."

William swallowed. "It must have."

He knew that his eyes had been emitting light, but he'd thought that she hadn't noticed, and he'd been glad that he hadn't needed to thrall her to forget what she'd seen. With how precious Kaia's mind was, he was afraid to get in there and cause even the slightest damage. Thankfully, she explained the glow away and he hadn't been forced to thrall her.

"You wanted to talk more about security," he changed the subject.

"Right. I got distracted by this magnificent view." She looked at him and not the ocean. "You said that the guys working in security were idiots, which probably meant that they aren't the sharpest tools in the shed, but you also said that you trust them. What if they are as trustworthy as you believe they are, but they blurt out something about the research we are doing in the wrong place, and at the wrong time? Someone who wants to find out what you are working on could overhear, and that someone might get motivated to infiltrate the lab or its computers and steal the information."

"Don't worry about it. I've got all angles covered."

"That's not good enough. That stuff is alien technology, and it's biological in nature. If those are instructions for how to build human bodies, people would kill to get their hands on them. It scares me."

She was so amazingly close to the truth that the short hairs on the back of William's neck prickled.

"How did you figure that after one day of investigating?"

Kaia shrugged. "For now, it's just a hunch, but I'm usually right. You were impressed by the research papers I published, right?"

"Very impressed. The subject matter was well researched, the calculations impeccable, and the findings were very well substantiated. I couldn't find fault with any of your methods or results."

She smirked. "Would it surprise you to know that it didn't take me more than a couple of months to submit for review and that I didn't have to make any revisions before my papers were published?"

"It would. That rarely happens." They reached an outcropping that created a natural enclave protected from the wind. "It often takes years to publish a paper in a respectable journal." He led her to the enclave and sat down with her on a flat rock shaped like a bench.

"The reason the articles took me so little time and didn't need revisions was that I knew what would work and what wouldn't." She scooted closer to him, and he wrapped his arm around her. "Gilbert has a nose for crooks and fakes, and I have a nose for science. The funny thing is that we are not related."

58

KAIA

William took her hand. "You're probably the smartest person I've ever met, and I've met my share of very smart people. Did you ever hear of Perfect Match?"

"The virtual fantasy studios?"

He nodded.

"Who hasn't? Their commercials are all over. What about them?"

"I helped the founders work out the kinks in their programming. Those guys are brilliant, and the machine they invented blew my mind." He smiled down at her. "I think it was the first time in my life I was jealous because they came up with an idea that was more revolutionary than any of mine."

"But they needed you to work out the bugs, so you were smarter than them."

He shook his head. "It's much easier to find mistakes in someone else's work than to create something original. They were too close to it to see where the problem was."

William's modesty was one more thing Kaia loved about him. Was she in love with him, though?

She'd never been in love before, so she didn't know the difference between love and sexual attraction or infatuation. Furthermore, he was sending her mixed signals, and she didn't know where she stood with him.

Yesterday, he'd told her that kissing was all he would allow until the project was done, and today he'd been a little distant. But then he had taken her for a walk along the coastline, which could count as a romantic gesture, and he led her to this secluded spot that was perfect for making out.

Did he just want another kiss, or did he want more than that?

Kaia was all for more, their proximity and William's unique masculine scent sending heat down to her center, but she wasn't going to push him. It was bad when guys did that to girls, and it was equally bad when the pressure came from the girl.

That being said, she could hint at wanting more and let William decide whether he was ready or not.

It sounded ridiculous even in her mind. He was thirty-two, most likely not a virgin, and yet he was more skittish than a sixteen-year-old girl.

Talk about role reversal.

Maybe she was a little too masculine for a woman? Spencer had scared the crap out of her with that aura reading of his. Thankfully, he hadn't said anything about it being manly.

Snuggling closer to William, she lifted her face to his and smiled. "Guys usually bring girls to spots like this to make out."

"This wasn't my intention." He smiled, and his eyes zeroed in on her lips. "But now that you brought it up, I won't be able to stop thinking about kissing you." He lifted his finger and rubbed it over her lower lip. "You have the most kissable lips of any woman I've ever been with."

A surge of jealousy turning her vision red, Kaia narrowed her eyes at him. "You make it sound as if you've kissed scores of women. How many are we talking about?"

"Enough to know that none had lips as succulent as yours or had even a fraction of your appeal. You are one of a kind, a precious jewel."

Clever man, showering her with compliments to take her mind off the subject of his previous lovers.

"I would have never pegged you as the Don Juan type. When did you have time to kiss all those other lips?"

He laughed. "And I would have never pegged you as a relentless temptress and a jealous monster." He dipped his head and feathered a kiss over her lips. "Although I enjoy your jealousy more than I should, let's not talk about any lips other than yours."

Oh, so now he was eager for a kiss.

Maybe she should throw more jealous tantrums at him to goad him into making love to her.

"Are you going to talk, or are you going to kiss?"

Just as before, he moved faster than was humanly possible, lifting her off her butt and settling her in his lap, and this time, he didn't wait before fusing their mouths.

Kaia groaned, the tension she'd felt all day long finally finding a release in William's arms.

As his tongue dueled with hers and his hands roamed over her back, she did what she'd been too shy to do the day before and snaked her hands under his shirt to touch his skin.

He was so warm and nearly hairless, and under the slight padding covering his abdomen and chest, she felt hard muscles.

Feeling brazen, she roamed a little higher and thumbed his nipples. They hardened immediately into two little pebbles, and as a growl started low in William's chest, he deepened the kiss, devouring her.

Her own nipples stiffened inside her lightly lined bra, aching to be touched, and as she pressed her chest to his in a futile attempt to relieve the ache, she hoped he could feel them and get the hint. But if he didn't, she was just going to take his hands and put them where she wanted them.

59

WILLIAM

Kaia was going to be the death of him. Well, not really since he was immortal, but the sweet torment she was causing him combined with his guilt over taking what she was so freely offering was slaying him.

She was temptation and sin personified, and William was salivating to get his mouth on those hard tips she was pressing into his chest.

With a groan, he yanked her T-shirt up over her chest, pulled the flimsy bra cups down, and closed his palm over one generous swell.

The shuddering moan Kaia uttered in response undid him.

It was as if she'd been starving for his touch, and now that he'd finally given in to her silent pleas, she fell apart with relief.

"Kaia," he murmured against her lips as he plucked at her nipple, eliciting another delicious moan from her.

"Yes," she murmured back. "Whatever it is, the answer is yes."

Fates, if only he could live with the guilt of accepting that yes.

He had to put his mouth on those sweet berries, though. Despite the vow he'd made to her and to himself to limit their passion to kissing until the end of the project, he just couldn't say no to that.

It didn't matter that they were outside and that it wasn't even dark yet, and it made no difference that someone might walk in on them. He needed to get a taste and bring her a few moments of bliss as much, if not more than, he needed to take his next breath.

Letting go of her mouth, he dipped his head and kissed one turgid peak, then the other, and then came back for the first and sucked it into his mouth.

It was delicious, and the sounds she made were even more so. Kneading, plucking, and lightly pinching one nipple with his hand, he sucked and licked the other.

Kaia threaded her fingers into his hair, holding him to her, and as she ground her bottom over his hard shaft, he could feel her sweet feminine center through the thick fabrics of their jeans. It was quite evident that she was ready for him if he decided to take her, but he would never forgive himself if he did.

Compared to him, she was a child, and he was a pervert for succumbing to his baser needs.

Kaia didn't act like a child, though. She was all woman. Reaching with her hand between her legs, she rubbed the seam of her jeans in sync with the gyrating motion of her bottom over his erection. Her lack of inhibition was the sexiest thing, and he was so close to erupting in his pants and letting his fangs elongate that he doubted his ability to prevent either. The only thing capable of cooling his fervor was the thought of walking back to his bungalow with a big wet stain on his groin.

When a powerful climax shook Kaia's entire body, and she threw her head back, his restraint nearly snapped, but he gritted his teeth and managed to force himself back from the brink.

Partially.

He hadn't erupted in his pants, but his fangs had elongated, and he was struggling to wrestle them back.

Releasing her nipples, he tugged the bra cups up, the T-shirt down, and wrapped her in his arms. Cocooning her in his embrace, he rocked her gently until her tremors subsided.

"Wow," she whispered into his chest. "I didn't know I could orgasm so hard just from nipple play."

William chuckled. "Glad to be of service." He rested his chin on the top of her head to prevent her from looking at him.

Without reaching release, wrestling his fangs to retreat was a monumental struggle, and even though the sun hadn't set yet, and the glow from his eyes wouldn't be noticeable, he preferred to wait a few moments before letting her look at him.

"What about you?" Kaia murmured.

"What about me?"

She gyrated her hips over his shaft, nullifying his efforts to force his fangs to retreat. "You didn't climax."

"I don't have to." He kept his chin over the top of her head. "But I would appreciate it if you didn't grind your perfect bottom over my erection. I'm trying to regain control."

"I like you better without it."

He snorted. "If you have any mercy in your heart, don't make me walk back to my bungalow with a big wet stain on my pants. I'd rather you bury me out here in the sand."

"I wouldn't do that. But I can think of a very easy way to prevent a stain." She reached for the top button of her jeans.

He put a hand over hers to stop her. "Don't. This was more than enough."

"For today," she added.

"Until the project ends," he corrected.

"We shall see about that."

60

KAIA

Funny how sex worked so differently for women than it worked for men. Guys reached their climax, and that was it for them. They were happy. Kaia had orgasmed like a firecracker during her too-brief interlude with William, but instead of feeling sated and relaxed, she'd gotten recharged with enough energy to power all of Safe Haven and several neighboring towns.

It hadn't happened immediately.

William had walked her to her bungalow, they'd kissed again at the door, and then he'd said goodnight and continued to his own place. The energy had started building back up when she'd gotten into her room and the replay had started.

Standing in the shower, she imagined William doing the same over at his place. He hadn't climaxed when she had, and she had no doubt that he'd gotten right to it as soon as he entered his bathroom.

Closing her eyes, she saw him bracing a hand against the shower wall, the other fisting his erection, his hand going up and down his shaft as he imagined that he was inside of her.

Had he climaxed already? Or was he still at it, his hand movements synchronized with hers?

Kaia closed her eyes, dipped her finger into her heated core, and then gently rubbed the magical spot at the apex of her thighs. With her other hand squeezing her breast, she imagined that William was with her in the shower, touching her, kissing her, filling her…

Kaia exploded with a tormented moan leaving her throat, but she wasn't done. The sexual energy still pulsing through her needed to be released, and it took another round until her body calmed down. Heck, it got so depleted of energy that she lacked the strength to stand and had to sit on the shower bench to finish washing.

After she was done, she got dressed in a pair of loose shorts and a sleep camisole and padded to the kitchenette to make herself a cup of tea to take to bed. The door to Kylie's room was closed, but Kaia could hear music playing.

Hopefully, it had been loud enough to cover for her bathroom activity. She wasn't ashamed or even embarrassed about her self-pleasuring, but it wasn't something she wanted to share with Kylie.

Still, she wanted to talk to someone about her feelings toward William, and the only one she could do it with was Cheryl, who was too young to hear about Kaia's sexual frustrations.

Could she talk with her mom?

Her mother wasn't a prude, and she knew that Kaia wasn't a virgin, but she might worry that William was taking advantage of her because he was older and he was her boss, but mostly because Kaia wasn't home.

Heck, she'd only arrived at Safe Haven yesterday. Her mother would be shocked to learn what she'd been up to. She wouldn't believe that Kaia had been the instigator and would accuse William of coercing her young daughter.

It was better not to tell her.

Putting the tea on her nightstand, Kaia lay on the bed and stared at the ceiling. Imagining how her mother would view the situation helped her understand William's position.

People might point fingers at him even though he had done nothing wrong, and if she truly cared about him, which she definitely did, she would let up and wait until the project was over. Everyone would be much more amenable to them having a relationship when they were no longer working together, and Kaia was back home.

Would she manage to survive on just kisses for that long?

She would have to, for William's sake, but it was so damn frustrating. The age difference was irrelevant, and so was their workplace situation, but people liked to put things in neat little boxes and frown at anything that didn't fit the norm.

Heck, she had been no different until she'd met William. She'd even told him that Anthony couldn't have been her boyfriend because he was too old for her, but that hadn't been the reason at all.

She liked Tony, but she hadn't been attracted to him. There had been no chemistry, at least not on her part. Tony just hadn't had that extra something that she found so appealing in William.

William was a giver. He was caring, selfless, and always looked out for others.

Tony hadn't been any of those things. He'd been selfish, driven, and conceited, but he had a great sense of humor, and he hadn't minded being friends with the freaky kid while the others had pretty much shunned her.

She wondered what Tony would have thought of William. He probably would have sneered at her choice and asked if she was looking for a daddy figure.

Maybe she was?

Nah. That was baloney. She didn't need a father figure because Gilbert had assumed that role, and she'd accepted him wholeheartedly.

But the truth was that Gilbert, William, and her father had more in common than met the eye, so maybe she liked the fatherly types?

They said that girls married men who were similar to their dads and guys married girls who were similar to their moms, so there was that.

When her phone rang with the familiar FaceTime ringtone, Kaia smiled and lifted it to her face. "Hi, Mom."

"What are you doing in bed so early? Are they working you to the bone out there?"

"Not at all. We took an hour break for lunch, and we were done at five-thirty and went to get dinner."

"How is the project going?"

"Great, but I can't tell you anything about it."

"I know. How are you getting along with your teammates?"

"We spent today mainly brainstorming ideas, and tomorrow we are going to dive in deeper."

"You look relaxed, and you sound happy, but I'm going to make you even happier. Eric can fly us over early on Saturday and fly us back Sunday night. We can spend the entire weekend with you."

It did make her happy, but not as much as it should have. If she spent the entire weekend with her family, she wouldn't spend it with William, and she was going to miss his company.

"That's awesome. I didn't expect you to come back so soon. You said that you couldn't make it here more than once a month."

"The truth is that I didn't plan on it, but Eric called and said that he has one of his jets available for the entire weekend and that he can fly us, so I jumped on the opportunity." Her mother chuckled. "I think he wants to see William's assistant again. The two of them hit it off."

"I noticed. Darlene is really nice. After I had my meltdown when you left, she gave me a hug and told me to call her whenever I felt lonely and needed to talk to someone."

That was an idea that Kaia hadn't thought of before. She could talk with Darlene about William. The two were friends, and Darlene might know things about him that would help her understand him better.

"Did you take her up on her offer?"

Kaia shook her head. "There was no need. I acclimated faster than I thought I would. I'm getting along well with William and with my teammates. Last night, I watched the chick flick that Cheryl recommended with my roommate."

"Is there a movie theater in the area?" her mother asked.

"We watched in our bungalow. They have all the latest movies on their servers."

Her mother smiled. "I'm so glad that you are finding your place there. You need to spread your wings a little."

"Yeah. I'm glad that I took this job. It's a fascinating project, and I got to meet some very interesting people. Did I tell you about the paranormals we share the dining hall and gym with?"

"You mentioned them yesterday."

"I know a lot more today than I knew yesterday." Kaia pushed up against the pillows. "Do you want me to tell you about them?"

"Sure. If it's not part of the secret."

"I don't think it is."

61

WILLIAM

William's day had passed in a blur of activity, saving him from dwelling on his crumbling defenses and how fast things were progressing with Kaia.

The girl was a force of nature on all fronts, and he had a feeling that the project would be finished much faster than he'd expected. In the two days she'd been working on decoding the journals, she'd already managed to translate words written in the gods' language, which he had no idea how she could have possibly done, and she cracked the first set of schematics, figuring out exactly what they meant.

So far, she hadn't figured out more than he had already known, but given that he could read at least some of the language, it was nothing short of awe-inspiring.

"Are we done for today?" he heard Corinne ask.

"I need a little more time," Kaia said. "But you can go ahead. I'll join you in the dining hall later."

They couldn't leave without him opening the lab's door for them, and the scanner that they thought scanned only his iris also scanned them to make sure they weren't taking anything out of the lab.

He pushed to his feet and walked out of his office. "I'll escort you upstairs." He turned to Kaia. "Are you sure that you want to stay? I can come back for you, but I suggest that you call it a day and come with us to eat dinner."

Chewing on her lower lip, she looked at the sheets of paper strewn over the table. "I need to organize this mess before I leave."

"I'll help you," Corinne offered.

Kaia nodded. "Thank you. I didn't feel hungry until William said the word dinner, but it hit me full force now."

"That's because the food here is not filling," Owen grumbled. "I would give my left testicle for a juicy hamburger with fries."

William's mouth salivated.

Would it be a huge security risk if he took the team out for a proper dinner?

The nearest town was an hour's drive away from Safe Haven, and he would need to take a couple of Guardians with him, but they would be happy to get a real meal as well.

"All done." Corinne put the neat stack of papers on Kaia's desk.

William scooped it up. "Give me a moment to put them away."

No one could get into the lab and take the papers, but he didn't want to leave them lying around. It took him less than a minute to put them in the safe in his office.

As he and his team went through the second door at the top of the stairs, his phone rang, and when he pulled it out of his pocket and saw the name, he rushed them out through the third door before answering.

"Hold on for one moment," he told Lokan, and looked at Kaia. "I have to take this. I'll meet you later in the dining room."

When she nodded, he went back into the building and waited until the door closed behind him. "I'm with you. What did you find out?"

"My servant snooped around, and what he found out was that someone resembling your guy's description and going by the name of Tony had been brought in about a year ago, but he left shortly after arriving. I sent him to check the departure ledger, and his name wasn't there, so he didn't leave the island. He could be dead, or he could be imprisoned, or it could have been some other Tony. They don't record last names in any of the ledgers that are accessible to servants."

"Do you have access to the ones that contain the full names?"

"I do, but I'm not scheduled to visit for another five weeks."

"Do you think it's significant that Tony is a bioinformatician? Does Navuh have a need for one?"

"I don't think so. The guys he brings in to breed the Dormants are young, in their mid- to late twenties, and smart. Those are the only criteria he cares about. He doesn't care if they are physicists or psychologists as long as their IQs are high, and they have a proven record of academic success."

Leaning against the wall, William let out a breath. "I have a feeling that it might be significant that a bioinformatician was brought to the island. Maybe Navuh decided to crack the immortal code. With all the scientists he lures to the island, he could open a research facility."

Lokan chuckled. "You are giving him too much credit. He's not that sophisticated. That being said, Losham is. I'll give him a call and check what he's up to. The thing about Losham is that he likes to brag, so he might share with me his latest schemes."

"Given that a year has passed since Anthony was taken, those schemes were hatched a while ago."

"True. Anything else I can do for you?"

"Not that I can think of. Thanks for the help."

"No problem. I'm happy to assist in any way I can."

As Lokan ended the call, William put the phone in his pocket. Was it worth mentioning to Kian that Navuh had had a bioinformatician brought to the island? And perhaps Turner as well?

William wasn't sure, but when in doubt, it was always prudent to err on the side of caution.

62

KIAN

"William." Kian held the phone to his ear as he closed his office door. "How is the research going?"

The project had only started the day before, so he wasn't expecting any groundbreaking discoveries, but if William was calling him this late, he might have some news.

"Better than expected. Kaia was worth every moment I invested in recruiting her and all the concessions I made for her."

"Glad to hear that." Kian took the stairs down to the lobby. "Turner wasn't happy when I told him that you allowed Kaia's family to accompany her to Safe Haven, and he even dug deeper into their background. Did you know that Eric Emerson was a fighter pilot in the Air Force?"

"It was in the security brief that Karen Locke's employer had prepared. The entire family passed the security check with flying colors. Did Turner discover anything worrisome?"

"Not really, which is why I didn't call you. What's up? I know that you are not calling me because you miss me."

William chuckled. "The truth is that I expected to be miserable away from my lab and my crew, but I'm enjoying it here. Having Darlene and Max with me is a big plus, and I love being right next to the ocean. It's a nice change of scenery."

Kian waved at Wendy and Wonder, who were heading home as

well. "Wait until it gets cold. You are not going to like it as much then."

"I hope the project will be done by mid-fall, and it seems likely that it will. Although, I'm still not sure what we are supposed to do with what we learn from those journals once they are deciphered."

"We'll worry about that then." Kian quickened his strides, eager to get home and sweep Allegra into his arms. "Anything else you want to talk about?"

"Yeah, there is. Can you think of any reason Navuh might need a bioinformatician?"

The short hairs on the back of Kian's neck stood up. "Why do you ask?"

"Kaia's friend was also recruited for a secret project that was supposed to take a few months, but it has been a year since anyone has heard from him, and his family thinks that he's dead. I asked Roni to do some snooping, and he found out that Anthony had booked a flight to the Maldives, but he hadn't booked a connection or a return flight. We know that the Maldives is one of the hubs that the Doomers use, so I asked Lokan to check if the guy was on the island."

"You shouldn't have done that. A missing human is not worth risking Lokan for."

William was silent for a long moment. "It was important to Kaia, and I basically bribed her to join the program with the promise to look into her friend's disappearance. After talking to Roni, I contacted Lokan to see if he could think of any reason Navuh might want to get his hands on a bioinformatician. He couldn't think of any and offered to look into it. He's also going to call Losham to see if he's up to anything."

"That's even more dangerous."

"I assumed that Lokan wouldn't have offered to help if he thought that it was too risky, but he was more than happy to help and promised to send his servant to snoop around the Dormants' enclave."

Kian slowed down his steps. "Did he find the guy there?"

Usually, the brains were kept on the island only until they

impregnated a Dormant, and then they were shipped out. They assumed that the women were pros, sent to pleasure them, and they had no idea that their seed was being stolen and they were fathering children.

"Someone there remembered a guy who matched Anthony's description and went by the name of Tony, but since they don't use last names, we can't be certain that it was the same guy."

"So, he's no longer there?"

"He's not, but he didn't leave the island. The servant checked the records, but no one named Anthony or Tony was listed in the departures log. Lokan said that he must be either dead or imprisoned."

"There might be a third option. Is Anthony a good-looking guy?"

"He's young, and I guess some would call him handsome. Why?"

Kian had a suspicion that he wanted to investigate, more to satisfy his curiosity than any useful investigation. The guy wasn't his responsibility, and if Kaia's friend had let himself be lured to the island with promises of free sex with beautiful women, he deserved what he'd gotten.

"Do you have a picture of him you can text to me? I want to see what he looks like."

"I'll do it right away."

A second later, Kian's phone pinged with an incoming message, and as he clicked it open, his suspicion was reinforced.

"Anthony has similar coloring to Navuh, and their facial bone structures bear some resemblance as well. We know that Navuh brings human servants who look like him to the harem for the immortal ladies to enjoy, so he can claim their children as his own. If he's breeding a new generation of warriors by pairing Dormants with smart men, it makes even more sense for him to do the same with breeding the immortal females whose sons he claims."

William let out a long-suffering sigh. "What am I going to tell Kaia?"

"Nothing for now. Kalugal's scheduled call with Areana is tomorrow morning. He could ask her if a smart guy named Tony arrived at the harem about a year ago."

63

KAIA

Kylie rose to her feet and picked up her plate. "Are you going to wait for William? He might not show up at all." A hint of a smile tugged at her lips. "He's so scatterbrained that he might have forgotten that he told us he would join us later, and went home."

Kaia bristled at the rude comment, but she wrestled her temper down. "William is not scatterbrained. He's brilliant, and sometimes his mind races ahead of him, so he appears distracted, but I assure you that it works like a well-oiled machine."

Kylie waved a hand in dismissal. "It was a poor choice of words. I meant that he spaces out. Although with how much he likes to eat, it's unlikely that he forgot about dinner, and if he did, his growling stomach would remind him. He's probably still stuck on that phone call."

Kaia nodded. "Maybe it was from his other lab, and he had to solve a problem for them. I'll wait a little longer, and if he doesn't show up, I'll call him."

Kylie looked around the empty dining hall. "The kitchen staff probably want to call it a day and go home."

"I'm sure that they'll keep the place open for William." And if the cook made a fuss, Kaia would fill a plate for him and take it to his place.

Kylie shrugged. "You're probably right. I'll see you later." She put her plate and utensils in the dirty dishes bin and walked out the door.

Leaning back, Kaia cast a sidelong glance at the serve-out window, glad to see that no one was giving her the hairy eyeball for not vacating the premises and letting them close up for the night. Perhaps she should ask them to prepare a plate for William before they put everything away and finished cleaning up. Pushing to her feet, she walked up to the window.

Only the cook was there, her two helpers already gone, and when she noticed Kaia standing at the window, she walked over. "What can I do for you?"

"Not for me, for William. He is running late, and I don't want him to miss dinner. Are you in a hurry to close up? Should I get a plate for him and bring it to his place?"

Maggie wiped her wet hands on her white apron. "You can if you want, but you don't have to. I'll put all the leftovers in the refrigerator, and he can come later and warm himself a plate whenever he wants."

"Are you going to leave the place open for him?"

She should have realized that William probably had the code for the lock.

"The kitchen is never closed," Maggie said. "If anyone is in the mood for a snack in the middle of the night, they can come in and get it."

"I didn't know that. Thanks for telling me."

"You're welcome." Maggie smiled. "The coffee dispenser is also left on all night, and I leave a basket of fruit out."

"That's very nice of you. Thank you."

A plate with cookies would have been even nicer, but Maggie had to follow Safe Haven's health protocol.

At least there was coffee, and it wasn't bad, so it wasn't totally nuts.

Kaia walked over to the dispenser and poured herself a cup. Perhaps she could still take a plate for William, using it as an excuse to go to his bungalow.

Ever since their make-out session yesterday, she'd been fantasizing about seducing him. William had no idea what he had done by giving her that incredible orgasm. He had awakened a ravenous monster who needed more and wouldn't rest until she got it.

Thankfully, deciphering the journals and what she was uncovering was so fascinating and all-consuming that she hadn't been bothered by carnal thoughts throughout the day. But now that her mind was free to wander, the cravings she'd managed to subdue last night had returned with a vengeance.

Glancing at the door, she made up her mind, rose to her feet, and walked up to the counter. "I think I'll take a plate for William after all. Can I come into the kitchen and prepare it myself?"

Maggie shook her head. "I'll prepare it for you. I need to finish cleaning in here."

"Thank you." She waited by the counter as Maggie filled up a plate, covered it with a lid, and brought it out to her.

"Remind him to return the dishes tomorrow morning."

"I will. Thank you, and goodnight."

Maggie smiled. "Enjoy your evening."

"You too."

If Kaia's plan succeeded, she was going to enjoy the evening very much indeed.

64

WILLIAM

As William opened the lab's topmost door, the sun was already setting. How long had he been on the phone? It hadn't felt like an hour had passed, but as he glanced at his watch, he was surprised to see that it was after seven.

Dinner was most likely over by now, but he knew he wouldn't stay hungry. Maggie never threw away the leftovers until the next morning, saving them in the refrigerator for those who missed dinner or got the munchies in the middle of the night.

He'd been guilty of both.

With Ronja and Darlene's help, William had gotten better about his food intake, but he still had a hard time fighting the urge to stuff himself whenever he was stressed. It wouldn't be the first time he'd reheated a plate in the microwave and ate alone in the dining hall, and most times, he didn't mind that. On the contrary, he enjoyed the peace and quiet.

Not this time, though.

He regretted the missed opportunity to spend time with Kaia and talk about things that weren't related to their research and get to know her better. Though given how consumed they both were by the secrets waiting for them to decipher, they probably wouldn't be able to help themselves.

That seemed to be their theme in more ways than one. He still couldn't believe that he'd let himself get carried away last evening.

How could he have been so careless?

He'd bared Kaia's body in full daylight, where any passerby could have seen them, and he feasted on her nipples like a savage.

Except, even though guilt was eating at him, he couldn't bring himself to regret it. Every delicious moment of it was etched in his memory—the way she'd reacted with such unabashed abandon, the sounds she'd made, the way she'd climaxed, the way she'd looked after they'd been done.

Well, she'd been done. He'd been in agony, but it was worth it.

He'd enjoyed giving Kaia pleasure more than he'd enjoyed receiving it from any other woman.

Fates, he was a pervert.

He sucked in a breath as he saw the object of his obsession walking toward him with a covered plate in her hands.

"You missed dinner." She smiled shyly. "So, I got you a plate to eat at home." She handed it to him.

"Thank you." He didn't know what to do next.

Should he invite her to join him?

Should he just smile back and say goodnight?

Should he tell her what he suspected had happened to her friend?

"I thought that we could go to your place and talk about the research." She glanced around before leaning closer to him. "I didn't want to say anything in front of the others, but the stuff I'm decoding is blowing my mind. They haven't realized what they are working on yet, and if you want to keep it that way, I need to know. It will seriously limit the help I can expect from them."

Looking around, William was glad that they were alone. It wasn't a topic to discuss in public, but he didn't want to take her back to the lab where they would be closeted together, and he didn't want to take her to his place either. Things might get out of hand again.

"We can talk in the dining hall."

"Maggie is still in the kitchen, and the cleaning staff is probably there already, mopping the dining room. Besides, there are security cameras in there as well, and we need privacy." A mischievous smirk lifted one corner of her mouth. "I didn't find any cameras in my bungalow, so I assume that there are none in yours either."

"There aren't."

Damn, the girl was scrambling his brain. He knew that there were cameras in the kitchen and dining hall and some on the outside of the building as well. He'd just forgotten about it because he couldn't think straight with her standing so close to him.

"Then let's go." She threaded her arm through his and started walking. "Did Roni find out anything new about Anthony?"

What was he supposed to tell her?

Even if he could tell Kaia that her friend might be being held captive on the Doomers' island and used as a breeder of a new generation of smart immortal evildoers, she wouldn't believe him.

"We are still investigating."

"We? Is there anyone else besides Roni looking into it?"

"Yeah, but I can't say more about it. The source has to remain confidential."

Kaia tilted her head. "In what way is that different than Roni? I don't know who he is, where he is, or what he does. You can tell me about the other sources in the same way."

"Roni works with me. The other two sources are part of my organization, but even mentioning them could put them in danger. That's why I can't tell you anything about them."

"I get it. They are informers."

In a way, Lokan and Areana were precisely that. Only they were much more.

"You guessed right."

"Who do you suspect took him? Do you still think that it has something to do with drugs?"

Again, in a way it was because that was what the Brotherhood did these days to finance its operations.

"Drugs and prostitution."

Her eyes widened. "I hope that you don't think that Tony is involved in that. He might be a prick sometimes, but he's not evil."

"I didn't say that he was. I suspect that he's a victim, not a perpetrator."

65

KAIA

Kaia's throat was suddenly dry, and her words came out in a whisper, "In what way? Why would they use a scientist for prostitution? He isn't even that good-looking."

She'd heard that it wasn't only women who fell victim to trafficking, but for the men, it usually meant slave labor, not slave sex. For the most part, women didn't hire male prostitutes, but given that an estimated ten percent of men preferred other men, it was possible that some of them were willing to pay for it, and a small percentage of them were psychos who didn't care whether the guy they were bonking was offering himself willingly or not.

Heck, some of them might even enjoy forcing themselves on a reluctant victim, the same as some thrived on hurting women.

Regrettably, there was no shortage of evil people who made life miserable for the rest of the human population that was mostly good, or at least neutral.

Kaia couldn't understand how people could be so evil, not from a woman's perspective and not from what she remembered from the male point of view of her previous life. It took someone seriously twisted to rape another person.

God, poor Tony.

How was she going to save him?

William regarded her with sad eyes. "I don't know any of this for a fact. It's all speculation, and you shouldn't get needlessly upset. Your Tony might be somewhere on the beach in the Bahamas, getting a tan while sipping on margaritas with paper umbrellas. Perhaps he met a fascinating, beautiful lady while working on his special project, and they decided to live on the money they'd just made and enjoy life. Maybe he was paid so well that he figured he never needed to work again."

Did the longing she saw in William's eyes hint that he'd been describing his own fantasy and projecting it onto Tony?

Was that what he wanted for the two of them?

William might fantasize about spending a few days in the Bahamas with her, but she doubted that he wanted to quit his job and live on the money he'd made so far.

He was too driven, not by ambition, because he didn't care about status or prestige, but by the burning curiosity to discover new things, create new technology, or come up with ways to improve people's lives.

She knew that because she was the same. Maybe that's why she was so drawn to him.

When they passed by her and Kylie's bungalow, Kaia cast a furtive glance at the windows, glad to see that the shutters were down.

"Do you want to let Kylie know that you are going to my place?" William asked as he opened the door to his bungalow.

He must have caught her glancing at the windows and misinterpreted it. He thought that she was worried about being alone with him, while her concern had been Kylie seeing her walking into his place and gossiping about it tomorrow.

"Maybe later." She followed him inside and pulled out a chair next to the small round table in his living room. "I would rather avoid her questions and speculations."

"As you wish." William took the lid off the plate before putting it in the microwave. "So, what did you want to talk to me about?"

"I think that your first theory was right, and we are dealing with alien technology. I was able to decipher several of the symbols with the help of the schematic drawing. When it occurred to me that they might be molecules, things started falling into place. I deciphered the symbols for oxygen, carbon, hydrogen, nitrogen, calcium, and phosphorus. Do you know how?"

"I can't wait to hear that." He took the plate out of the microwave with his bare hand and carried it to the table.

"Isn't the plate hot?"

"Not really." He put it down and pulled out two more empty plates from the cabinet along with utensils for both of them.

Sitting down, he pushed the loaded plate she'd gotten for him to the center of the table. "Dig in."

"I've already eaten. I'm not hungry." She pushed the plate toward him, and it was scalding.

Was the guy so distracted that he hadn't noticed his fingers getting burned? Or was he playing macho and didn't want to admit that he was hurting?

She glanced at his hands, but they both looked fine. Maybe he wasn't sensitive to heat.

"I'm still waiting to hear how you did that."

"Right." She leaned back in her chair. "First, I should start by saying that I figured out what the symbol for percentage was. We've already deciphered their numerical symbols, so when I got that, it was a game-changer. I copied one of their tables, and when I substituted their numbers for ours and then replaced their symbol for percentage with ours, I immediately knew what I was looking at. It was the chemical composition of an average human body in terms of elements and compounds. Oxygen is the most abundant at sixty-five percent, carbon is next at eighteen percent, then it's hydrogen, followed by nitrogen, calcium, and phosphorus. The rest are small amounts of other trace elements and metals." She looked into William's eyes. "I think that those journals contain information about human biology. The thing was that the next table had symbols that didn't represent anything that should be in a human body, and that table was on the same page as the other one. I'm still trying to figure out what it's about."

66

WILLIAM

William wasn't surprised that Kaia had figured that out. What he was astonished by was that she'd done it in two days.

"First of all, congratulations. You are unbelievable. And secondly, you are right about not revealing your suspicions to the others. It would seem that these aliens left us blueprints to build a human body."

Kaia's eyes widened. "You are brilliant. I didn't think of that. I thought that they investigated humans to learn more about us." She waved a hand. "With all the stories about alien abductions and medical examinations, I thought that maybe there was a kernel of truth in them. When I was a kid, those stories scared the bejesus out of me. I thought, what if they abducted me? But then I figured that advanced aliens wouldn't need to kidnap humans to learn what they were made from. They would have scanners that would tell them everything they wanted to know without them having to even touch a human."

If William wasn't beating himself up for steering Kaia in a direction he should have kept her away from, he would have been amused by her story. He could imagine the young Kaia pondering the probability of alien abduction and realizing that the stories didn't make sense.

He might have to thrall her later and remove that suggestion from her mind, but he hated messing with her brain. Unless it was absolutely necessary, and there was no other way to control what she knew and what she took away with her from the research, he wasn't going into her head.

Maybe he could just redirect her mind to think in other directions.

Getting to his feet, he collected his plate and put it in the tiny sink in the kitchenette. "What other alien theories did you examine as a kid and debunk?"

"Let me see." She pushed away from the table and moved to sit on the couch, patting the spot next to her for him to join her. "I was fascinated with unidentified submerged objects. I imagined an underwater alien base in the deepest ocean trenches, but I haven't been able to debunk that yet. Many of the sightings were reported by very reliable witnesses, like navy officers and pilots, so we can't assume that they were all nuts. There are places so deep in the oceans that even our most advanced equipment can't get down to them and check whether anything or anyone is hiding in these depths."

She scooted closer until her thigh was touching his, and that small contact was enough to cause him great discomfort.

Clearing his throat, William moved his thigh an inch away. "What about unidentified flying objects?"

"Same thing, but with a twist. Many were reported by air force pilots, radar operators, and the like, so they can't be dismissed either, and their velocity and maneuverability defy the laws of physics as we know them. As for where they are hiding, I have two theories. One is that unidentified submerged objects and unidentified flying objects are one and the same, and they hide in the deepest regions of the sea, and my other theory is that they have an underground base on the dark side of the moon. Until both are debunked, I'm willing to go out on a limb and accept that not only are we constantly visited by aliens, but that they also live among us and always have." She gave him a bright smile. "As proven by those journals you found. What I don't know is why they are here and what they want. As far as I know, they are not interfering in human affairs, so maybe they are here only to watch."

If Kaia only knew how close she was to the truth, she would be ecstatic. Maybe one day she would discover it for herself, but she wouldn't learn it from him.

Not unless she was a Dormant.

Could her incredible mind be considered a paranormal ability?

And what about the undeniable pull between them?

Except, he'd been wrong before. Hannah had worked in Amanda's lab, was incredibly smart, both Syssi and Amanda had liked her a lot, and he'd felt a connection with her as well. It hadn't been as powerful as what he felt with Kaia, but then Hannah hadn't been forbidden fruit.

She hadn't been so young, she hadn't been his subordinate, and he hadn't had to work as hard to resist her when he'd needed to. Hannah's brain had been no less precious to him than Kaia's, and he couldn't bite her as often as he would have liked because he'd been reluctant to thrall her too frequently.

Thankfully, he had great self-control, and he'd often pleasured Hannah without biting her or even flashing his fangs, but he wasn't sure he would be able to do the same with Kaia.

In fact, he was certain that he couldn't.

But maybe if he was careful, his thrall wouldn't cause any damage. The only time he'd entered her mind was when they'd first met, and that had been a long time ago. He could probably thrall her again safely, but that was the devil on his left shoulder talking.

The angel sitting on his right shoulder demanded that William stay strong and resist temptation.

67

KAIA

"As fascinating as the subject of alien visitations is, I still have work to do, and it's getting late." William got to his feet. "I'll escort you to your place."

Kaia stifled a groan. She'd expected him to do what he thought was honorable, but she'd hoped his desire for her would overpower his need to follow the rules he'd set for himself.

William didn't have a poker face, and she could read his emotions as clearly as if he was actually expressing them out loud and sharing his inner struggles with her.

He'd been waging war with himself since the moment he'd invited her into his bungalow, wanting her to stay, craving her, but he'd decided to be a damn gentleman and do the right thing.

Or the wrong thing.

Kaia had a very different opinion on what was right and what was wrong, but since she'd promised herself not to push him, she couldn't call him out on his bullshit. Or maybe she should? If she didn't take the initiative, months would pass until she got him to take her to his bed, and she couldn't last that long.

To hell with that.

She might be only nineteen, but she knew that life was fleeting, and every moment wasted was a moment lost forever. She had no intention of wasting the moments of her life on being timid and dancing around someone else's misguided opinions and sensitivities.

And if that meant taking risks and stepping on toes, she was willing to accept the consequences.

"I don't want to go." Kaia crossed her legs and looked up at him. "Do you really have work to do, or is it an excuse to get rid of me?"

He swallowed, his Adam's apple bobbing up and down. "I don't want to get rid of you, and I always have work that can't wait. But whether I do or don't, you shouldn't be here."

"Why not? I've read very carefully over the contract I signed, and there was no clause prohibiting fraternizing between teammates, and that includes you. There was no clause about fraternizing with the boss either. If we both want me to be here, there is no reason for me to leave."

Letting out a resigned breath, William sat back down on the other side of the couch. "I guess work can wait a little longer. Can I offer you a cup of tea?"

"Coffee would be better."

"Coming up." He rose to his feet and walked over to the kitchenette.

Now what?

Resigned was not the emotion Kaia had been going for, and she didn't know how to turn things around and get William in the mood for making love.

Should she take her shirt off? Would that be a big enough clue for him? Or did she need to go to his bedroom and get naked for him to get a hint?

When he returned with two cups of coffee, she gave him her sweetest smile. "You know what I've just realized?"

He lifted a brow. "What's that?"

"I know very little about you, while you know everything there is to know about me." Well, except for one thing, but that had no bearing on their relationship. "You said that in order to take this thing between us a step further, we need to get to know each other, but you never talk about yourself. I don't even know where you live when you are not working on deciphering alien science."

A ghost of a smile lifted one corner of his lips, and when he took his glasses off to wipe them with a corner of his shirt, the sight of his blue eyes took her breath away. They seemed to be glowing with an inner light.

Was he an angel? Or maybe an alien?

Kaia stifled a snort.

It would be just her luck to meet a hot alien who needed help finding his way back home. Was Darlene an alien too? Or did he have her under his thrall because he needed a human prop to perfect his human act?

"I'm originally from Scotland, but I've lived in Los Angeles for many years, and that's where my permanent home is."

That didn't sound too otherworldly.

"What about relationships? Have you ever been married?"

He shook his head.

"What about girlfriends?"

He nodded.

The guy who usually talked up a storm had turned mute when asked personal questions, but that wasn't going to deter her.

"How many, and have you been in love with any of them?"

William smiled. "I feel like I'm being interrogated."

"That's because you are. I'm shortening the entire getting-to-know-each-other period by not beating around the bush."

"I thought that I was in love once, but in retrospect, I wasn't. I liked her a lot, though, and then she moved away, and we lost touch."

Kaia narrowed her eyes at him. "You aren't going to tell me how many girlfriends you've had, are you?"

"Other than Hannah, none are worth mentioning. She was the only one I had feelings for, and I told you about her. What else would you like to know?"

Kaia wasn't done with questions about his ex-girlfriend, but she knew when it was time to retreat and regroup, and when it was time to push forward, and she needed to give it a rest for now.

"What kind of music do you like to listen to?" she asked.

"Instrumental, mostly classical."

"Nothing contemporary?"

"It's not that I don't like it, but lyrics distract me from my thoughts, so I prefer instrumental music. There is always something I need to figure out, and I don't have time to listen to someone singing about their broken heart."

"Makes sense. So, I guess you don't watch movies either."

"I do, but rarely. I've seen all the *Star Wars* movies, *Guardians of the Galaxy*, *Wonder Woman*, *Lord of the Rings*, and the *Harry Potter* movies."

"The boy who lived." She laughed. "Those are some of my favorite movies as well. In the music department, though, my horizons are broader. I like the oldies like the Red Hot Chili Peppers, Night Wish, and even older ones like Queen and Pink Floyd."

68

WILLIAM

"It's almost midnight." Kaia leaned her head on William's arm. "Is your bungalow going to turn into a pumpkin when the clock hits twelve?"

It took him a split second to get the reference. "Aren't you confusing fairytales?"

They'd been talking for hours, and apparently Kaia's mind lost some of its sharpness when she was tired. If she fell asleep on his couch, William would be relieved but also disappointed.

"Yes, I am." She looked up and smiled at him. "I'm about to kiss the prince, and I don't think he's going to turn into a frog."

William had known that this moment was coming, and evidently Kaia wasn't tired enough to forsake her seduction plan.

She'd thought that she was being very clever, but he'd seen right through her so-called let's-get-to-know-each-other excuse and had made all kinds of promises to himself to turn her down gently. Except, on some subconscious level, William must have accepted the inevitability of what was about to happen between them, knowing that he wouldn't be able to resist.

"I'm no prince, but you are definitely a princess." He hooked a finger under her chin. "My princess." Dipping his head, he took her lips in a gentle kiss and wrapped his arm around her.

The moan she released into his mouth was one of longing mixed with relief, the sound making him feel guilty for denying her for so long. Except, it hadn't been long at all.

Kaia had arrived on Sunday, and it was only Tuesday, or rather Wednesday morning. He had succumbed to her charms practically without a fight.

But what choice did he have?

To deny her would hurt her feelings and sabotage the project, and keeping her at arm's length was causing them both pain. He'd hoped she would back off and wait patiently for a more appropriate time, but that wasn't in Kaia's nature, and he was done fighting the insane attraction between them.

"William," she murmured against his lips. "Take me to your bed."

The word bashful was not in Kaia's vocabulary, and he was glad that it wasn't. It made her what she was—a force of nature, a goddess of science, a woman to be reckoned with.

"Your wish is my command, my lady."

As he lifted her into his arms and carried her to the bedroom, Kaia wound her arms around his neck and purred like a satisfied kitten. "You're so strong. I love how easily you can carry me."

"You're light as a feather."

She threw her head back and laughed. "What a sweet liar you are. But I don't mind." She tightened her arms around his neck and tilted her head up to kiss him.

Sitting on the bed with her on his lap, he took over the kiss. She melted into him, and as a needy groan escaped her throat, William's immortal instincts screamed for him to take care of that need, to satisfy his female, and to claim her as his own.

He delved deeper with his tongue, dueling with hers and preventing it from entering his mouth and discovering that his canines had elongated and that their sharp points could draw blood.

With a warning growl, he squeezed her tighter to him, but her need was so great that she didn't heed the warning and reached under his shirt. The feel of her hands roaming over his naked skin obliterated the last of his resistance, and as the dam burst inside of him, he snaked his hand under her T-shirt to cup her breast over her bra.

She trembled, crying out as he pulled the bra cup down and dipped his head to take the succulent berry between his lips.

This time they weren't out in the open where anyone could see them. There was nothing stopping him from baring her completely and taking her as he'd yearned to do since the first time he'd seen her.

When she clutched at the back of his head and held him to her breast, his eyes rolled back in his head, but he couldn't just let himself revel in the pleasure of holding her in his arms, smelling the intoxicating aroma of her arousal, and suckling on her breasts. He had to take care of his princess, and she was aching for him to touch her where her need was the greatest.

Reaching down, he rubbed his fingers over the seam of her jeans, his shaft getting impossibly hard as he felt her heat through the thick fabric. Her moans grew frantic as he pressed his thumb to the apex of her thighs, and with her hips gyrating faster and faster over his erection, he was just as close to climaxing as she was.

Kaia was so ready for him that he could have taken her right there and then, but he wasn't going to. He would pleasure her with his hands and his tongue, bringing her to one climax after the other, but as much as he wanted to make her his, he wasn't going to claim her tonight.

69

KAIA

Kaia trembled from the intense pleasure, but it wasn't enough. William's mouth sucking on her breast and his fingers rubbing that most sensitive spot through her jeans was a sweet torment, and she could climax just from that, but tonight, she wasn't going to settle for just kissing.

She wanted it all.

When he released her breast and lifted his head to take her lips, she pushed on his chest, and as he tumbled down on the bed, she knew she wouldn't have been able to do that unless he'd allowed it. Despite his soft appearance, William was insanely strong, and if she wasn't already beyond turned on, that would have done it for her.

Kaia followed, lying over him and rubbing her aching sex against his rock-hard erection. Impatiently yanking his shirt apart, she didn't care that buttons were flying everywhere. The growl leaving William's throat was not one of anger over the shirt's destruction, but of hunger that she was eager to satiate.

Rolling her under him, he settled between her thighs, gripped her wrists, and pinned her hands above her head. "Naughty, naughty girl," he tsked.

"Are you going to punish me?" she teased.

"I am." He dipped his head and nipped her ear.

When he released her hands and slid down her body, Kaia smiled.

She'd never had anyone pleasure her with his mouth, and if that was how he was going to punish her, she would get naughty as often as she could.

As he kissed her center through her jeans, she reached down, intending to shove her jeans off, but he batted her hands away and yanked them down her hips, pulling them off along with her skimpy panties.

"Ohh," she moaned as he blew air on her heated flesh.

"Beautiful," William murmured before lightly kissing her lower lips. "Did you ever have anyone lick your gorgeous pussy?"

Kaia almost climaxed just from hearing him say that. She'd never have expected prim and proper William could ever talk dirty.

"No," she whispered. "You're going to be my first."

His head whipped up, and he looked at her in alarm. "Are you a virgin?"

She laughed. "Just a cunnilingus virgin and eager for a change of status."

His worried expression evaporating, he smirked. "Not as much as I am eager to change it." He dipped his head and treated her to a long lick that had her hips shooting up.

"Stay still, my naughty princess." He gripped her thighs, pinning them down. "Close your eyes and enjoy."

Kaia wanted to watch, but William's tone brooked no argument, and she had a feeling that if she didn't comply, he would stop what he was doing.

Besides, it was sexy as hell to be ordered around by him, but only in bed.

"Yes, master," she teased when she closed her eyes and let her head fall back on the mattress.

Her reward was a flick of his tongue over that most sensitive spot that had her seeing stars behind her closed lids.

As he went on to feast on her, licking, nipping, and nuzzling, she was helpless to do anything other than moan, not even able to undulate her hips because he was pinning them down, but that just added to her arousal.

Then he let go of one side, and a moment later, he thrust his tongue into her sheath while his thumb pressed over the center of her desire. As the orgasm shot up and exploded out of her, she screamed his name.

He kept licking and thrusting until the tremors subsided.

Her eyes were still tightly closed as he climbed over her and took her lips in a scorching kiss, the zipper digging into her sensitive flesh, making her realize that he still had his pants on.

"William," she murmured against his lips.

"Shhh, it's okay." He pumped his hips over her, rubbing his hard length against her mound. "Keep your eyes closed, princess."

She was too blissed out to object, but she couldn't understand why he wasn't getting rid of his pants and filling her up with that magnificent erection she could feel through his pants.

Reaching down, she yanked on the waistband, but he caught her hands again and pinned them over her head while kissing her hard enough to bruise her lips.

Kaia wanted to tell William that she needed him inside of her, but he was possessing her mouth and holding her hands, and his big body was pinning her under him. There was nothing she could do other than surrender.

70

WILLIAM

The devil on William's left shoulder was riding him hard, whispering in his ear that Kaia wouldn't be satisfied with the orgasm he'd given her, that she needed to be claimed as much as he needed to claim her. But the angel on his right shoulder pleaded with him to exercise restraint, to get off her and run into the bathroom before she saw his fangs and his glowing eyes, and he was forced to thrall her.

Hell, he didn't even have a condom, and if his suspicion was correct and she was a Dormant, he would induce her transition without her consent, and she would never forgive him for that.

As she released a strangled mewl into his mouth, he realized that he was crushing her with his bulk, and as he lifted off her and braced on his forearms, she sucked in a breath.

"I want you in me, William," she hissed. "If you are not inside of me in two seconds, I'm opening my eyes."

How the hell did she know that this was the most effective threat she could use on him? And why did her assertiveness chase the angel off his shoulder, leaving only the devil behind?

"Keep your eyes closed," he commanded as he lifted just enough to push his pants down and kick them off him.

The smile lifting her lips was full of satisfaction, but he wiped that smirk off her face with one brutal thrust, burying himself inside of her.

Her orgasm had prepared her for him, but she was tight, and when she cried out, he had a moment of panic and stilled immediately. But then that satisfied smile returned to her lips, and she lifted her long legs, wrapping them around his waist and gripping his ass with her hands.

"You're mine." She dug her fingers into his flesh and arched her hips, getting him to go even deeper.

"I'm yours," he growled against her ear. "And you're mine."

He was out of control, and if she opened her eyes right now, she would see him in his full immortal glory, his fangs fully elongated, and his eyes blazing blue light.

Keeping his head down, his cheek tucked against hers, he reached between them and circled his thumb over her clit.

"William," Kaia moaned his name.

As his thrusts became faster and stronger, he had to remove his thumb, and as he felt his seed rising in his shaft, he pushed the slightest of thralls into Kaia's mind, preparing her for what he was about to do next.

Licking her neck, he pulled out of her and fisted his erection, and as he sank his fangs into her neck, he came all over her belly and her thighs. She climaxed under him, the venom inducing a chain of orgasms that went on and on for nearly as long as he kept spilling on top of her.

When it was all done, and Kaia was soaring on the clouds of bliss, he withdrew his fangs, licked the puncture wounds closed, and lay on top of her for a moment to catch his breath.

Pulling out and finishing outside had been a feat William doubted any other immortal male could have accomplished, but he wasn't proud of himself for achieving the impossible.

He imagined the angel on his right shoulder shaking his head at him in disapproval, while the devil on his left shoulder was dancing a victory dance and flipping the angel off.

They had both acted recklessly, just for different reasons. Kaia didn't know that he couldn't give her sexually transmitted diseases or get her pregnant, and even if she was on the pill, she should have made sure that he put a condom on. She was young and impulsive, and perhaps she could be forgiven, but he was tempted to treat her to a good spanking for how irresponsibly she'd acted.

Except, knowing her, it would only encourage her to be even naughtier. It hadn't escaped his notice how throaty she'd sounded when she'd asked him if he was going to punish her.

Brazen, assertive Kaia yearned to yield control, and he was more than happy to play along.

But then, he wasn't blameless either. He didn't have the excuse of youth and impulsivity, and he shouldn't have allowed things to progress so quickly between them. Perhaps he should let Kaia spank him, although he doubted she would enjoy it as much.

The image put a smile on his face, but then the reality of what he'd done slapped it off his face.

The thralling Kaia would need at the end of the project was substantial, and the responsible thing would have been to avoid thralling her until then. By giving in to his impulses and her insistence, he was endangering not only her but also the safety of the project.

71

KAIA

An obnoxious beeping noise woke Kaia from the best dream ever, but her annoyance was quickly replaced by a fuzzy warm feeling as she registered the arm draped around her and the warm body pressed against her back.

She was in William's bed, in his arms, and it was much better than any dream. Well, since the dream had been about him, it was nearly as good, but the real thing was always better.

"Good morning." She turned around and kissed him on the lips. "Or is it still night? What time is it?"

He opened his eyes and smiled. "I thought that I was dreaming, but you are really here."

She chuckled. "Funny, I dreamt about you too, and then that annoying beeping started, and I woke up. What was it?"

"My alarm." He sighed. "I'm supposed to be in the gym at five, but I think I'm going to skip it today." He pulled her closer against him. "I might never get out of bed at all."

"I wish we could stay here all day and snuggle, but I need to get to my bungalow before Kylie wakes up and starts the gossip train." She kissed him again and then pushed on his chest. "I need to pee."

He grumbled something under his breath but let go of her.

She found her clothes folded neatly on the nightstand and pulled the T-shirt and panties on before padding to the bathroom.

After she'd passed out, William must have cleaned her up and collected her clothes because she remembered them being carelessly tossed on the floor.

After taking care of her bladder and brushing her teeth with her finger, she padded back to the bedroom and sat on the bed. "Wake up, sleepyhead."

Instead of opening his eyes, he yanked her down to him and wrapped her in his arms. "You are way too cheerful for someone who slept only two hours."

"I'm happy." She couldn't stop smiling. "But I don't want to do the walk of shame. I'd rather sneak into my room and tell Kylie that we were working on the project, and I fell asleep on your couch."

A frown tugged on his brows. "Are you embarrassed about spending the night with me?"

"Never. I'll shout it from the rooftops if you are okay with that, and I'll tell everyone that we are officially together. I'll also move my things in here and sleep with you every night."

He smiled. "I would like that."

That was a surprise. He'd been so concerned about having a relationship with her because she worked for him, and now he didn't mind telling everyone about it?

"Really? That's a big departure from where you were just yesterday."

"Things have changed, and I have no intention of hiding our relationship. I'm going to get mercilessly teased and accused of cradle robbing, but I can live with that. You are not a shameful secret, my princess Kaia. If anything, you are a great prize to be proud of."

"That's music to my ears." She relaxed against his chest. "Are you going to tell Darlene that you're not joining her today for a swim?"

"I'm just not going to show up." His hand traveled down to her bottom, and he gave it a hard squeeze. "You should get a good bare bottom spanking for being so careless."

If not for his serious tone, she would have thought that he was teasing. "What do you mean by careless?"

"You're impulsive. You didn't verify that I had a condom, and that's careless. I happen to be clean, but allowing a guy you've just met to have unprotected sex with you is irresponsible."

Talk about spoiling the mood. From floating on clouds, she'd tumbled down into detention.

"I'm on the pill, so pregnancy prevention was covered, and you are too much of a dork not to be clean. I knew that I had nothing to worry about."

"A dork, eh?" He playfully slapped her bottom. "I'm a nerd, not a dork. Even an old lecher like me knows the difference."

She laughed. "You are both a dork and a nerd, but so am I, so we are in it together. You are also a sexy hunk of a man, not an old lecher or a cradle robber. And you are mine. But I still need to get to my room, shower, and put on fresh clothes before going to breakfast."

"Not yet. Stay for a little longer."

72

WILLIAM

William lingered in bed long after Kaia left to shower and change, basking in the afterglow of the best lovemaking he'd ever experienced despite pulling out at the last moment.

Kaia hadn't commented on that, so perhaps her memories of those final moments were fuzzy thanks to his venom and the slight thrall he'd managed right before he'd bitten her.

Waking up with her in his arms had been phenomenal, but if he wanted many more mornings like that, she needed to move in with him, and that would make some waves. He needed to come up with a strategy to deal with the responses to their relationship.

People were going to snicker and make comments, but he could handle it. The question was whether Kaia could. Even those who didn't know how old he really was would frown on their relationship.

A thirteen-year difference was a big deal for humans at any age, especially when the girl was as young as Kaia.

Her stepfather was going to kill him, or at least try, and so would the uncle. Hopefully, that wouldn't ruin things for Darlene, who had high hopes for the guy.

Perhaps he should propose to Kaia?

Would her family still be angry if they were engaged?

And why did the prospect of calling her his fiancée appeal to him so much?

Closing his eyes, William did something so atypical that it could only mean that he was in love. He prayed to the Fates, beseeching them to make Kaia his mate. Well, first she had to be a Dormant, and then his mate. Or was it the other way around?

When his phone rang, he expected it to be Darlene berating him for not showing up for their swimming session again, but as he lifted it, the picture on the screen was Kian's.

His anxiety spiking, William pushed up on the pillows and accepted the call. "Good morning, Kian."

"Good morning. I hate being the bearer of bad news, but I just got off the phone with Kalugal. He asked Areana about Tony, and she confirmed that he's in the harem, which means that he's not getting out. No one ever does."

William swallowed the bile rising in his throat. "So, your hunch was right. Is he at least being treated well?"

"Of course, he is. The harem is Areana's domain, and she takes care of her people." Kian cleared his throat. "Was Anthony Kaia's boyfriend?"

"No, he wasn't. They were just good friends."

"Good. Areana told Kalugal that Tula took Anthony as her lover, and she refuses to share him with the other immortal ladies."

"That's one hell of a coincidence. Is he happy there?"

"Kalugal didn't comment on that. Obviously, he's not suffering, and he's under Navuh's compulsion to donate his seed the natural way, but he's a young man who had a bright future to look forward to, and it's been taken away from him. He can't be too happy."

"Can we rescue him? We can do it the same way we extracted Carol from the island."

"I feel bad for the guy, but I'm not risking our people and a war with Navuh to rescue a human."

"Yeah. You're right. I shouldn't have even suggested it. I just don't know what to tell Kaia."

"Don't tell her anything. As far as she's concerned, you couldn't find any more information about her friend. Case closed."

William didn't want to lie to Kaia. He was already lying to her about too many things.

"I'll think of something. Thank you for calling me right away."

"You're welcome. I'm sorry I didn't have better news for her."

After Kian ended the call, William got out of bed and padded to the bathroom. Turning the water on in the shower, he got under the spray, braced his hands on the tiled wall, and hung his head. While the hot water sluiced down his back, he tried to come up with a way to tell Kaia about Tony without lying to her, but at the same time not telling her about the island and how he knew about it.

If Tony was Tula's lover, then perhaps the story about him finding a girl and enjoying his time with her was not such a big departure from the truth. It would be a lie by omission, and that wasn't as bad as a complete fabrication.

But knowing Kaia, she would ask questions that he couldn't answer, so maybe Kian was right that the best strategy was not to tell her at all.

73

KAIA

"Good morning." Kylie had a knowing smirk on her face as she walked into their small living room. "Where were you last night? I went to sleep after one in the morning, and you weren't here yet."

As a dozen different considerations flashed through Kaia's mind, she took a long moment to answer. She didn't want to hide her relationship with William, and he didn't want that either, but despite what she'd told him about shouting it from the rooftops, she wasn't the type of girl who freely shared details about her sex life with her friends. It was nobody's business.

"I was with William." She lifted her phone and pretended to be absorbed in her sister's Instatock channel.

"I thought so." Kylie walked over to their coffee maker, stuffed a pod into the slot and a mug under the spout, and then leaned against the counter with her arms crossed over her chest and that annoying smirk still playing over her lips. "Working late on the decoding, I presume?"

The sarcastic tone aggravated Kaia, and the answer dancing on the tip of her tongue was that she'd had mind-blowing sex with a spectacular man and had woken up in his arms this morning, which had also been an amazing experience, but it was none of Kylie's business.

"Among other things." Kaia put her empty coffee cup in the sink. "I'm heading out to get breakfast. Are you coming?"

"Yeah." Kylie took the freshly brewed cup of coffee and brought it to her lips. "I just need a few sips."

Tapping her foot on the floor, Kaia waited for her to finish drinking even though she would have liked nothing better than to walk out the door and leave her nosy roommate behind.

She'd hoped to have a better relationship with Kylie, perhaps even form a real friendship that they could maintain after the project was over and they returned to the Bay Area, but there was something about her roommate that just rubbed her the wrong way. Kylie wasn't horrible, but she wasn't bestie material either.

Not that Kaia had ever had a bestie. Tony had been her closest friend, but he was a guy and much older than her, so he didn't really count. Besides, he was gone, so the only one left was Cheryl. Her sister was four years younger than her and had no prior life memories, but she was a very old soul. Cheryl was level-headed and direct, and Kaia could always count on her to tell her the truth and watch her back.

Perhaps she could call her later and share the wonderful news about her and William. Not about the sex, of course. She would only hint at that, but about them officially becoming a couple.

"I'm ready to go." Kylie put her cup in the sink.

As they walked out the door, she threaded her arm through Kaia's and leaned closer to whisper in her ear. "So, what were the other things you and William did last night?"

"We talked." Kaia smiled sweetly at her.

Thankfully, Kylie wasn't stupid and got the hint. "Fine. If you don't want to talk about it, it's your choice." She tilted her head to look up at Kaia. "Did you know that the Safe Haven community practices free love?"

"I've read about it. Good for them, but it's not for me. I'm too possessive to share."

"Yeah, I don't like to share either. I can't imagine falling in love with someone and watching him with another woman, but I wouldn't mind just having fun for a while and choosing a different guy each night. And what's even better, it's ladies' choice with them. The men have to wait to be invited. They can't initiate, but they can try to impress the ladies to get an invitation. How cool is that?"

Kaia opened the door to the dining room. "I can see the merit of that, and kudos to them for empowering women, but it's not for me. I'm a one-guy girl, and I want my guy to be a one-girl man." She waved at Darlene, who was sitting with Eleanor and three of the paranormals.

William wasn't there yet, and she wondered whether he was still sleeping. Had she exhausted him so thoroughly last night?

The thing was that she couldn't remember what happened from the moment right before she'd blacked out from bliss, and it bothered her. It had been literally mind-blowing sex because her mind had shorted out, and stuff like that just didn't happen to her.

74

WILLIAM

William was struggling to keep the information Kian had shared with him from Kaia. He'd even skipped breakfast so he wouldn't have to face her in a social environment, but once their workday ended, he would have no more excuses. He had to come up with something that he could tell her that wouldn't be a complete lie but would also give her hope and not devastate her.

He was a smart guy, and he should be able to think of something before Kaia lost her patience and demanded answers.

Sitting across the desk from her and keeping it bottled inside of him was pure hell.

As Kaia lifted her head and looked at him, William forced a tight smile. Seeing his pinched expression, she lowered her head and went back to the stack of photocopies he'd printed for her to work on, but not before he'd caught the pained look in her eyes.

After what they'd shared yesterday, she'd probably expected smiles and covert kisses, not a nervous wreck who was giving her the silent treatment. He'd even left the door to his office wide open so they were in plain view of the other team members.

William hoped that she would take it as his attempt to act professionally during work hours, and not as his reaction to their intimacy of last night and this morning.

If it hadn't been such a reality-altering experience, and he wasn't falling in love with her, it would have been much easier for him to lie to her or to pretend that he didn't know what happened to her friend. It would have been just one more thing he couldn't talk about because the clan's security demanded it.

But Kaia was his mate, he could feel it in every fiber of his being, and he would be very surprised if he was wrong. And if he was right, he had to tell her the truth about everything anyway, so why wait and live with the torment?

"I need to make a phone call." He got to his feet.

Kaia lifted her head and looked at him with those big sad eyes of hers, cementing his decision. "I can leave if you need privacy. I can use a coffee break." She was out the door before he had a chance to object.

As she closed it behind her, he dropped back into his chair and let out a breath before picking up his phone and calling Kian.

"William," the boss answered in his usual gruff voice that people took to mean that he didn't have time for them. "Anything new with the decoding?"

"Plenty, but that's not what I'm calling about. I think that Kaia is a Dormant and that she's my mate. I'm going to tell her everything tonight, including what I know about her friend."

There was a long moment of stunned silence. "What makes you think that she's a Dormant? Does she have any paranormal abilities?"

"Not as far as I know, unless her uncanny ability to translate the gods' language and genetic coding counts. It's like she was born with the knowledge, but that could be attributed to her brilliance. The others don't have a clue about what they are working on. Well, I'm exaggerating. They have a vague idea, but since only Kaia has access to larger portions of the manuscript, she's the only one who has the big picture."

"What about affinity?" Kian asked.

"That's actually a good indicator. Eleanor and Darlene like her a lot, and that's not because Kaia is such an easily likable girl. She's assertive and direct, and she's quick to anger, which doesn't endear her to her teammates. But that could also be because of envy. She's a kid, and she's smarter and more accomplished than the three of them combined."

"You sound like you are in awe, not just in love."

"I am, and I feel like an old lecher lusting after a nineteen-year-old who works for me, but as Kaia pointed out, I need her much more than she needs me, so she's in the position to coerce me, and not the other way around."

Kian chuckled. "I like her already. But that doesn't mean that you should tell her everything. You can give her the general overview about immortals and Dormants and get her consent to induction, but you can't tell her about obtaining the information about her friend. That would endanger Lokan and Areana, and especially Areana. Navuh wouldn't kill his mate over this, but he would confiscate her means of communications with us, and we can't let that happen. He could even retaliate by hurting those she loves, and one of those is Tula, Wonder's sister."

"How is Kaia going to jeopardize their safety? For the next two weeks, she's not going to leave Safe Haven, and in that time, we will know whether she's a Dormant or not. And with the security systems we've put in place, no one can get to her either."

"What about her family? They are coming to visit her this weekend."

Onegus must have updated Kian about that, but it wasn't an issue either.

"She's already under compulsion not to reveal anything about the research. I can ask Eleanor and Emmett to include this as well."

"You can't tell Eleanor and Emmett about Areana. They don't know that we can communicate with her, and if they don't know that, how are they going to compel Kaia not to reveal it?"

"I don't have to give them any details. I'll find a way for them to form an umbrella compulsion. Besides, I won't mention Areana by name. I will just tell Kaia that we have a source in Navuh's harem."

"I don't like it," Kian grumbled.

"I have no choice. I've bitten her once already and had to thrall her. I don't want to do that again. Her brain is too precious to mess with, not just to me but all of us. She holds the key to the translation."

"Fine. Just be careful."

As relief washed over William, he closed his eyes for a brief moment. "Thank you."

"Don't mention it, and by that, I mean, don't mention it to anyone ever. I can't believe the concession I'm making for you. If it was anyone else…"

"I know. I'm special, and I'm truly grateful."

75

KAIA

William was acting strange, and the only explanation Kaia could think of was that he regretted last night.

But he'd been so loving this morning. And what about all that talk about her being his great prize and him being proud to win her?

What, or who had changed his mind?

She glanced around the table at her teammates. Kylie was scribbling on her yellow pad, Corinne was trying to figure out the chemical composition of one of the materials that William had partially translated, and Owen was working on a spreadsheet. None of them looked guilty or were giving her weird looks, so they weren't the culprits.

Perhaps Darlene had told William to back off?

The woman seemed to like her, and Kaia liked her back, so the only reason for Darlene to do that was if she thought that William was taking advantage of her. But if the two were old friends, she should know that William would never coerce anyone into doing what they didn't want to do. He was a good man.

The door to his office opened, and as he stepped out, William immediately zeroed in on her as if none of the others were there. "I need to talk to you." He walked over to the table and offered her a hand up.

That was it. He was going to tell her that they couldn't continue whatever they'd started and would have to limit their interactions to the lab. Or something like that.

Swallowing the lump that had formed in her throat, she took his hand and tried to suck in a breath, but all she got was a trickle of air.

"It's okay," William murmured quietly as he led her to the lab's door. "There is no reason for alarm."

Her panicked expression probably made him think that she was expecting bad news from home, not from him. But what if that was what he'd come to tell her?

"What happened? Is my family okay?"

"I didn't hear anything to indicate otherwise. The thing I need to talk to you about has to do with what we are working on."

Kaia didn't believe him.

When they were outside the lab, she turned toward the bungalows, but William took her hand and guided her in the opposite direction. "We are going to the lodge."

"Why?" After the first day, they had been told not to go there because a new retreat had started, and they were not supposed to mingle with the guests.

"We need to talk with Eleanor and Emmett."

That was even stranger. "They are not supposed to know what we are working on. What do we need to talk to them about?"

Maybe they had been the ones to turn William against having a relationship with her?

"It's related to your contract." He sounded exasperated.

She hoped he wouldn't try to pull that one on her. Kaia had an excellent memory, and she'd read the entire contract carefully.

Tugging on his hand, she forced him to slow down. "There was nothing in there about prohibiting relationships between team members. I would have remembered if there was."

William stopped, turned to her, and before she knew what was happening, his hand cupped her nape, and his lips smashed over hers in a scorching hot kiss.

He kissed her like a starving man, like he couldn't get enough of her, and as she put her hands on his chest and melted into the kiss, he wrapped an arm around her and pulled her into his body.

When she had to come up for air, he let go of her and looked into her eyes. "I'm not trying to get rid of you. The opposite is true. I want to keep you with me for as long as I can."

As his meaning sank in, Kaia's eyes widened. So that's what he needed Emmett and Eleanor for—witnesses for their marriage contract.

"I like you a lot, William. I might be even falling in love with you. But I'm not ready to get married after knowing you for three days."

He laughed. "We are not going to the chapel or the courthouse. We are just going to the lodge. Can you wait patiently for a few more minutes instead of jumping to conclusions?"

"I can't help it." She let him lead her at an even faster pace. "That's what I do. I gather clues and put them together. I do it even in my sleep. How do you think I can decipher that alien language?"

76

WILLIAM

As William knocked on Emmett's office door, Eleanor opened it and smiled. "Good afternoon. Please, come in."

"Welcome." Emmett spread his arms in his prophet pose, the long sleeves of his robe fluttering in the breeze blowing through the open window. "Please take a seat."

When William had called ahead and explained what he needed them to do and why, both Emmett and Eleanor had congratulated him and wished him and Kaia the best of luck, and there had been true warmth in their voices.

Eleanor rolled her eyes at her mate. "You can drop the theatrics, Emmett. Your flock is not here to witness it."

William didn't mind. As long as the compulsion worked, Emmett could pretend to be an angel and flap a pair of fake wings. It would probably be an improvement over his Moses act.

The guy pouted. "How did I end up with a grouch like you who doesn't appreciate a good act? I'm a performer. I need an audience."

"You have it." Eleanor leaned and kissed his bearded cheek. "Every day, almost all day long. I want to see the real Emmett from time to time."

"My love." The guy beamed at his mate.

The two were an odd couple, and right now they seemed to have forgotten that William needed their services.

Looking confused, Kaia leaned closer to him. "What's going on?"

"Emmett and Eleanor are a loving couple, but they are two very different people. Emmett likes to live on a stage, while Eleanor is more down to earth."

Kaia still looked confused, but she nodded.

Eleanor patted her mate's arm. "We have a job to do."

"Right. Do you want to go first?"

"Sure." Leaning against Emmett's desk, Eleanor crossed her arms over her chest and her feet at the ankles. "The reason you are here is that William is ready to reveal more secrets to you, and he needs our help to ensure that you don't breathe a word of what he's about to tell you to anyone, and that includes Emmett and me."

Kaia turned to him with an offended expression on her beautiful face. "You could've just asked. I would have never broken your trust. Besides, I've already signed a confidentiality agreement."

He took her hand and leaned toward her. "It's not entirely up to me, and the lives of many people depend on that information remaining a secret."

"Then why tell me at all? I don't want to know something that means life or death to people. I don't want that kind of responsibility."

"You're smart," Eleanor said.

William had a plan, and he knew precisely how he was going to play it. "It's about Tony."

Kaia's head whipped around to Eleanor. "Where do I sign?"

The woman chuckled. "It's not a written agreement. It's a verbal one. You will not repeat anything William tells you is a secret to anyone but him, and only when you are sure that no one else can hear you. You will not write it, mime it, or communicate it in any other fashion either. Now, repeat what I said and swear an oath."

Kaia looked as if she wanted to say something else, but she did exactly as Eleanor had commanded her instead. When she was done, she looked at the woman with narrowed eyes. "Are you also a hypnotist like Emmett?"

"I am. And just to cement it, Emmett is going to repeat what I just did."

William was surprised. Emmett's compulsion hadn't worked as immediately and as strongly on Kaia as Eleanor's. Perhaps she was the stronger compeller?

Turning to him, Kaia rubbed a hand over her temple. "How do they do that? I wanted to ask that question before repeating what Eleanor said, but I couldn't. It was like a compulsion."

"Because that's precisely what it was," Emmett said. "Eleanor is a strong compeller, but I'm even stronger, and the doubling of our powers will ensure your silence."

William was no longer sure that Emmett was right about being the stronger compeller, but this wasn't the time to comment on it.

Kaia looked like she was about to bolt, but Emmett stopped her with a simple command. "Sit down."

Her bottom hit the chair with a thwack.

Later, William would have a word with Emmett about his Doctor Evil performance. There was no need to scare Kaia, and he could have just done the compulsion the way Eleanor had done it.

"Ignore his theatrics." William squeezed her hand. "He will do exactly what Eleanor did, no more, and no less."

77

KAIA

*A*s they left Emmett's office, Kaia stopped right outside the door and turned to William. "That was the weirdest hour of my life, and I've had a few that I didn't think could be topped." Like standing naked in front of the mirror, looking at herself through the eyes of a man, and touching her own breasts. "But I have a feeling that things are going to get much weirder than that."

"You have no idea." He took her hand and brought it to his lips for a soft kiss. "But don't worry. The rest of it is going to be much more pleasant. I apologize for Emmett's unnecessary theatrics. I don't know what has gotten into him." He lowered her hand and led her down the corridor toward one of the lodge's side doors.

"You said that the secret had to do with Tony."

"It does, but I can't tell you about it without explaining a few things first, and those are not the type of things I can tell you out here." He opened the door and held it open for her. "Let's go to my bungalow."

Kaia smirked. "I have no objection to that, but aren't you forgetting something?"

He frowned. "What?"

"The other team members. They are stuck in the lab, and they can't get out without you opening the door for them. Thankfully, lunch was delivered before we left, so they are not starving."

"Right." William rubbed the back of his neck, with a sheepish smile lifting the corners of his lips. "We need to stop by the lab and let them out. Everyone gets the rest of the day off. I bet they are going to love that."

"No doubt." Kaia leaned into him as they kept walking. "You really should scan another person's eyeball so someone else can open those doors." She narrowed her eyes at him with a mock stern look. "Talk about irresponsible. If something happens to you, how are we supposed to get out?"

"You are right. I'll get Max to lend me his eye." He winked at her.

"You seem so different from the way you were this morning. I was sure that you were regretting what happened between us."

Remembering the private phone call he'd needed to make, the puzzle pieces fell into place. "You called someone and asked permission to tell me the truth, didn't you?"

"Yes. And the reason I was in such a dreary mood all morning was that I couldn't tell you all the things I wanted to, and it was eating away at me. There should be no secrets between people who love each other."

Love? Was he telling her that he loved her?

In a way, he'd already said that in so many words this morning.

Did she love him back?

How could anyone be in love with someone after knowing them for three days?

William stopped in front of the lab door. "Do you want to come in with me? Or do you want to wait out here?"

"I'll come with you. I need to organize my papers."

She'd left them on William's desk in a neat stack, and since he'd locked the door behind him, it wasn't necessary, but she didn't want her teammates to start asking him questions about her without her being there.

When he opened the third door, Corinne gave him a glare worthy of a stern matriarch. "I was starting to worry that you'd abandoned us here."

"I would never do that." He sent an overt smile Kaia's way. "I came to get you out. Everyone gets the rest of the day off."

"What's the occasion?" Owen asked.

"I have a headache." William didn't even bother to sound convincing. "I need to lie down and have my girlfriend rub my temples." He wrapped his arm around Kaia's shoulders.

Corinne shrugged. "If you want to dig your own grave," she murmured under her breath, "it's no skin off my nose."

William pretended that he hadn't heard her, but Kaia's skin wasn't as thick as his, and Corinne's jab hurt. It implied that William was manipulating her to get her in his bed, or that she was manipulating him to later extort him with threats to sue him for sexual harassment. It cast a sleazy light on both of them.

She was tempted to say something biting back, but William squeezed her shoulder reassuringly, and she decided to let it go.

Her teammates would get used to them being a couple, and in a day or two it would be old news, and everything would return to normal.

Or so she hoped.

78

WILLIAM

On the way to his bungalow, William had thought long and hard about the way he was going to present things to Kaia. She had an open mind, and after dealing with the journals and what they contained, she wouldn't dismiss his story as the ramblings of a madman.

He didn't expect to encounter too much disbelief from her.

Nevertheless, he was nervous as he put down two glasses of water on the coffee table and sat down next to her on the couch.

"Everything I'm going to tell you from now on is a well-guarded secret." He took her hand and clasped it.

She nodded. "I wouldn't tell a soul even without the hypnotic compulsion. It wasn't necessary."

He believed her, but he hadn't had the luxury of trusting his instincts on that.

"I got the boss's approval to let you in on the biggest secret in the world under the condition that you undergo compulsion to never reveal it."

"The biggest?"

He smiled. "After I tell you what it is, you can tell me if you think it is the biggest or not."

Kaia let out a breath. "Just get on with it, then. I can't stand the suspense."

He nodded. "I'll start with a brief overview, and after I'm done, you can ask me to elaborate on the parts you want more information on." He sucked in a breath. "The mythological gods were real people, and they had children with humans who were born immortal. The immortals had the gods' powers to manipulate human minds, but to a lesser extent. When those immortals took human mates, though, their children were born mortal. It was later discovered that the children of female immortals carried the immortal genes in a dormant state and that there was a way to activate them. Most of the gods perished in an attack launched by one of their own, but a few survived, and some of the immortals and humans who carried the godly genes survived as well."

Kaia regarded him with interest, and so far, she didn't look as if she was about to declare him insane and walk out the door, which was encouraging, but he hadn't gotten to the part of him being one of those immortals.

"The survivors split into two opposing camps. The one I belong to is headed by a benevolent goddess whose mission is to continue her people's work and help humanity progress and evolve. The other camp is headed by the immortal son of the god who murdered the other gods, and his mission is to rule supreme over an enslaved humanity. Lately, he decided to improve the quality of the immortal warriors he breeds on his island, so he started attracting smart young men to breed the dormant females he keeps enslaved there."

William lifted his glass and took a sip of water before continuing to the part she would find most relevant. "Your friend is one of those smart young men, but unlike the others who have no idea that their seed is being stolen and go home after their sex vacation is over, he's been sent to Navuh's personal harem because of his slight resemblance to the despot. That way, Navuh can claim that all the children born to the immortal females he keeps there are his. Anthony is alive, and he's treated well, but he's never going to leave that island."

For a long moment Kaia just gaped at him, then she leaned down, took her glass, and drank half of it in one go. "If anyone other than you would have told me this story, I wouldn't have believed it. But I know that you are not crazy, and you are not prone to making up fantasies either. So, my question is, how do we get Tony out?"

William's heart swelled with pride and a big smile spread over his face. "I knew you wouldn't freak out and run away screaming that your boyfriend is a madman."

She narrowed her eyes at him. "I have many more questions for my so-called boyfriend, starting with how old you really are, but for now, I want to know what can be done for Tony."

William's smile wilted. "Nothing, I'm afraid. The island is home to about twenty thousand immortal warriors, and my clan is tiny in comparison. Even if Tony was one of us, we wouldn't have dared to start a war with Navuh to get him out."

That wasn't entirely true, but to tell her more meant exposing Areana and her role in Carol's extraction, and he'd promised Kian not to do that. Besides, it had no bearing on his relationship with Kaia, and Anthony was an unlucky human, not a clan member.

Kaia let out a breath. "At least he's alive. Do you know that for sure?"

"They don't use last names on the island, so I can't be a hundred percent sure, but I doubt that they have another scientist named Tony who also matches your friend's description."

"I assume that you have an informant on the island."

He nodded.

"Can he pass a message to Tony? Just so he knows that he hasn't been forgotten?"

"I'm not sure. I'm not the one who's dealing with the informant, and I doubt my boss would authorize it."

That part was close enough to the truth. William was no longer in charge of communications between Areana and Annani or Kalugal at the pre-agreed times. That job had been assigned to one of the guardians back at the village.

"Is your boss the goddess?"

"The goddess is the head of our clan, but she leaves the day-to-day management to two of her children. Her son is my boss."

"How many kids does she have? Were their fathers human?

Where does she live?" Kaia chuckled. "Don't tell me that it's on Mount Olympus."

79

KAIA

"It's not on Mount Olympus." William's eyes shone with that inner light Kaia now knew she hadn't imagined. "She lives in a place called the sanctuary, and no one knows how to get there except for her Odus, who fly her people in and out of there."

"The Odus?"

William took his glasses off and reached for a corner of his shirt to wipe them with, but then stopped and put them on the coffee table. "Immortals don't need glasses. I wear them to protect my eyes from the computer glare, and since I spend most of the time in front of the screen, I usually don't bother taking them off." He smiled. "I feel naked without them." He took in a long breath. "The Odus are what you would call cyborgs, but the technology to build them was banned on the gods' home planet. Seven of them were either sent or brought to Earth, and they belonged to our Clan Mother, the goddess. She assigned one to each of her five children, whose fathers were indeed human, but one of her sons was killed, so his Odu returned to her. Not too long ago, the one taking care of her surviving son gifted him with a surprising birthday present. A trunk of handwritten journals containing the blueprints of how to build an Odu. That's what you've been working on. We are trying to decipher the gods' scientific language."

So that was where the journals came from. Now everything clicked into place, painting a fantastic picture that she had no doubt was true. If she wasn't embarrassed to show her excitement, Kaia would have danced in a circle singing, 'I knew it.' She'd always suspected the mythological gods had been aliens, but she couldn't come up with a reasonable explanation for why they had disappeared. William had provided her with the missing piece of the puzzle that had finally unlocked the mystery and confirmed her suspicions.

"Did you try to take one apart to see how it worked?" she asked.

William's eyes widened with an expression of horror. "The goddess wouldn't allow it, and even if she did, I wouldn't have dared. The Odus are like members of our family, and to open up one of their brains would have been like operating on one of my cousins without knowing if I could put them back together again."

"I get it." She leaned back. "Are they sentient?"

"I believe so. They are constantly learning, but their creator limited their ability to learn. They were supposed to be domestic servants, and I assume that was done so they wouldn't become dangerous, but they were used as weapons nonetheless, and that's why the technology to make them was destroyed, and they were decommissioned."

"Can I meet one? I mean an Odu?"

"Perhaps. It depends on a few things."

"Like what?"

William chuckled. "You never cease to astonish me. The questions you ask are not the ones I prepared answers for. Aren't you wondering why I told you all of this?"

She was, but then other questions intruded, and she'd lost her train of thought. "At first, I thought that you told me all this because of Tony, but since there is nothing that can be done for him, it didn't serve any purpose other than to let me know that he's alive, but you could have told me that without revealing all the background story. Was it because of what I was decoding? Was I getting too close to figuring out what those schematics were for?"

He shook his head. "That's not it at all, but it will certainly help you now that you know the big picture. I told you the brief history of gods, immortals, and Dormants because I suspect that you carry the godly genes, and if you do, being intimate with me might activate them. I didn't want to do that without your consent."

So far, everything William had told her had sounded logical, but now he'd managed to stun her.

Kaia lifted her hand. "Wait a minute. Are you telling me that I can turn immortal?"

"Yes."

"How?"

"Look at my teeth."

He smiled wide, and for the first time ever, she noticed that his canines were longer than usual, and as she looked closer, they elongated in front of her eyes.

"What the heck, William? Why do you have fangs? Are immortals vampires?" Her hand flew to her neck. "Did you drink my blood?"

He laughed nervously. "We don't drink blood. Immortal males inject venom, which delivers incredible orgasms and has healing properties, so you have nothing to worry about on that account. But when that happens during sex with a Dormant, it can induce her transition, and that's something to worry about. Not for you because you are so young, but for older Dormants, it might be dangerous."

"What if I'm not a Dormant? What would it do to me?"

"The venom has euphoric, aphrodisiac, and healing properties. It gives you orgasms, trips to fantasy land, and a wonderful sense of well-being when you wake up."

She'd experienced all of that with him, which meant that he'd bitten her, which meant that he could have already induced her.

Panic seizing her, she touched her neck again. "You've bitten me."

"I did."

"We had sex. You could have induced my transition already."

His cheeks reddening, William shook his head. "To induce a Dormant, two things have to happen at once. One is unprotected sex, meaning insemination, and the other is the venom bite. You don't remember it, but I pulled out before climaxing. If you don't want to be induced, using a condom would prevent it."

Kaia barked out a laugh. "So that's why you were so angry about me not insisting on you using a condom." She wagged her finger at him. "You were the one who acted irresponsibly. If you didn't have a rubber, you shouldn't have had sex with me at all." Another laugh escaped her throat. "Talk about sexually transmitted diseases. I could have caught immortality from you."

80

WILLIAM

As Kaia collapsed in a fit of giggles, William realized that she must have reached the limit of what she was able to absorb and pulled her into his arms. "It's all too much at once, and you didn't get enough sleep last night. Maybe you should take an afternoon nap, and we can continue talking about it when you are rested."

Hiccuping, Kaia wiped the tears from her eyes and let out a sigh. "Maybe I'm still inside the trip your venom sent me on. But wait, that doesn't make sense. I can't be inside the trip if this is not real because I wouldn't know about it. But maybe you slipped something into my water?" She leaned over, lifted the glass off the table, and sniffed it. "Smells fine, but that doesn't mean anything." She extended her tongue and lapped at it like a dog. "It tastes fine too."

She was losing it.

"I really think you should take a nap." He got to his feet with her in his arms, walked over to the bedroom, and put her down on the bed. "Do you want me to undress you?"

"Please do." She eyed him with amusement dancing in her eyes. "But you have to get naked too. I didn't get to see you fully nude last night."

He was relieved to hear her sounding bossy as usual and in control of her emotions.

"I'm shy." He took off her flip-flops and dropped them on the floor.

"No, you're not." Kaia stretched her arms over her head. "You are a scion of gods, an immortal. How can you be shy?"

"I was just joking." Not really, but he would go with that.

"But if you are immortal, and so were the gods, how did they die?"

"Gods and immortals can be killed. It's just a little harder to do. Immortality means that we don't age and we don't get sick."

"Fascinating. How old are you?"

"Too old for you." He pulled her jeans down her hips. "I've told you that already."

"I'm an old soul."

"Not as old as me." Leaving Kaia's T-shirt and underwear on, William pulled the blanket over her, kicked his shoes off, and lay next to her over it.

This wasn't about sex, and despite her bravado, Kaia was exhausted, overwhelmed, and she needed warmth, comfort, and sleep.

"Give me years," she insisted. "I want to know."

"I'm over three hundred years old, which is considered young for an immortal but ancient compared to you."

She lifted the blanket. "Get in here but take off your pants first."

"Yes, ma'am."

He did as she commanded and pulled her into his arms. "You don't need to decide anything right away. You are young, and there is no rush. We can use condoms until you tell me that you want to give immortality a go."

She lifted her eyes to him. "If there is no rush, why did you tell me now?"

"Because I can't make love to you without biting you, and to make you forget that I need to thrall you. One thrall is harmless, but more than that can cause damage, and you are too precious to me to risk it."

"Am I precious to you? Or is it my brain?"

"Both. But given how uniquely gifted you are, I'd rather err on the side of caution and not thrall you at all."

"What about what Emmett and Eleanor did to me? Isn't that dangerous to my precious brain?"

"It's not. Compulsion works differently, and not all immortals can do it. In fact, very few can, and I'm not one of them. That's why I needed their help."

"Good." Kaia yawned and closed her eyes. "I don't mind playing kinky games with you and letting you boss me around in bed, but only when I want it. I would hate it if you compelled me to do things I didn't want to do."

"I would never do that." He kissed the top of her nose.

For a moment, he thought that she'd fallen asleep, but then she asked, "The kinky games or the compulsion?"

He laughed. "I'll play any game you fancy, but I will never compel you unless the security of my clan demands it."

"I get it. I would do anything to protect my family as well." She cupped his cheek and leaned up to kiss his lips. "And I would do anything to protect you too."

His heart surged with emotion. "Why?"

"Because I'm falling for you, my handsome, immortal prince."

Dear reader,
Thank you for reading the ***Children of the Gods***.
As an independent author, I rely on your support to spread the word. So if you enjoyed the story, please share your experience with others, and if it isn't too much trouble, I would greatly appreciate a brief review on Amazon.
Love & happy reading,
Isabell

COMING UP NEXT
THE CHILDREN OF THE GODS BOOK 63
DARK WHISPERS FROM AFAR

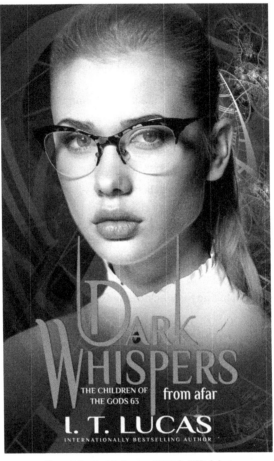

To read the first 3 chapters JOIN the VIP club at ITLUCAS.COM —To find out what's included in your free membership flip to the last page.

Also by I. T. Lucas

THE CHILDREN OF THE GODS ORIGINS
1: Goddess's Choice
2: Goddess's Hope

THE CHILDREN OF THE GODS

Dark Stranger
1: Dark Stranger The Dream
2: Dark Stranger Revealed
3: Dark Stranger Immortal

Dark Enemy
4: Dark Enemy Taken
5: Dark Enemy Captive
6: Dark Enemy Redeemed

Kri & Michael's Story
6.5: My Dark Amazon

Dark Warrior
7: Dark Warrior Mine
8: Dark Warrior's Promise
9: Dark Warrior's Destiny
10: Dark Warrior's Legacy

Dark Guardian
11: Dark Guardian Found
12: Dark Guardian Craved
13: Dark Guardian's Mate

Dark Angel
14: Dark Angel's Obsession
15: Dark Angel's Seduction
16: Dark Angel's Surrender

Dark Operative
17: Dark Operative: A Shadow of Death
18: Dark Operative: A Glimmer of Hope
19: Dark Operative: The Dawn of Love

Dark Survivor
20: Dark Survivor Awakened

21: Dark Survivor Echoes of Love
22: Dark Survivor Reunited

Dark Widow
23: Dark Widow's Secret
24: Dark Widow's Curse
25: Dark Widow's Blessing

Dark Dream
26: Dark Dream's Temptation
27: Dark Dream's Unraveling
28: Dark Dream's Trap

Dark Prince
29: Dark Prince's Enigma
30: Dark Prince's Dilemma
31: Dark Prince's Agenda

Dark Queen
32: Dark Queen's Quest
33: Dark Queen's Knight
34: Dark Queen's Army

Dark Spy
35: Dark Spy Conscripted
36: Dark Spy's Mission
37: Dark Spy's Resolution

Dark Overlord
38: Dark Overlord New Horizon
39: Dark Overlord's Wife
40: Dark Overlord's Clan

Dark Choices
41: Dark Choices The Quandary
42: Dark Choices Paradigm Shift
43: Dark Choices The Accord

Dark Secrets
44: Dark Secrets Resurgence
45: Dark Secrets Unveiled
46: Dark Secrets Absolved

Dark Haven
47: Dark haven Illusion

48: Dark Haven Unmasked
49: Dark Haven Found
Dark Power
50: Dark Power Untamed
51: Dark Power Unleashed
52: Dark Power Convergence
DarkMemories
53: Dark Memories Submerged
54: Dark Memories Emerge
55: Dark Memories Restored
Dark Hunter
56: Dark Hunter's Query
57: Dark Hunter's Prey
58: Dark Hunter's Boon
Dark God
59: Dark God's Avatar
60: Dark God's Reviviscence
61: Dark God Destinies Converge
Dark Whispers
62: Dark Whispers From The Past
63: Dark Whispers From Afar

PERFECT MATCH
Perfect Match 1: Vampire's Consort
Perfect Match 2: King's Chosen
Perfect Match 3: Captain's Conquest

The Children of the Gods Series Sets

Books 1-3: Dark Stranger trilogy—Includes a bonus short story: **The Fates take a Vacation**
Books 4-6: Dark Enemy Trilogy —Includes a bonus short

STORY—THE FATES' POST-WEDDING CELEBRATION
BOOKS 7-10: DARK WARRIOR TETRALOGY
BOOKS 11-13: DARK GUARDIAN TRILOGY
BOOKS 14-16: DARK ANGEL TRILOGY
BOOKS 17-19: DARK OPERATIVE TRILOGY
BOOKS 20-22: DARK SURVIVOR TRILOGY
BOOKS 23-25: DARK WIDOW TRILOGY
BOOKS 26-28: DARK DREAM TRILOGY
BOOKS 29-31: DARK PRINCE TRILOGY
BOOKS 32-34: DARK QUEEN TRILOGY
BOOKS 35-37: DARK SPY TRILOGY
BOOKS 38-40: DARK OVERLORD TRILOGY
BOOKS 41-43: DARK CHOICES TRILOGY
BOOKS 44-46: DARK SECRETS TRILOGY
BOOKS 47-49: DARK HAVEN TRILOGY
BOOKS 51-52: DARK POWER TRILOGY
BOOKS 53-55: DARK MEMORIES TRILOGY
BOOKS 56-58: DARK HUNTER TRILOGY

MEGA SETS
INCLUDE CHARACTER LISTS

THE CHILDREN OF THE GODS: BOOKS 1-6
THE CHILDREN OF THE GODS: BOOKS 6.5-10

TRY THE CHILDREN OF THE GODS SERIES ON **AUDIBLE**

2 FREE audiobooks with your new Audible subscription!

FOR EXCLUSIVE PEEKS AT UPCOMING RELEASES & A FREE COMPANION BOOK

Join my *VIP Club* and gain access to the VIP portal at
ITLUCAS.COM
(or go to: http://eepurl.com/blMTpD)

Included in your free membership:

- **FREE** Children of the Gods companion book 1
- **FREE** narration of Goddess's Choice—Book 1 in The Children of the Gods Origins series.
- Preview chapters of upcoming releases.
- And other exclusive content offered only to my VIPs.

If you're already a subscriber, you'll receive a download link for my next book's preview chapters in the new release announcement email. If you are not getting my emails, your provider is sending them to your junk folder, and you are missing out on **important updates, side characters' portraits, additional content, and other goodies.** To fix that, add isabell@itlucas.com to your email contacts or your email VIP list.

Made in the USA
Las Vegas, NV
21 June 2022